CLOSE TO HOME

BEAR & MANDY BOOK ONE

L.T. RYAN

with

K.M. ROUGHT

LIQUID MIND MEDIA

THE BEAR & MANDY LOGAN SERIES

Close to Home

Under the Surface

The Last Stop

Over the Edge (Coming Soon)

1

Katie disappeared two days before our thirteenth birthday.

It felt like such a significant number back then. *Thirteen*. We would finally be teenagers. Our parents would have to take us seriously. We were one step closer to adulthood, where we could make our own decisions. Stay up late and eat whatever we wanted for dinner.

Those are the kinds of things you care about when you're thirteen.

And there was no better way to assert our independence than to run away. Neither of us enjoyed living at home. Katie's father was always working, and her mother was absent, even when she was there physically. We couldn't describe what was wrong with her back then, but now I know she was an addict. Alcohol. Pills. Daytime talk shows. She could function when friends and family were around, but when it was just her and Katie, she didn't bother to pretend.

Her mom kept up the act around me at first. But once she realized I had no one to tell her dirty little secrets to, she dropped the pleasantries, and I faded into the background along with her daughter. When you're twelve, you're still a child. Insignificant. As long as we didn't interrupt her programs, she let us do whatever we wanted. And they had such a big house to explore.

Or at least it felt that way to me. I lived in a trailer with my father, whichever girlfriend he was seeing at the time, and my two older brothers. Sometimes I got mad at Katie for hating her life because at least her parents loved her. There was no doubt in my mind that my dad hated me. He never missed an opportunity to say it to my face.

But as angry as I got at Katie for not appreciating the life she had, I knew how she felt. The loneliness. The despair. An incessant need to disconnect your brain just to get through another day. It just eats at you. All we wanted was to leave home. Never look back. Katie looked young, but with some makeup, I could pass off as fifteen. Which was almost sixteen. I could start working, and we could build a life of our own.

These were the demented dreams of a couple of twelve-year-old girls. It never would've worked, but back then, we had a secret that could change everything. The sort of thing that makes you feel powerful. It warps your sense of reality. You're willing to take all sorts of risks just to see your dreams come true.

When Katie didn't show up at school, I thought maybe she had admitted she was sick. She never skipped school if she could help it, but she'd been sluggish and disoriented the last few weeks. I figured maybe she had asked her mom to stay home.

But when I walked to her house after the final bell, there were two cop cars in her driveway. I could hear crying from the porch. This is how I knew her mother cared. My father wouldn't have shed a tear.

I knocked on the door, and a police officer opened it. He looked down at me, wondering for just a second if I were Katie. But we looked too different. Where she was fair, I was sallow. Where she was bright, I was dark. Where she giggled and danced, I turned inward with an anger no child should feel at that age.

"Can I help you?" His voice was kind but firm, as though impressing upon me that this wasn't an appropriate time and maybe I should turn around and run home.

I stood firm. "Where's Katie?"

"What's your name?"

"Where's Katie?" I asked again. "Why wasn't she at school?"

"Are you one of Katie's friends?"

"Yes." I puffed up my chest. "I'm her best friend."

The man gestured for me to come inside. I kicked off my shoes like we were supposed to and glared at the officers who hadn't bothered to follow the rules. I felt bigger than them. More responsible. More respectful of the mandates put in place by Katie's father. Almost-thirteen was a hell of a drug.

I sat down in a chair across from Katie's mom. There was a half-empty wine glass next to an ashtray with a dying cigarette. I scrunched my nose. My father smoked, and I hated the smell. The way it wrapped its fingers around my lungs and squeezed. The way it choked the life out of you, one breath at a time.

"Has Katie been feeling okay the last couple of days?" the police officer asked.

I dragged my focus from the cigarette to look him in the eyes. "No. She's been sick."

"I mean," he said, "has she been feeling okay *mentally?*"

Katie was always happy, even when she was sad. She turned her feelings outward to help people, where I turned them inward to hurt myself. "She's been fine." Somehow, it felt like a betrayal to tell this man that Katie wasn't happy at home. "Normal."

"Has she ever talked about running away?"

It was the last question I expected, and my face showcased my surprise. How did he know about our secret? There was no way Katie would ever tell someone, especially not a police officer. But what other explanation could there be? No one knew but us, and we never wrote our plans down. If she didn't tell him, how could he have possibly found out?

The officer knelt in front of me. My father had instilled a fearful respect for the police into me from a young age. This man's eyes were kind. They say the eyes are the window to the soul. I wanted to trust him. And I desperately wanted to know what had happened to Katie.

"You're not in trouble," he said.

I hated the way my body flooded with relief.

The officer continued. "But I need you to tell me whether Katie wanted to run away."

My eyes flicked to her mother. She wasn't paying attention to us. She was too busy feeling sorry for herself. When I looked back at the cop, he was staring expectantly at me. I swallowed the bile that had risen from my stomach.

"She wouldn't have left without me."

The officer blew out a breath. I had confirmed what he suspected, and that was all he needed to know. "Where were you going?"

"Downtown."

"Anywhere specific downtown?"

I shook my head. Those weren't the kind of details we concerned ourselves with. The city's center provided opportunity. That's all we needed to know. But they wouldn't find Katie there.

"She wouldn't have left without me."

He wasn't listening. He and his partner exchanged glances, and I saw everything I needed to know in that moment. They thought Katie had run away, that she had hopped a bus, and gone downtown. It would be a race to get to her before something bad happened.

I imagined Katie walking the streets of downtown without me, but it was impossible. We were a pair. Inseparable. And she'd been too sick the last few days. She'd stumble down the hallway, and I'd have to hook my arm through hers to keep her moving. She'd fall asleep in the middle of class, and I'd poke her with the end of my pencil to jolt her awake. She'd clutch her stomach and ask to be excused to the bathroom where she could throw up in relative privacy.

Back then, we didn't know what it meant. Did she eat something bad? Is this what getting your period feels like? Was it just a bug that needed to work its way through her system? Our secret kept us from telling anyone, for fear they would read our mind and discover what we were planning.

Even at that moment with the cops there, I hesitated to tell them more. If she strolled through the door, and I had revealed our entire plan to the adults, then we'd never be able to live out our dreams. And it would upset Katie that I took that away from her.

I jumped off the chair when the door opened, convinced this was Katie returning home. She could tell them it was just a joke, that she got a little lost, but she was home now, and we could go back to our daydreams.

But it wasn't Katie.

It was her father.

And when his gaze glossed over the officers in his living room, me standing there with wide eyes, and his wife crying, he didn't look confused or startled or upset. He looked like a man who carried a lifetime of burdens on his shoulders.

Two days later, when I turned thirteen, they still hadn't found her. By then, I knew thirteen wasn't a magical number that would fix all our problems. Being a teenager was worse than being a child. It came with higher expectations and more responsibilities, and still no one wanted to listen to what I had to say. They were convinced she had run away.

But I knew better.

She wouldn't have left without me.

2

BEAR STEPPED ON THE HEAD OF THE SHOVEL AND DUG IT DEEPER INTO THE earth. He pushed down on the handle and scooped up a pile of dirt, dumping it to the side. Rinse and repeat. The manual labor felt good, even if he was more used to digging graves than flower beds.

He was grateful that his legs worked.

Grateful that every day got easier.

There were still moments when he found himself lost. Adrift in the sea of his own mind. He'd stumble over a word, or his knee would give out and he'd have to catch himself on whatever piece of furniture was close by. But those days happened less often now. He might not be as strong as he once was, but when it came down to it, there was no doubt in his mind he'd be able to defend himself or Mandy.

The squeal of brakes made him turn. A bright yellow school bus sat at the end of the driveway. When the doors opened, Mandy bounded down the steps. She looked up, and Bear waved his whole arm over his head like it'd been years since they last saw each other instead of just a few hours. He could feel her eyes roll from where he stood. A smile crept across his face.

"You're so lame," she said once she'd made it to the top of the driveway.

"Lame?" He pretended to be affronted. "No one's ever called me lame in my life."

"To your face."

"That hurts." He pulled her in for a hug, and she didn't resist. "How was school?"

She shrugged when he finally let go of her. "School."

"Sounds about right."

Mandy pointed to the holes in the garden. "How are the peenies?"

"*Peonies.*" He chuckled. "They're fine. They won't bloom till spring, though."

"Lame."

"Just like me." He leveled her with a look. "Is that your new favorite word?"

"Perhaps."

Bear eyed her sagging backpack. "Got a lot of homework?"

"Just math and English." She hung her head. "And history and biology."

"Better get to it then. You're lucky. I was gonna make you help me."

Mandy held up her hands. Her fingertips were covered in alternating blue and purple nail polish. "I just did my nails this morning. No way I'm getting them dirty."

"Where did you get nail polish?"

"At the grocery store." She must've seen the scrutiny in his face, because the rest of her words tumbled out of her mouth. "They only cost, like, a dollar."

"It's not the money." They weren't exactly hurting for it. "You could've asked if you wanted some."

"I know." She said it too fast. "But you would've gotten the wrong kind."

"There are kinds?" He scratched his beard and remembered too late he was wearing dirty gloves. "I thought there were just colors."

Mandy rolled her eyes, bounced as she hitched her bag up on her shoulder, and reached for the front door. "Exactly my point."

"Do your homework," he shouted after her. "You're cooking dinner." When she gave a muffled affirmative, he added, "And I'm not lame!"

Bear stood there for a moment, but didn't hear a response. He knelt to plant the peonies, his mind wandering to the nail polish. It wasn't a big deal, and he was glad she'd bought them instead of stealing the items. But what else wasn't she telling him? Maybe it was nail polish now, but tomorrow it could be something else. Something bigger.

Sasha's voice crept into his head as it often did when he panicked about Mandy. *Don't smother her. She'll just resent you for it later.* Easier said than done. Mandy had been to hell and back. He didn't want to be the reason she returned. Then again, she was fourteen now. She wasn't helpless. He had made sure of that. He doubted there was a kid in that school who could harm her. But that didn't mean the idea of her not needing him didn't hurt.

When the peonies were planted, Bear brushed himself off, grabbed his shovel, and walked around to the backyard. They'd been there for a month, but he'd hesitated to make their house a home. He'd cut ties from everyone, including Jack. He didn't delude himself into believing they wouldn't know how to find him. Clive had his number, and it was only a matter of time before the phone would ring. Bear had been clear about his thoughts on any of them reaching out, but when did he ever get his way?

He and Mandy had moved to a house just outside of Rochester, New York. It was more than big enough for the two of them. Living life out of hotel rooms meant it felt like a luxury to have a two-bedroom all to himself again. Fixing it up gave him something to do while Mandy was at school. And today's project was the garden.

Mandy had wanted him to plant the flowers in a rainbow, so he did. It didn't matter what it looked like. He just wanted to keep his hands moving. Figured it would help with his recovery from having the brain tumor removed. Plus, the nicer the house appeared, the more his neighbors would think he was just a single dad raising his teenage daughter.

Perception was everything if they were to survive Mandy's teenage years.

The backyard was another project altogether. That would be his domain. He wanted a vegetable garden so they wouldn't have to go into town as often. Self-sustainment. He'd plant garlic and onions and tomatoes and cucumbers. Anything and everything to keep them fed. Plus, he could teach Mandy what the plants looked like in case she ever needed to forage for food.

There was a strip along the right side of the backyard that butted up against the tree line. It'd be perfect for a vegetable garden. It'd get a good amount of both sun and shade, plus he had already measured the hose, and it'd reach to the very end. Now it was just a matter of digging up the earth and creating a bed for the vegetables to thrive.

Bear's muscles screamed in protest as he jammed the shovel into the earth again, but he ignored the pain. Sweat beaded along his forehead as he continued to outline the size and shape of the bed, then dig out the center so he could till the garden and add fertilizer. He'd be able to plant some vegetables in the fall, but the garden would really take shape in the spring. It was strange to think he'd be in the same place until then. How long had it been since he'd had a home address?

It was unsettling to consider living in the same place for any length of time, but he had gotten the immunity they had promised him. Plus, they had wiped his records clean. And Mandy's. She deserved to go to school and make friends and live life as a teenager. It was the best he could do for her, given the circumstances.

Even though she didn't know everything, Mandy seemed to understand. Sasha's death had devastated them both, and they'd spent more than a few sleepless nights crying and trading stories. Mandy's ability to bounce back amazed Bear, but he had to question how much of it was real and how much was bluster. She was a tough kid, but there was still a lot she didn't understand about the world. Hopefully, going to school would kick her off in the right direction.

Somewhere between thinking about Sasha and wondering what Mandy's future would bring, Bear's shovel struck something solid. It reverberated up his arm and made his teeth rattle. He looked around the yard like someone was waiting to step out of the shadows and offer him an answer to his questions. But when no one presented themselves, he kept digging.

The shape of whatever was beneath the soil spilled beyond the rough outline of his garden bed. He kept digging. The sun lowered in the sky, and the surrounding air cooled in response. Sweat still soaked him from head to toe. He could feel it dripping off his forehead and stinging his eyes. It evaporated from his back and sent goosebumps scurrying along his arms.

It didn't take him long to realize he had hit an old concrete septic tank cover. He knew where the current septic was buried, which meant no one had used this one in at least a decade. No one had mentioned something buried here. Was there a reason? The likely answers were laziness or negligence. Nevertheless, curiosity got the better of him.

Bear grabbed a crowbar from the garage and used it to pop open the cover. What would he find? Nothing alive, that was for sure. The remnants of human waste, bacteria, and a headache. He'd have to cover the tank back up tomorrow and find another place for his garden. But it didn't hurt to look.

You were never too old to hope you'd find buried treasure in your backyard.

The sound of the top grating against concrete echoed across the yard. As soon as Bear lifted the top out of the way, a rancid smell hit him that invaded his nostrils and burned his eyes. Ten-plus years of desiccation would make anybody tear up. Some things were meant to stay buried.

Bear pulled a flashlight out of his pocket and peered into the hole.

"What the hell?"

Rainwater, debris, and a buildup of bacteria couldn't hide the bones jutting up above the surface. He'd seen enough dead bodies in his day to know they didn't belong to an animal.

Before Bear could decide what to do, Mandy stuck her head out the back door and called for him. "Dinner's ready. I burned the garlic bread. Again."

"Yeah. Be there in a minute."

She took one step out of the house. "What's that?"

"An old septic tank." He pocketed the flashlight and reseated the cover. "I'll deal with it in the morning."

Mandy scrunched up her nose. "That's disgusting." She backed away as Bear approached the door. "You need a shower."

He looked down at his muddy hands. "I think you're right. Don't eat all the burnt pieces. You know they're my favorite."

"You're so weird," Mandy said, but with a hint of affection.

"I thought I was lame?"

"You can be both, you know."

Bear grunted and trudged upstairs to the shower. The last thing he needed was another dead body on his hands. It had to have been over a decade since the person had died. Would another few years matter? He could leave the poor schmuck down there until it was time to move on. Then it would be someone else's problem.

As Bear turned the handle for the shower and waited for the water to warm up, he sat on the edge of the tub and looked down at his mud-caked hands. Dirt was better than blood, and he didn't miss a life of looking over his shoulder. Not that the habit was easy to break. He'd always be worried about someone finding him or Mandy. And calling the cops to his house to check out some human remains was less than ideal.

But what kind of example would he be setting for Mandy if he didn't do something about it?

3

BEAR HAD WAITED UNTIL MANDY GOT ON THE SCHOOL BUS BEFORE calling the police. Not that Mandy couldn't have handled it. She'd seen worse in her short life. But they were supposed to be lying low, and the less she knew, the less he had to worry about.

He watched from a second-story window as the sheriff's vehicle pulled into the driveway and crept toward the house. Sixty seconds passed before a woman stepped out, looked around, and approached the front door. From his vantage point, he couldn't get a good look at her features.

The doorbell rang. Bear didn't move. He watched the street to see if any of the neighbors were peering through their blinds. When he realized he was the only one being nosy, he left his perch, lumbered down the stairs, and opened the door.

The sheriff was an attractive red-haired woman with dark eyes and a smattering of freckles across her face. She had an athletic build. He figured her to be a decade younger than him. She peered up at him, taken aback by his height.

"Riley Logan?"

He reached out a hand, which she shook without trepidation. "Call me Bear."

"Bear." She looked him up and down. "Because of your size, I take it?"

"'Cause I'm as cuddly as a teddy bear."

"Right." Her face remained passive, but there was a twinkle in her eye. "My name is Josephine McKinnon. May I come in?"

Bear remained still and quiet for a moment. He hadn't given a second glance to a woman since Sasha's murder. It had only been a few short months, though his life had changed in every way since. This woman standing in front of him stole his breath. A complication he didn't quite understand because of his grieving. A complication he couldn't have in his life. Not now.

"Mr. Logan?" McKinnon tilted her head and smiled. "Bear?"

He shook his head. The thoughts of what McKinnon would look like out of her uniform dissipated. "I'd rather just take you around back, if it's all the same to you."

She hesitated for a fraction of a second, and Bear saw her gaze flick over his shoulder to the inside of the house. But when he stepped forward through the doorframe, she backed away and gestured for him to lead.

"On the phone, you said you found human remains?"

"That's right."

"In an old septic tank?"

"Yes, ma'am."

"How do you know they're human?"

They rounded the corner of the house, and Bear made a beeline for the hole on the other side of the yard. "Too big to be an animal."

"Could be a deer."

"Hunted all my life. I know what a deer looks like. This ain't no deer."

They stopped next to the tank. Bear picked up the crowbar he'd placed nearby. When he popped the lid, he took a step back and gestured for the sheriff to take a look. They both waved away the smell, not that it did any good. They'd have to acclimate to it.

McKinnon pulled out a flashlight and clicked it on. She squatted down and allowed the light to flood the inside of the tank. Bear heard her suck in a breath when she found what she was looking for.

"It stinks," she whispered.

"They didn't mention this when I bought the place."

"People who hide bodies usually want them to remain hidden."

Bear laughed. "Our working septic has been around for at least ten years, so I imagine this one is older. Don't know how a body ended up in there, but between the groundwater seeping in year after year and the tank being closed off, it's done nothing but rot for at least a decade."

"I see a thigh bone and a foot." She looked up at him. "You're right. Definitely human."

"Like I said," he replied. "Ain't no way it's a deer."

McKinnon crept closer and shone her light around the edge of the cover. Bear hadn't been able to see it in the fading sun last night, but in the middle of the day, his eyes caught the shine of a clump of hair attached to the edge of the lid. "Lucky us." McKinnon pulled out a baggie and a pair of tweezers. "Must've gotten caught between the metal and the concrete. The seal kept it from degrading."

"Lucky us."

McKinnon stood. Bear could hear her knees creak. She tucked the baggie into her vest pocket. "Walk me through how you found this."

"Pretty straightforward." He pointed to the area he'd outlined in the grass the night before. "Was planning to dig a vegetable garden there when I hit this thing. Didn't know what it was, so I kept digging."

"A vegetable garden, huh?" She raised an eyebrow. "You don't strike me as the type."

Bear shrugged. "I'm a man of many surprises."

"I bet you are." McKinnon tapped her notebook as she looked over at the outline of the garden, then back up at Bear. "How come you didn't call it in last night?"

Bear had his excuse ready. "It was late. I have a daughter. Didn't want her to see. Figured that poor soul's been in there a while. Another day wouldn't hurt."

"You're new in town."

Bear grinned. "Is there a question in there?"

"Where are you from?"

"A little bit of everywhere."

"That's not an answer."

Bear shrugged again. "It's the truth."

"Where were you before this?"

Bear stared her down before he answered. He gave her credit for not looking away. "Overseas."

"And you chose Upstate New York to settle down?"

"Good a place as any. I like my space." He wasn't trying to be subtle as he spread his stance.

McKinnon put her hands on her hips and peered into the hole again, then up at the sky. "Might rain tonight. We should wrap this up sooner rather than later."

"I'd appreciate that. For my daughter's sake." It wasn't his only reason.

"How old is she?"

"Fourteen."

"They're fun at that age, aren't they?" She shook her head. "They love you and hate you, depending on the hour. You've got your hands full."

"You have no idea." Bear chuckled despite the situation. He could handle Mandy now, but in a couple of years, that was going to change. She was a spitfire. "But she's a good kid. I'm trying to keep her away from all this."

"So, you said." McKinnon brought out her phone. "We're a small sheriff's department. I'm gonna have to bring the state police in on this."

Bear's stomach clenched. It was the last thing he wanted to hear. "Look, I appreciate that, but I don't love the idea of Staties traipsing across my lawn."

"Why?" She looked up at him with a smile, but there was a hardness to her eyes. "You got something to hide?"

"It's a small town. People talk."

"That they do." McKinnon blew out a breath. "Unfortunately, I don't have any officers to spare. Considering this may be a homicide from over a decade ago, we're gonna need manpower. I empathize with your situation, but—"

"—your hands are tied." He held his hands up and pressed his wrists together.

"Pretty much." She tapped a few numbers on her phone but didn't press the dial button. "I'll try to get them out of your hair as soon as I can, all right? Unless you've got any other bodies hiding out around here."

"Plenty of skeletons in the closet, but no bodies that I'm aware of."

McKinnon stepped away to make her call.

Bear cursed under his breath. This was the last thing he needed. The idea of a bunch of New York State Troopers lining his driveway was enough to raise the hair on the back of his neck. He was supposed to be lying low. For a second, he wondered if this was all part of Clive's plan —get Bear a house with a body in the backyard and then frame him for the murder. It's not like Clive didn't have the resources to pull that off.

Bear shook the thought from his head. It made no sense. If Clive wanted Bear dead or in prison, he would've done it before sending him to Rochester. And even if he did, Clive wouldn't do that to Mandy. Leaving her out on the street. The guy could be an asshole, but he wasn't heartless.

When McKinnon returned, she wore a grave expression. "They're on their way. I'll need you to stick around and answer some more questions."

Bear sighed. "Don't suppose it'd be a good look if I had a beer in my hand when the troopers showed up, huh?"

McKinnon chuckled. He liked that she had a sense of humor. "No, I don't suppose it would."

"All right then," Bear said. "Coffee it is."

4

Mandy didn't like school, but still it fascinated her. She'd never been around so many kids her age. There was a constant learning curve. She soaked up information from every interaction and stored it in the back of her mind for future reference. Bear was always telling her to stay vigilant, and she instinctively knew that went double for when she was at school.

Ninth grade was no joke. Every class offered her another window into the world, and she found her brain bogged down with questions she didn't know the answers to. She had more real-world experience than any of her classmates, but for some reason, none of what Bear had taught her helped her pass her English exams or the pop quizzes every week in math class. That was partly why she hated sitting through an entire day of useless information—she already knew it wouldn't help her survive out in the real world.

But there was one highlight to her days at Crossroads High School, and that was Laura Lynn Weinberger. Despite her unfortunate name— or maybe because of it—Laura Lynn was one of the nicest people in school. On the first day of classes, she walked right up to Mandy and introduced herself. Mandy blew her off at first. Never trust anyone who is too nice to you, Bear had told her. But the next day, Laura Lynn sat down at her lunch table and offered half of her turkey and cheese sandwich. It felt like such a luxury compared to Bear's sloppy PB&J.

The two had been friends for only a few weeks, but Mandy couldn't imagine getting through the day without the other girl. Laura Lynn had other friends in other social groups, but she chose to spend most of her time with Mandy.

"You're different," Laura Lynn had said when Mandy asked her why. Mandy had taken offense at first, but Laura Lynn just shrugged. "You make things more... interesting."

Mandy liked that. She knew she'd have to hide her true self from her classmates—there was no way they could know who she really was or what she'd been through as a child, losing her family, being abducted, surviving—but at least she could show Laura Lynn part of the real her.

Today, Mandy had stolen two lollipops from the nurse's office on her way into school. They weren't supposed to have any candy in the hallways, but Mandy didn't care. Didn't they know there were worse things she could be doing? As Mandy unwrapped her cherry lollipop and stuck it in her mouth, Laura Lynn slipped hers into her backpack.

Laura Lynn stopped short and drummed her fingers on the nearest locker. "Oh no."

"What?"

"Pete and Jamie." She pointed down the hallway. "They're right next to my locker."

"So? We'll tell them to move."

"You can't just tell them to move." Laura Lynn said this slowly, as though Mandy barely understood English. "They'll beat us up." She gasped. "Look. See what happens?"

A boy with thick glasses and a button-down shirt was pressed up against the lockers, courtesy of Pete and his goons. Jamie was holding one of Marcus' arms while Pete had an arm across the boy's neck. There was another boy Mandy didn't know, and he jeered from a safe distance. He kept looking around, making sure no teachers would spot them.

When Mandy took a step closer, Laura Lynn grabbed her arm and hissed, "No, don't do it."

Mandy shook her off. She hadn't been at the school long enough to call Pete her true arch nemesis, but he was a contender. The first day she got there, he spread a rumor that her mom had been an alcoholic and that was why she wasn't around. How he had already found out that it was just her and Bear, she had no idea. But ever since then, she'd been looking to settle the score.

Pete now had Marcus' face pressed up against the lockers. The boy had a tear streaming down his cheeks, and Jamie was pointing and laughing at him. Pete looked like he thought he was king of the world.

Mandy was about to change all that.

She tapped on Pete's shoulder. The other boys hadn't seen her approach. He was so shocked someone had dared to interrupt him; he released his grip on Marcus. But he still held the other boy by one of his wrists.

"Hey," she said. "Let him go."

Pete looked over his shoulder. He threw his head back and laughed. "What are you gonna do about it? Go cry about it to your mom."

"I will once you let him go." Mandy shook off the barb just as easily as she'd seen Bear do countless times. She'd learned from him that violence was acceptable only after all other avenues had been explored. "Come on, Pete. It's not worth it."

Pete let Marcus go, but the other boys still had him trapped. "What's not worth it?"

"Getting beat up by a girl."

Pete smirked and looked at his friends like, *can you believe her?* "And who's going to beat me up?" He looked over Mandy's shoulder. "Laura Lynn?" He sneered her name. Laura Lynn was popular because she was pretty and her family was rich, but some of the kids saw her kindness as weakness. "Is she going to have her daddy pay me off?"

"Just let him go," Mandy said. "And we can settle this outside."

The other boys snickered, and Pete took a step closer. "Why wait? Let's do it right here. Right now."

Mandy didn't bother giving him another warning. Two was enough. When he raised his arm as if to slap her, she grabbed his right wrist with her right hand and yanked it across her body with all her might. She put her left hand on his shoulder and pushed as hard as she could. Her speed surprised him. He yelped and tripped forward, allowing Mandy to shove him into the lockers face first, just like he'd done to Marcus.

"I told you to leave him alone." Mandy leaned in closer to his ear and whispered. "I tried to warn you. Don't mess with my friends."

Pete only whimpered. Mandy couldn't help but feel satisfied at hearing the sound.

There was an audible silence. Then an ear-splitting screech ripped through the air. "MISS LOGAN."

The boys scattered, and Mandy let go of Pete. He started crying, but there were no tears. When Mandy turned around, she found herself face to face with Mrs. Turner. The woman was only a head or so taller than Mandy, but the tight bun on top of her head added several more inches. She was probably in her sixties, but she looked ancient and severe. All the kids were afraid of her.

"What in the world do you think you're doing?" Mrs. Turner asked. She was red in the face.

"He was trying to beat up Marcus, ma'am."

Mrs. Turner looked from Pete's tear-stained face to Marcus'. She turned back to Mandy. "Be that as it may, violence is never the answer. What would your father say?"

Mandy shrugged. "He'd probably just critique my form." Mandy thought better of her answer and added, "Ma'am."

5

BEAR THREW OPEN THE DOOR TO CROSSROADS HIGH SCHOOL WITH enough force that it bounced off the concrete wall and hit his heels as he walked through. But he didn't feel it. All he saw was red. He thought the drive over would have been enough to calm him down, but it merely allowed him time to stew in his anger.

Moments after the New York State Troopers arrived at his doorstep, Bear got a call from school saying Mandy had been caught fighting. They hadn't given Bear any additional information, just a single demand: Meet them at the school within a half hour to discuss Mandy's punishment. He'd agreed and hung up the phone, turning to face a curious Sheriff McKinnon.

Bear had given the sheriff the short of it, apologizing for having to leave. He didn't like the idea of the cops poking around while he wasn't there, and he was more than aware it wasn't a good look, but what else could he do? The school hadn't given him a choice. He wasn't about to risk Mandy's future because he had a stick up his ass.

Didn't mean he was happy about it.

Mrs. Turner met him at the front office. He knew exactly the kind of teacher she was. By the book, no wiggle room for circumstances. These kinds of teachers didn't even like children. They just enjoyed wielding power over people smaller than themselves. Liked the idea of shaping kids into subservient pod people. Don't bother letting students think for themselves. They should obey their elders and follow the rules—no exceptions.

"Mandy was completely out of line," Mrs. Turner said. "There is no justification for her actions."

Bear brushed past the teacher and shouldered his way into the main office. "I'll be the judge of that."

He heard Turner *tsk* behind him, but she wasn't in charge of the situation. Principal Amos was. Bear had met the man on Mandy's first day of school and decided he was a good enough guy. He had a round waist but a skinny face and thin ankles, like a spinning top. A thick walrus mustache was at war with his beady eyes, and it was winning. The man had a quiet demeanor that Bear took as a sign of intelligence.

"Mr. Logan." Amos stuck out his hand. "Thank you for joining us."

"Of course." Bear shook the principal's hand and then turned his gaze to Mandy. She shrunk under his scrutiny, but he was only looking for signs of mistreatment. Though he was happy to see she was the apparent winner, he kept his scowl. "You mentioned a fight?"

"There is no justification for Miss Logan's actions," Mrs. Turner repeated. She squared off against Bear, and he had to give her points for bravado. "It is never okay to strike another student."

Bear turned his back on her and addressed the principal. "I'd like to hear Mandy's side of the story."

"She is a child," Turner said behind him. "She'll lie to get out of it."

"Can you excuse Mrs. Turner and send her back to class?" Bear looked back down at Mandy. "What happened?"

Mandy sat a little straighter in her chair. She didn't break eye contact. "Pete, Jamie, and another kid were picking on Marcus. They pushed him up against the lockers. He was crying and in a lot of pain." She swallowed audibly. "I walked up to Pete and told him to knock it off. He refused. I gave him another warning, and when he tried to hit me, I pushed him up against the locker. Didn't mean to hurt him. I was just trying to defend myself. Oh, and save Marcus."

Bear turned to the principal. "Were there witnesses?"

"Several," Amos said. "They corroborate her story."

"So, what's the problem?"

Turner huffed. "The problem is she struck another child."

"It was self-defense." Bear finally leveled the full weight of his stare on Mrs. Turner. "This Pete kid's a bully. It's not the first time Mandy has mentioned him. I'd wager a guess there's a thick folder around here with his name on it. Why haven't you done anything about the problems he's causing?" When all Turner did was sputter, Bear turned back to Amos. "Give her a month of detention. I'll make her do extra chores at home, and she'll write an apology letter to Pete and his parents." He looked down at Mandy. "And we'll have a long conversation about how we handle bullies."

Amos sputtered. "A month? We were going to suggest two weeks of—"

"A month." Bear pushed past Turner and gestured for Mandy to follow him. "And I expect Pete to receive the same punishment."

He waited at the door, but when neither the teacher nor the principal could find any further words, he shouldered his way back out to the hallway and into the fresh air of the parking lot. Mandy trailed behind him, jogging to catch up.

When they reached his truck, Bear unlocked the doors and fit himself behind the wheel. He waited until Mandy had climbed inside before turning to her. She wore a grin on her face. "What are you so happy about?"

"That was awesome." She was breathless. "I bet no one's ever talked to Turner like that."

"*Mrs.* Turner. You'll show some respect." Bear didn't enjoy the way the grin slid from her face or how tears filled her eyes, but he didn't back down. "That was unacceptable. Have you not listened to anything I've been telling you?"

Mandy threw her hands in the air. Her voice shook. "Of course I've been listening. You've been telling me to stand up for myself and make sure I stay vigilant. And to not let anyone push me around." Her voice caught, and the tears were as much frustration as betrayal. "What did you expect me to do, Bear? Let him beat up Marcus?"

Bear pinched the bridge of his nose. "No, of course not. But now you've got a target on your back."

"Pete's hated me from day one." She sniffled. "And so has Mrs. Turner. I haven't done anything wrong."

"There will be many people who dislike you for no reason. You just gotta shrug it off. They're not worth your time."

"Marcus would disagree."

Bear let out a breath of air. She got him there. "I'm glad you stood up to Pete. And I'm sure Marcus is grateful, too. But we can't afford for you to get kicked out of school, all right? This isn't lying low."

Mandy slumped in her seat. "I know." She sniffled again. "I'm sorry."

He ruffled her hair and then started the engine. "I really thought they were going to suspend you."

"I think the only reason they didn't is because they're afraid of you." She grinned but stopped short of giggling. "Do I really have to do all that stuff?"

"You bet." Bear shot her a look just in time to see her roll her eyes. "And if you say—"

"Lame," she finished.

He shifted into drive. He was still pissed, but Mandy understood the situation. And she'd spend the next month making up for it. No use rubbing salt in the wound. "You hungry?"

She looked at the clock. "It's not even four yet."

He shrugged. "Man's gotta eat."

Mandy's eyes lit up. "Can we go to Georgie's?"

"Yes, but don't get the wrong idea." Bear pulled out of the parking lot and swung the truck left, heading back into town. "This is not a reward. I was already going to go there before you suggested it."

"Then why'd you ask?"

"Gotta at least make it look like you have a say."

Mandy crossed her arms over her chest, but there was a smile on her face. "Whatever."

Georgie's was a local diner that hadn't changed since 1957. From the tables to the curtains to the staff, it'd been under the same family's supervision for over sixty years. George Hill Sr. had followed his dreams late in life, and he'd died a fortunate man over twenty years ago. His son continued the legacy of cheap food and friendly atmosphere, all in a place where local gossip ran rampant.

Bear hadn't been a fan at first. He wasn't looking to get on anyone's radar, and this was the place where you went to get noticed. But Junior's food won him over. You couldn't beat good diner food. The greasier the better. Burgers, brats, and bacon. It was enough to give any man a heart attack, but Bear figured it was worth the risk. Plus, a single cup of coffee could keep you sustained for three days straight. Jet fuel.

But it was the man himself who had really sealed the deal. Bear saw a little of his future self in Junior, if he was lucky enough to live to his age. The younger Hill didn't have time for games, and he'd call you out on it sooner than he'd save your feelings. But if you were good to him, he was good to you. And that kind of loyalty bought you a lot in a town like this.

Mandy pushed through the door and sat herself in the corner booth. She'd saved the seat facing the door for Bear, but he could tell she was getting itchy having her back to the room. She was a quick learner, at least. Hell, that was part of the problem, wasn't it?

Caroline Hill was George's wife and the best waitress Bear had ever come across. She could read minds and have your drink order on the table before you even opened your mouth. Plus, she always gave Bear an extra helping of bacon. And she doted on Mandy. The girl had stars in her eyes every time she looked up at Caroline.

"Good afternoon, you two." Caroline placed a steaming mug of coffee down in front of Bear and a glass of cherry Coke—made with real juice and topped with a handful of cherries—in front of Mandy. "The usual today?"

"Yes, Miss Caroline," Mandy chirped.

Bear chuckled. "Thank you, Miss Caroline."

"I'll get that right in for you." Caroline looked at Bear over the top of her glasses, which she wore on a chain around her neck. "You doin' all right there, Riley?"

He held her gaze for a moment and realized the entire town already knew about the cop cars at his house. "Just fine, Miss Caroline. How about you?"

She took in his answer for a moment before pushing her glasses to the top of her head. "Oh, you know. Same ol'. We're still down to one grill. Junior's breaking his back trying to fix it, but he can't get a handle on it." She leaned in and lifted an eyebrow, doubling the wrinkles on her forehead. "Don't tell him I said that."

"Say the word," Bear offered, "and I'll have a look at it."

"Deal. I'll even throw in a couple dinners on the house. How's that sound?"

"Sounds great." He sipped his coffee and felt it stimulating his mind. "You can even tell him I'm desperate for work. That'll make him feel better."

Caroline bobbed her head and walked away to take drink orders from a new table. Bear looked around the diner, surprised he could name almost everyone in there. Jackie was the local drunk. He was a Vietnam War vet and harmless. Bear was pretty sure he subsisted on vodka and coffee—he never saw Jackie eat. Shirley and Janice sat in the corner, knitting and sipping on mimosas. Every once in a while, they'd look at Bear and put their heads together and whisper and smile. He didn't mind the ego boost. Charlie and his son Walter both worked at the big pharmaceutical company that basically ran the town. And then there was little old Bernie, who practically lived at the diner. People would come in just to chat with him and hear his stories. Rumor had it he used to work for the FBI. Bear was friendly but tried to steer clear of him when he could. Can never be too careful.

When their plates arrived, Mandy dug in despite having said it was too early for dinner. Bear wanted to bring up the incident at school again but refrained. When she sat down to write her letter, he'd have another chat with her. Press too hard too early, and she wouldn't hear a word he said.

The mundane sounds of the diner were comforting. Life went on, no matter what kind of mess Bear inched toward. A few other patrons glanced his way, but he couldn't tell if it was because he was still the newest guy in town or because of what was going on back at his house. Or maybe he had bacon in his beard. Who knew?

Bear wiped his mouth with a napkin and tossed it onto his empty plate. When Caroline came by with the check, he noticed she'd knocked off an extra five bucks. He tipped twice as much. While he appreciated the gesture, he didn't need help. Especially from the Hills. It was hard enough running a diner in a small town. People would complain if they raised the price of coffee by ten cents a cup. They didn't need to be offering charity to someone who didn't need it, no matter what the situation looked like.

The ride home was silent. Mandy played on her phone. Bear considered taking it away as part of her punishment but decided against it. He'd make her clean out the basement over the next month. That'd be punishment enough.

As they got closer to the house, Bear's grip tightened on the wheel. There was little chance the cops had cleared out by now. Sure enough, when he pulled his truck into the driveway, there was barely enough room for him to park in front of his own house.

Mandy looked from the patrol cars and then up at Bear. She had one eyebrow raised and an inquisitive grin playing around her mouth. "So, what did *you* do today?"

6

As soon as they got home, Bear made Mandy sit at the dining room table and do her homework. She didn't bother to protest because they both knew it would've fallen on deaf ears. His anger at the situation had dissipated, replaced by the anxiety of their current problem.

Bear decided Mandy's punishment would start tomorrow. Tonight, he threw together a casserole from leftovers in the fridge and washed as many dishes as he could lay his hands on—all so he could stand at the back window and watch the State Police work.

Every hour, Sheriff McKinnon would knock on the back door and give him an update. Mandy wouldn't look up from her schoolwork, but her pencil would stop moving across the page while she eavesdropped. As much as he wanted to keep her out of the situation, he was glad she paid attention. But they'd have to work on her definition of *subtle*.

The troopers had removed the skeleton from the tank. It looked like all the bones were there, no visible sign of the cause of death. McKinnon had said one of their experts predicted the body to be a female about Mandy's age. Bear's heart squeezed at the thought of not knowing where his daughter had been buried for a decade or more. He would've done everything in his power to find her.

They found no more hair, but they drained the tank, taking the detritus away in plastic bags and collecting the water in case it contained trace elements that could help them solve the case. They took hundreds of pictures of the tank, the surrounding area, and even the house. Bear was in at least a dozen of them, peering out the window like some sort of specter.

After they removed the body and transported it to the coroner in the next town over, the police fanned out and explored the woods surrounding the house. No one was delusional enough to believe they'd find anything after all this time, but they wouldn't be doing their jobs if they didn't at least try. Bear had no reservations about the quality of their searches. They were being thorough.

After the sun had gone down, Bear caught McKinnon in a furious debate with one of the troopers. He was a tall, bulky man with a bald head and a thin mustache. He kept glancing over at Bear, but whenever he'd make for the house, McKinnon would step in his way. Bear knew the discussion was serious when she put one hand on her hip and wagged the other in the man's face. He finally relented, and the pack of cars retreated down the driveway and dispersed into the night.

Bear met McKinnon at the back door, and this time he didn't resist when she asked him to let her in. He sent Mandy up to bed and grabbed two beers out of the fridge. He set one down in front of the sheriff, and she drained half in one go.

"Thanks," she said, wiping her mouth.

"No problem." He pointed at the casserole. "Hungry? "

"After that?" She grabbed her stomach and winced. "Not a chance. Take another beer, though."

"Fair enough."

There was a beat of silence as Bear pulled another one out for her. He caught McKinnon looking around the kitchen. It didn't appear to be curiosity laced with suspicion. Rather, genuine interest in the kind of house Bear kept. But McKinnon wouldn't find any evidence about the case or otherwise. The place was minimalist, if not barren. If she asked, he could pass it off with the excuse that they had only just moved in. But that line wouldn't work forever.

"What was Mr. Clean so upset about?" Bear asked. "Did you steal his bucket and mop?"

"Who?" McKinnon stared at the fridge, which was covered in magnets Mandy had collected from other states over the years. "Oh, Officer Hart?" She frowned. "He wanted to interview you. I said I'd take care of it. He didn't like that very much. I told him he was here because we needed help, not because I was handing the case over to him."

"Why?"

McKinnon dragged her eyes from the magnet collection. "Huh?"

"Why didn't you want him to interview me?"

"Because you wouldn't have given him any answers. He'd waste his time, and you'd get angrier at the situation. We lose enough people around here. Don't wanna go chasing off new folks who seem half-normal."

"What's the other half?"

She grinned. "That's what I'm tryin' to figure out."

"You think you'll do better at questioning me?"

She shrugged. "My chances are higher." Her gaze returned to the fridge. She pointed. "You been to all these places?"

"And a lot more." Bear sipped his drink. "You from here?"

McKinnon looked surprised by the return volley. "Nah. Grew up in Mississippi."

"New York must be culture shock."

"The city, maybe. Only thing that shocks me 'round here is the cold." She frowned. "People are the same wherever you go."

Bear noted the sadness in her voice. "That's bleak."

She looked up at him. "You disagree?"

"No," he said. "I don't."

She studied him for a moment. "Don't like me very much, do you?"

"Actually, I do." He sat across from her and set his beer down. The condensation collected on the table's surface. He made a mental note to buy coasters. "But I don't like cops very much."

"Why not?"

He gave a half laugh. "You think most people do?"

"Not sure. I think most people respect a cop's authority, whether or not they like them."

"Respect or fear?"

"Touché." She took a sip, then looked him dead in the eye. "But the people who don't respect their authority are the ones who have something to hide. And the people who don't fear that authority definitely do."

"And you think I fall into the latter category?"

"Can't imagine you're afraid of much, but I think you have something to hide." She didn't break eye contact. "Then again, most of us do. Just feel like your secret is bigger than the average, uh, bear's."

Bear smiled as he resisted shifting in his seat. There was no way he would let her in on the fact that she was hitting close to home. "You know I had nothing to do with that body out back."

"Yup."

"Then why do you have to know where I came from and what I'm doing here? It's irrelevant."

"Because I'm trying to figure out if I can trust you." She tipped her bottle back and drained the rest of her beer. "You're smart. Observant. You're military." She winked when his eyebrows shot up. "Don't act so surprised. You all have a certain look. It's hard to hide. My guess is people are lucky to have you on their side. I'm sure that little girl buried out back would be happy to have you working for her."

"I'm not trying to get involved."

"You're involved, whether you like it or not. Sooner we figure out what's going on, the sooner we can get out of your—" Her phone buzzed. She looked down at the number and frowned. "Excuse me. I have to take this."

As the sheriff stepped into the other room, Bear finished his own beer and rinsed out the bottles. He placed them next to the sink, making another mental note that he needed a recycling bin. He put it on the same list as the coasters. There were so many odds and ends they needed, he could hardly keep track of them in his head. Owning a house was an exhausting, never-ending list of chores.

He heard McKinnon's muffled conversation through the wall, but couldn't pick out any words. The wind rattled a window in the living room. A creak in the floorboard upstairs told him Mandy was making her way from the bathroom to her bedroom, settling in for the night. The house popped as though it were stretching out its limbs after a long, hard day of standing upright. He could relate.

McKinnon reentered the room. Her jaw was clenched, and the crease between her eyebrows had deepened to a ravine. She didn't meet Bear's eyes when she spoke. "I gotta go."

"Everything okay?"

"Not sure." She slipped a card out of her pocket and set it on the table. "This is my number if you find anything else. I'll follow up with you soon." She finally looked up. Straight into his eyes. "Please think about it. Helping, I mean. Your daughter isn't much older than that girl out there. Her parents deserve to know what happened to her, even after all this time. If you think of anything that might point us in the right direction, no matter how crazy it sounds, call me." A sad smile found its way to her face. "I'll try to rein in the questionings, but old habits and all that, ya' know?"

"Yeah," Bear said. "Old habits."

7

THE NEXT MORNING, BEAR WATCHED MANDY GET ON THE SCHOOL BUS before walking out the back door and surveying the yard. There had been a dozen people traipsing across his property yesterday, and they'd left an impact. Footprints, additional upturned earth, and a pair of latex gloves. He shook his head. So much for the integrity of a crime scene.

Bear snatched up the gloves, then grabbed his rake and put all the loose debris from the yard into a garbage bag. The troopers had taped off the immediate area around the tank with yellow caution tape. Even though they had gathered what they could, they had instructed Bear not to cross the line or disturb anything else.

McKinnon had been right about the rain. Around midnight, a storm had swept through. The troopers had the wherewithal to close the tank's lid before leaving for the night, but Bear figured there had to be an extra inch of rainwater inside. Now that it was dug up, it'd be difficult for the elements not to affect it further.

As he was contemplating what to do about his vegetable garden, his phone rang. He had programmed McKinnon's number into it last night, despite swearing to himself he wouldn't get involved. But it looked like she wasn't giving him a choice. He picked up right before it went to voicemail.

"Mr. Logan? It's Sheriff McKinnon."

"Sheriff." He didn't bother keeping the resignation out of his voice. "What's happening?"

"I wanted to apologize for last night." She sounded like she was navigating uncharted territory, like she wasn't used to apologizing to potential suspects, however unlikely their guilt might be. "For leaving so abruptly."

"You have nothing to apologize for." Bear could feel her tension through the phone. Curiosity got the better of him. "Everything okay?"

"That's why I was calling." Her tone was higher than last night, and the words rushed, almost slurred together. "Wondering if you'd have coffee with me."

"Is this a proposition, Sheriff?" He joked, despite the situation. "Or is it under the pretense of arresting me?"

"Neither." McKinnon didn't sound like she was in the mood for jokes today. "I have something I wanted to run by you. If you've got a minute."

Bear hesitated. He could feel himself walking closer to the point of no return. If he said yes, then he'd bury himself deeper in the case. If he said no, it might look suspicious. He wasn't sure which was worse, but there was something in McKinnon's voice that told him she was on her own precipice. He didn't want to be the reason she slipped and fell. "Yeah, I can do with some coffee."

Twenty minutes later, Bear sat across from McKinnon at a small coffee shop in town. It was the kind of café that carried all sorts of fancy mixtures and picture-perfect cupcakes. The barista almost didn't know what to do when he ordered his coffee black. McKinnon took hers with enough cream to turn it white.

"How's your day so far?" she asked when they sat down.

"Other than your boys ruining my yard?" He took a sip of his drink and shrugged. "Coffee's good."

"They're not my boys." She softened. "But I am sorry about that."

"I'm just annoyed I'll have to find a new spot for my garden."

"How did Mandy handle the news?"

Bear kept a straight face. "She's a tough kid. Curious. Wants to know what I'm going to do about it."

"What *are* you going to do about it?" McKinnon took a sip of her coffee, her eyes wide with intrigue.

He'd thought about that on the way over. "What do you know about the house? Its history? Everyone who lived there before me?"

"Not much. At least no personal stories. House had been on the market for a year or two before someone bought it, but they never moved in. Kinda assumed it was a second house for a bigwig who aspired to fix it up but never got around to it. Then you bought it."

"What about before that? Ten, fifteen years ago."

McKinnon wrapped both hands around her mug as though she could soak in every molecule of heat through her palms. "A man named Jeremy Olsen. He worked for HealTek, like most people 'round here do."

"That's the pharmaceutical company?" When McKinnon nodded, Bear asked, "What happened to him?"

"Died a couple years ago. Cancer." She leaned forward. "That's why I asked you here."

"To talk about Jeremy Olsen?"

"No, to talk about cancer. And teen suicide. The death rates for this county are astronomical."

Bear shrugged. "It's a small town. Largest hospital is forty-five minutes away. From what I've seen, only a few people are well off. Everyone else is working themselves to the bone just to survive and provide for their kids. That's bound to influence your health."

"It's more than that." McKinnon looked around. No one was paying attention to them, but she leaned in closer, and her voice dropped to a notch above a whisper. "I mean *astronomical*. We have one of the highest cancer rates in the United States. We've had a few journalists come out here and poke around, but after a few days, they leave."

Now Bear was interested. "Paid off?"

She shrugged. "Don't know."

"But you have a hunch."

McKinnon doubled down. "I don't know anything. Not yet anyway."

"You think this has something to do with the girl?"

McKinnon sighed. "There are a couple missing children's cases from ten to fifteen years ago. She's likely one of them. Won't know until we test her hair, though."

"But?" Bear didn't enjoy having to pull the thoughts from the woman's head. "We both know you have your theories. Otherwise, you wouldn't have asked me to get coffee."

McKinnon looked around one more time. Bear recognized a few faces in the café, but he didn't know their names. It wasn't like going to Georgie's. This was a younger crowd. A few college kids home from school, catching up on their work over a croissant. He and McKinnon were by far the oldest in there. Even if she was younger, her sheriff's uniform would've ensured she stood out.

"Not here." She stood up. "Got something to show you."

Bear didn't move. He felt himself on the edge of the cliff again. The more his curiosity dragged him forward, the more he dug his heels in. He just wanted to keep his head down. Keep Mandy safe. Stay off the radar. But he could smell trouble from a mile away, and McKinnon was stirring it up. It saturated the surrounding air. He'd be lying if he said it didn't already have its stench on him.

Besides, he'd rather know what he was up against. If this was too big, at least he'd have a heads up before it went south. He and Mandy would be halfway across the States before it crashed down on the small hamlet. They'd be long gone. They'd be safe.

Bear stood up, too. "Lead the way."

8

Mandy and Laura Lynn occupied a table on the far side of the cafeteria, well away from their peers. They both had their backs to the wall—Mandy, so she didn't have to live with the tingle that raced up and down her spine if she couldn't see what was behind her, and Laura Lynn so she could observe her classmates and make passing comments about this person's new shoes or that person's favorite subject. She knew so much about people just by sitting and observing. Mandy made a mental note that her new friend would make an excellent spy. But she'd have to toughen up first.

Thoughts of spies and secret societies vacated her mind the second Marcus walked into the room. He scanned the tables, trying to figure out where to sit. Mandy stood on top of her chair and waved him over. He looked startled and even checked behind him to see if she was pointing to someone else. She shook her head and put her hands on her hips. He made his way to their table.

Laura Lynn stayed quiet, watching the interaction with wide eyes.

Marcus stopped short at the table but didn't sit down. "Uh. Hi."

"Hi." Mandy pointed to a chair. "Go on. Sit."

He slid his tray onto the table and plopped into his seat. His lunch consisted of a sandwich, an apple, some milk, and a bag of healthy-looking chips. Mandy looked down at her half-eaten peanut butter and jelly sandwich and sighed.

"You look scared," Laura Lynn said, staring at Marcus.

"Oh, well." He looked around the room, then back at Mandy. "You did kinda beat someone up yesterday."

"Yeah, but I'm not going to beat *you* up," she said.

Marcus scoffed. "I know that." He relaxed. "So, does this mean we're friends now?"

"Sure." Mandy shrugged, but it sent a thrill through her. She had just doubled her number of allies. "If you want to be."

"It's certainly in my best interest." Marcus wore another button-down shirt today. He looked like an old man stuck in a kid's body. He cleared his throat. "Thanks for yesterday, by the way."

Mandy shrugged again. "No big deal."

"But you got in trouble."

"I've been in worse." She hoped that made her sound mysterious and cool. It's not like it was a lie, either. "Just sucks I have to spend a month sitting next to Pete."

"He used to be nice," Laura Lynn said. "He gave me his orange Jell-O in second grade."

"Well, he's not nice now." Marcus took a violent bite of his apple. "He's a dick."

"Why does he hate you so much?" Mandy asked.

"I wouldn't let him cheat off me in math class." Marcus chuckled. A little dribble of juice ran down his chin, and he wiped it away with a napkin. "They would've figured out something was going on if he got all the answers right. I wasn't going to risk my grades for him. Why can't he just do the work like the rest of us?"

"His dad is mean." Laura Lynn's voice was far away. "My mom says he has a troubled home life."

"Yeah, well, doesn't mean he has to take it out on me." Marcus took another bite of his apple and chewed contemplatively before swallowing and turning his attention back to Mandy. "Speaking of trouble. What was going on at your house yesterday?"

Mandy looked away. "What do you mean?"

"All those cop cars? Everyone's talking about it."

Her head snapped up. "They are? What are they saying?"

"They said it was because you beat up Pete."

"I pushed him up against the locker. They're not going to send a bunch of state police to my door for that." She rolled her eyes. "That's so dumb."

Laura Lynn slid half her sandwich to Mandy. She didn't normally eat a lot, but she looked extra frail today. "So, why were they really there?"

Mandy wasn't sure what to say. On the one hand, she knew Bear would be angry if she talked about the bones. They needed to keep a low profile, and the fewer people who knew about the girl in the septic tank, the better.

On the other hand, Laura Lynn and Marcus were her friends. And they didn't have anyone to tell. Besides, she was bursting with the information she'd picked up the night before. She knew Bear wouldn't let her get involved, which meant she had to do her own investigation. And now she had *two* partners in crime.

"Bea—my dad found a body in the backyard."

"*What?*" they both hissed.

"Are you serious?" Marcus asked. He had abandoned his apple.

She nodded and leaned closer. They mirrored her movement. "He was out digging a garden and dug up this old septic tank. When he opened it up, there were bones inside. *Human* bones."

Marcus' eyes lit up. "Cool."

"Who was it?" Laura Lynn asked. "Do you know? Do you think your dad—"

"Not yet, and no. But the sheriff and some state troopers were over. I heard some stuff. They think the body's been in there at least ten or fifteen years." Excited as she was by all the action, it also made her sad. "Can you believe that? Not knowing where your kid has been for the last fifteen years. Not knowing if she's still alive or dead." When Laura Lynn and Marcus exchanged a look, she frowned. "What?"

"Do you know how many kids die around here? Or go missing?" When Mandy shook her head, Marcus continued. "A lot. Like, *a lot* a lot."

"How?" she asked. "Why?"

"Lots of reasons," Laura Lynn said. "Cancer. Running away. Murder. There are lots of stories like that. Kids going crazy and sent to insane asylums."

Marcus sat straighter in his chair. "I don't believe all of them. Jake used to try to freak me out by telling me if I didn't clean my room, all the kids from the mental hospital would escape and eat me alive." He glanced to the side and shook his head. "What an asshat."

"Who's Jake?" Mandy asked.

"My older brother. He's in college now." Marcus started in on his sandwich, talking through a mouthful of food. "But he said his friend's brother died that way. Some rare disease or something. Totally incurable."

"That's pretty weird," Mandy said.

"Maybe that's what happened to the girl in the septic tank," Laura Lynn offered. "Maybe she went crazy and fell in."

"And what?" Marcus asked. "Her parents just closed it up and forgot about her? I doubt it."

"Then it was probably murder," Mandy said. Another thrill went through her, but a twinge of fear followed this one. "We should look into it. Do our own investigation."

Laura Lynn and Marcus both looked down at their plates. Marcus was the first to answer. "I don't know about that."

"What?" Mandy felt confused. She had figured at least Marcus would be into the idea, even if Laura Lynn wasn't. "Aren't you a computer genius? You could help me solve the case! We'd be heroes."

"It's not worth it." When he looked up again, he was deadly serious. "A lot of people have gone missing over the years, Mandy. Not just kids. It's better to just keep your head down. Don't cause any trouble."

Mandy blanched. When she looked at Laura Lynn for support, she saw her friend nodding in agreement. Mandy sat back in her chair with a huff, the turkey and cheese sandwich untouched. So much for showing Bear she could take care of herself by solving this on her own.

9

Bear pulled his truck next to McKinnon's cruiser and put it in park. He hopped out and met her around the side of her car. "A graveyard? This is about to get real interesting, or real weird."

"Let's hope it gets interesting," McKinnon said.

The slam of her door echoed through the surrounding trees, and the two of them trudged their way up a set of steps to the cemetery. Bear had passed it a few times as he'd driven around town. It was the biggest within a twenty-mile radius, but it wasn't huge. The gravestones were crammed near each other, filling the entire plot of land to the brim.

There was a short wrought-iron fence around the perimeter and a plaque that read "April Meadows Cemetery" in block letters. A few trees were scattered around, along with a couple of larger headstones, but most of the markers were small and modest. The paths were skinny and winding, as though they had been an afterthought.

"What're we doing here?" Bear asked.

"Just observe." McKinnon walked through the stones with no apparent purpose in mind. "Tell me what you see."

"Why?" Bear felt the frustration mount in his chest. He didn't enjoy being out of the loop. "Why are you asking me?"

McKinnon stopped and turned to face him. He had to pull up short to avoid knocking her off her feet. "You're more than you say you are." Her expression was unreadable. "And I think you can help me." She paused. "I *need* you to help me. I'm not sure anyone else will."

Something in her voice softened Bear. This wasn't a person who wanted to dig into his past because she was curious about what he was doing here. She recognized a kinship—a newcomer who was smarter and more experienced than the Average Joe.

McKinnon must've seen Bear give in because she smiled and turned on her heel. They remained silent as she wound her way through the gravestones, and Bear went into Sherlock mode. He looked at every stone on either side of the path and gathered information, even if his brain didn't think it was relevant at first glance. There was no telling what McKinnon was looking for, so he stored it all in the back of his mind.

Bear first noticed the family names. A few of the founding families were in this plot, going back a couple hundred years. Schmidt, Müller, Zimmermann, and Richter. All German. The Richter plots were more ornate than the others, but the Müllers had the most headstones. Some names had changed over the years as families immigrated later —Smith, Miller, Zimmer—but Bear was willing to bet they were related.

Second, he noticed the dates. As McKinnon led him to the far corner of the cemetery, the years reached further and further back. She stopped at what seemed to be the first grave in the cemetery. Johann Richter, 1887. In loving memory.

Bear made a noncommittal sound of interest.

"What do you see?"

He studied her for a moment. She looked wary, almost scared. Like she knew something no one else did, and she was bursting at the seams to share. But that kind of trust in another human being often came with consequences. Especially if you'd just met that person the day before.

"Only the back quarter of the graveyard has headstones from the nineteen-forties or earlier." Bear pointed back toward the entrance. "Another quarter or so from before the nineteen-seventies. That's eighty years to make up fifty percent of the cemetery."

"And?" McKinnon sounded like a teacher whose student was *this close* to working out the right answer for himself.

"That means the other half of the graveyard has stones from nineteen-seventy to present day. Forty or fifty years." Bear was pacing now. "And the dates are off."

"Off?"

"Most old gravestones show people dying before they hit fifty. Many people died early back then because of poor healthcare and sanitation. Not to mention working conditions." Bear stopped and looked at the sheriff. "But there are a lot of newer graves here, and a lot more people dying around the same age. The death rate is going up, not down. People are dying younger."

"Bingo."

Bear shook his head. "So, what does it mean? Why?"

McKinnon shrugged. "Hell if I know. Like I said, our death rates are astronomical. Did you know Union County, Florida, has the highest rate of cancer in the United States? Just over two hundred cases a year. We have half that and an eighth of the population. It doesn't make sense."

"You mentioned suicide rates, too? Illnesses?"

"Las Vegas, Nevada, has the highest rate of suicide annually. Just over thirty people per one hundred thousand residents. Do you know what the population of Las Vegas is? A little over six hundred thousand people. That means one hundred and eighty people are killing themselves a year in Vegas."

Bear was almost afraid to ask. "And here?"

"Twenty in the last year." She shook her head. "And it's not like it is in Vegas. Nameless people. Faces on the street. I knew every single one of those people. Mothers. Fathers. Children. *Children.*" There were tears in her eyes. "A twelve-year-old who didn't think life was worth living anymore. What kind of place is this if a middle schooler feels he'd be better off dead?"

Bear took a step closer. He wanted to put a reassuring hand on her shoulder but resisted. "What's going on, Sheriff? Why is this happening?"

"I don't know." When McKinnon looked up into Bear's eyes, he saw the kind of determination that could change the course of his stay in this small town. It was a choice—help or stay out of the way. "But I think it has something to do with that girl you found in your septic tank. Whatever happened to her has happened to others."

"She was murdered." Bear didn't want to dissuade her from following through on the thought, but he needed to keep them grounded. "It wasn't cancer. And it probably wasn't suicide."

"Lots of people go missing around here," McKinnon said. "Men, women, children. A lot more children than people would like to admit. Some people think they run away. That this town is cursed. They feel like those missing kids might be better off away from here."

"But you don't think they are."

"They're either dead or worse." She shook her head. "They've stepped out of one fire and into another."

"Are there any common links?" Bear asked. "Any patterns?" He gestured around the graveyard. "You've got plenty of data to look at. There's gotta be something that jumps out at you."

"That's the problem." McKinnon laughed, borderline hysterical. "There's information missing. Years of our records that don't exist." When Bear opened his mouth to ask about it, she held up a hand. "I know what you're going to say, but whoever did it, whether it's one person or many, covered their tracks. This office building burned down. That basement flooded. Someone stole them. A computer got hacked. A hard drive blew up." She leveled him a look. "Don't ask me how a hard drive blows up, because I don't know."

"Okay." Bear started pacing again. "So, you've got a conspiracy on your hands."

"Don't think I missed the way you say *you* and not *we*."

He shrugged. "Like I said, I'm just trying to keep my head down. I don't want any trouble."

"Trouble found you when you dug up that body." McKinnon looked sorry for him. "People aren't going to think you had anything to do with it, but you're new in town. Your name is tarnished. Small town residents will find any reason to ostracize outsiders."

"I'm not looking to make friends."

"What about enemies? People around here don't need an excuse to hate you. They'll do it on principle alone."

Bear sighed. "So, what are you going to do about it?"

"*Your* reputation?"

"*Your* conspiracy."

She shrugged. "I was going to ask you the same thing."

10

BEAR WAS HOME BY THE TIME MANDY CLIMBED OFF THE BUS AND RAN UP the driveway. He'd spent another half hour with McKinnon in the cemetery, but ultimately didn't give her an answer. He was sympathetic to the situation, but what could he do that she couldn't? She was the sheriff. She had more power to get answers than he ever would.

The situation still nagged at him. It tugged at the back of his mind like a needy toddler. Numbers swirled in his head—percentages of this and rates of that, birthdates and death dates, populations. He kept on until he found himself staring into space and trying to put it all together, like a puzzle with missing pieces. He knew McKinnon was on to something, but until they had some idea of the big picture, he had no way of helping her.

Not that he was ready to stick his neck out for her, he reminded himself. She was a good person—a good cop—and he could tell she cared about this town and these people. But this was supposed to be his retirement. His reprieve from the life he had led before this one. He wanted Mandy to go to a good school, learn how to be around kids her age. She deserved to live a normal life. And it was his job to give it to her.

As if on cue, Mandy burst through the front door, breathless and excited. He chuckled. "It's nice to see you so excited to do your homework."

"Yeah, yeah." She turned away. "I know the rules. But I had an interesting day at school."

"Did you?" This was a first. Mandy talked little about school, and Bear didn't press. He knew how hard it was to be the new kid. "What happened?"

"Made a new friend."

"Oh yeah?" He went to the kitchen and poured her a glass of water. "Who?"

"Marcus."

"The kid you saved from Pete?"

"Yeah." Mandy drained the glass before Bear even had a chance to put the pitcher away. "He's, like, a tech genius. He was telling us about all the computers he has. Even built his own."

"That's pretty cool." Bear filled the glass up again and handed it to her. "He's not committing any crimes, is he?"

"No idea." Mandy didn't seem all that concerned if he was, and Bear couldn't blame her. Their shared definition of criminal activity was more than a little blurry. "He's really smart. Knows a lot of stuff."

Bear didn't miss the way her cheeks were flushed, and he didn't think it was just from the run up the driveway. But he wasn't ready to talk to her about boys and crushes. He had enough on his plate. "That's very impressive. Knowing stuff."

Mandy ignored him. She stiffened. "I told him about the body." When Bear's eyes narrowed, Mandy held up her hand. "Everyone already saw the cop cars. They thought it was because I beat up Pete. They were going to find out sooner or later, Bear. All the parents will be talking about it, and the kids will hear it one way or another."

"Fair point," Bear grumbled.

"So, I told him about the body. And you know what he said? There are lots of people who go missing around here. A lot of kids who die of cancer and stuff."

Bear didn't let on that he knew more about what she was saying. "Yeah?"

Mandy's voice got quiet. "Laura Lynn thinks it's a sign."

"A sign of what?"

She shrugged. "Bad things. Do you think—" Mandy's voice cut off, and it surprised Bear to see tears in her eyes. "Do you think we deserve it?"

Bear guided her to the table, and they sat down across from each other. He wasn't always good at this stuff—the quieter part of being a dad. Usually, he went from zero to a hundred trying to protect Mandy. But sometimes it was just about checking for monsters under the bed.

Unfortunately, a lot of their monsters were real.

"Deserve what?" Bear asked.

"Bad things to happen to us."

"No. Especially not to you." Bear took her hand. "I've done a lot of things I wish I could take back, but I've always tried to make up for it. No matter what, I try to keep the balance in favor of the good guys. That's really the best we can do." He ducked his head to look her in the eyes. "And you know you haven't done anything wrong, right? Life dealt you a crappy hand, but that doesn't mean you deserved it."

Mandy nodded her head. "Do you think our house is haunted?"

He chuckled. "If it was, it wouldn't have been so expensive."

"What do you think happened to her?" Mandy took another sip of water. "The girl?"

"I'm not sure." Bear had always treated Mandy more like an adult than a kid. She was too smart to fall for the usual tricks, and he knew better than most that the world wouldn't be kind to her. The last thing he wanted to do was scare her, but he also wanted her to be ready for whatever came at them. "I think she was murdered."

"Why?"

He shrugged. "Don't know. Lots of different reasons. She saw something she shouldn't have. Maybe it was a message to her parents. Maybe it was an accident, and someone buried her to hide their mistake."

"Are you gonna try to figure it out?"

"Not sure that's a good idea."

"Why not?" Mandy frowned. "I thought we tried to help the people who couldn't help themselves. You know, keep the balance."

Bear sighed. She had him there. "We're also supposed to be—"

"Lying low." Mandy sighed. "I know. But what if that was me, Bear? Wouldn't you want to know what happened?"

"I'd stop at nothing to find you." Bear's voice was a growl, and he had to work to suppress the sudden anger that overtook him at the idea of someone hurting Mandy. "I'd do anything to get you back."

"I wish that girl had a dad like you." Mandy sounded sad. "Maybe she wouldn't have died."

Bear couldn't bring himself to tell her it didn't always work like that.

She sat up straight, a new light in her eyes. "What about talking to the neighbors? Maybe some of them have been around for a while. They could know something."

"I'm not sure that's such a good idea." He looked at the clock. It wasn't even dinnertime yet, so he couldn't use that as an excuse. "The more we get involved, the more trouble we invite to our doorstep."

"Marcus and Laura Lynn seemed scared, too." Mandy deflated. "They said it was better to stay out of it, or something bad might happen to one of us." She looked up, and her eyes were wide. "But I just want to help. And you always win, Bear. You always beat the bad guys."

He didn't know what to say. That one of these days, he was bound to lose? The numbers weren't on his side, and he was still recovering from his latest surgery. Or was he supposed to tell her he was tired? Tired of being on the run, tired of looking over his shoulder, tired of worrying about whether he'd wake up in the middle of the night with vengeance standing over him.

Bear didn't want to help because he wanted to be selfish for the first time in his life. He wanted to put himself and his daughter first. He wanted to relax. Finding the body in his backyard was a coincidence, but for all he had reassured Mandy, it felt a lot like retribution. He had a duty to help others, but for once, he wanted to look the other way.

Except there was no way he could tell her that. As she sat there with hope in her eyes, Bear felt the weight of the world pressing down on his shoulders.

11

BEAR USED HIS THUMB AND FOREFINGER TO SPLIT THE BLINDS. IT WAS A bright fall day with just enough chill in the air to make you want to sit down with a cup of coffee and read the newspaper. Autumn in Upstate New York was picturesque. The leaves on the trees were just turning, and there wasn't a cloud in the sky.

The irony of this perfect day was that Bear's new life was falling apart around him.

He hadn't expected it to happen so soon. Then again, he had no way of anticipating finding a body in his backyard. Paranoia had crept in, and he couldn't help feeling an unbearable itch to leave.

That morning, his house had been on the news. Two separate reporters—one from the local station and one from Rochester—had stood on the sidewalk outside his home and gathered footage for about an hour. Every fiber of his being wanted to chase them off. He resisted. For now. So far, the news had no information about the man who had found the body, and he was going to keep it that way.

Mandy had already left for school by the time the news story ran. He felt a pang of guilt for not giving her a better heads up that her entire school would be talking about what had happened at her house. But she was a smart kid. She'd already told her friends about the body because she knew this would happen eventually. She was thinking more clearly than he was.

When she asked if she could sleep over at Laura Lynn's house that night, he'd jumped at the opportunity. He was keeping up pretenses for Mandy, but without her around, he'd have a little more liberty to dig into the situation. Now that it was getting wider attention, he'd have to decide to make a move or get moving.

Bear's ears perked up as a car with a loud muffler approached the house. It was a red Honda Civic that had seen better days. It didn't slow down or turn into the driveway, so Bear stored it in his memory banks in case it made another trip down the street.

That morning, he'd caught four different vehicles slowing and staring at the house, like they could glean information from the siding if they made prolonged eye contact. One of the vehicles had actually pulled into the driveway, backed out, and then went back the way it came. Maybe someone really had needed to turn around, but given the size of the town, he doubted it. By this time, everyone knew what had happened there. If you hadn't seen it on the news yourself, then your friend had, and they couldn't wait to tell you all about it. Including their theory of who the girl was and what had happened to her.

Bear let the blinds slip closed and scratched his nails through his beard. He couldn't stop thinking about what the sheriff had showed him the day before. All those gravestones from the last fifty years. So many people dying young. If there was a reason, some sort of conspiracy, why hadn't anyone spoken up about it? Especially with all those kids missing.

Fear made people do crazy things. Like keep their mouths shut. If they knew anything about what happened to their neighbor's kid, they wouldn't say something for fear of what would happen to their own. But that kind of thinking only took the spotlight off you and yours. Some other poor sap would end up biting the bullet instead.

A dog barked outside, and Bear split the blinds again. A young couple with a cocker spaniel walked by, glancing up at the house. The woman pointed at the window. They must've seen him staring out because they ducked their heads and rushed off. For as much time as

Bear had spent home over the last month, he'd never seen them before. How far had they walked just to get a glimpse of the house?

He backed away from the window. The urge to get out intensified, even if it meant risking someone tracking him down or asking him questions. He was a ticking time bomb, and every second he spent inside meant the pressure continued to build. He wasn't doing himself any favors worrying about what would happen next. He was always better at taking action and dealing with the consequences.

Considering he'd have a night to himself, Bear jumped in his truck and headed to the grocery store. A nice steak, a couple of potatoes, and a bottle of vodka would do the trick. Not enough to make him sloppy, but enough to take the edge off. He'd relax tonight, get a good night's sleep, and then regroup tomorrow. Soon enough, he'd decide one way or another—stay and figure out what the hell was going on or leave and find him and Mandy a new place to settle down. Preferably a less eventful town.

As soon as Bear entered the grocery store, he knew it had been a mistake. Both cashiers, two blonde teenagers, silenced their gossip at the sight of him and followed his every move as he grabbed a basket and headed down the first aisle. He could feel their gaze boring into the back of his head. It seemed some people did know who lived in that house.

Bear ignored the looks and the whispers. He felt more comfortable sticking to the shadows, but that wasn't an option in a well-lit grocery store. Which meant he needed to get his stuff and get out. Go home. Eat. Drink. Sleep. Regroup.

His task list in mind, Bear grabbed the two largest russet potatoes he could find and tossed them into his basket. He added some onions and mushrooms to top his steak. If he weathered this storm, he wouldn't have to come to the grocery store for most of this stuff in the future. It'd be in his back yard, ripe for the picking. Too bad you couldn't grow steak from the dirt, too.

No one approached him until he was standing over beef cuts, trying to decide if he wanted to go big or go home. He saw the woman walk up to him from his side, but he kept his head down. She wasn't being subtle, and he didn't want to give her the satisfaction of thinking he had noticed her in any capacity.

It was only when she cleared her throat and tapped him on the arm that Bear looked up. She was about ten years older than him, with bottle-blond hair, a heavy face of makeup, and a wedding ring she hid behind her back as soon as she realized Bear had noticed it. One of her front teeth had a faint smear of lipstick.

"Hey," she purred. She batted her eyelashes like Bear couldn't see right through her performance. "My name is Sheila."

Bear didn't respond. He stared at her like he was mute.

She cleared her throat, some of her confidence draining away. "I just wanted to say I'm so sorry about what happened at your house the other day. What a tragedy."

"Why are you sorry?" He screwed his face up into a puzzled expression. "Are you the one who killed her?"

Sheila took a step back. "No, of course not."

"Oh. Then why are you apologizing?"

"I'm just, you know, sorry that it happened to you."

"No, you're not." Bear couldn't help but enjoy the way he'd thrown her off-kilter so easily. "I'll give you credit, though. You were the only one brave enough to come up to me. Everyone else is just whispering behind my back." He pointed at an elderly couple who startled and shuffled off in the other direction. Bear threw a pair of steaks into his basket. He didn't even care if they were a good cut or not. "But it's not going to happen, lady. I'm not interested."

"Interested in what?"

Bear looked her up and down, then brushed by her. "Any of it."

On his way to the registers, he rearranged his face into a scowl and broadened his shoulders so he'd look even bigger. The girl behind the counter didn't make eye contact with him. She scanned his items while the other one bagged his groceries, and he was out of there in less than two minutes. It was a good thing he had vodka at home, because he wasn't in the mood to stop anywhere else.

If Bear hadn't already thought leaving was a mistake, by the time he pulled into his driveway, he'd confirmed it. A man stood in his front yard, snapping pictures of the house on a professional camera. Bear launched himself out of his truck, barely putting it in park first, but the man was too fast. He blurred as he sprinted off to the woods. He knew where he was going, aiming for the street parallel to this one on the other side of the trees.

Bear grabbed his groceries and stormed through the door. He tossed the bag on the counter and worked his way through the entire house. There were no surprises waiting for him. He walked the perimeter of the backyard and found everything undisturbed. Then he spent the next hour walking from window to window, peering through the blinds to make sure no one else spent longer than ten seconds looking at his house.

He glanced at the clock. Just past one in the afternoon. It was going to be a long evening, and no amount of steak or vodka would make it better.

12

MANDY SAT IN LAURA LYNN'S BASEMENT WITH HER KNEES TO HER CHEST and her arms wrapped around her legs. They were watching some terrible horror movie about a zombie cowboy. Laura Lynn kept falling asleep. Her head would drift to the side until the screaming started, then she'd jolt awake and pretend like she hadn't missed a thing. Sure enough, two minutes later, she was asleep again.

But Mandy didn't mind. This was the first sleepover she'd ever had. It was exciting to have a friend like Laura Lynn, even if Laura Lynn didn't know everything about her. She wanted to tell Laura Lynn about everything she'd seen and experienced, but not because she wanted to brag. She wanted someone other than Bear to talk to. Someone her age who would be impressed and scared and sympathetic.

For all Bear did to keep Mandy safe, a lot of this stuff wasn't a big deal to him. Sure, she'd caught him anxious or afraid or angry, but he knew how to deal with it. Roll with the punches, as he liked to say. Even though Mandy felt older than her fourteen years, sometimes she wanted to act like a kid. She hated the fact that she had to sit with her back against the wall or keep people in her peripherals, or check every room in the house before she could settle down for the night. It was exhausting.

The zombie cowboy ripped someone's arm clean from its socket, and the man screamed in such a high-pitched voice it made Mandy giggle. Laura Lynn jolted awake again. She laughed along with Mandy, but her eyes were already drooping.

Mandy hit pause on the movie. "Okay, this movie was your idea, and you're not even watching it."

Laura Lynn groaned and pulled the blanket up over her head. She offered a muffled response, but Mandy couldn't make out any words.

Mandy pulled the blanket back down. "What?"

"I'm sorry." Laura Lynn looked like she meant it. "I'm so tired. I haven't been sleeping well lately."

"Why not? What's going on?" Mandy lowered her voice. "Is it your dad?"

Mandy had only met Laura Lynn's dad once, but she didn't like him. He was always stressed out and angry, and he took it out on the rest of his family. He never hit them, at least as far as Mandy knew, but he was mean. Laura Lynn's mother got the brunt of it, but Laura Lynn couldn't escape it either.

"I don't know." Laura Lynn put her arms across her stomach. "I just haven't been feeling very good lately. I keep getting cramps. Sometimes I throw up."

Mandy lowered her voice even more. "Is it your period?"

Laura Lynn shook her head. "No. No. Definitely not. I thought maybe it was something I ate but then it kept getting worse. Perhaps I'm allergic to something?"

"That's why you haven't been eating lunch." Mandy reached past Laura Lynn and grabbed her glass of water. "Here, chug this. I'll go get some more. You might be dehydrated."

Laura Lynn took a tiny sip and then hugged the glass to her chest. When Mandy narrowed her eyes at her, she took a few more sips before setting it down. "It hurts if I drink too much too fast."

"Have you told your mom about it yet?"

She shook her head. "Don't want to bother her with it. Figured it'd go away by now." She blew a piece of hair from her face and turned to

Mandy. She put on a brave look, but Mandy could see past it. "Anyway, how are you? We didn't really talk about school today."

Mandy looked away. Her first few classes had passed by in blissful ignorance, but when lunch rolled around, she couldn't ignore the whispers anymore. It felt like every single person had been talking about the body Bear had found in their backyard. She'd even heard people referring to her as Septic Tank Girl. It made Mandy want to punch something. Or *someone*.

And she almost did. Pete had apparently not learned his lesson the first time around because it felt like he was leading the pack. He spread insane rumors that people would realize were lies if they took more than two seconds to think about them. Like saying the girl was Mandy's sister or that Bear had buried the girl in their back yard and then felt so guilty, he called the police on himself. Most people didn't seem to believe the rumors, but they still spread them from person to person anyway. And it all led to everyone looking at her like she was a charity case. She hated that feeling.

"It'll blow over soon," Mandy said, more for herself than Laura Lynn. "They'll get bored, and something more exciting will happen, and they'll forget about me."

"More exciting than a dead body?" Laura Lynn winced and clutched her stomach tighter. After a few breaths, she seemed to relax. "I doubt it. Especially if Pete is out to get revenge. He'll do anything to make the whole school hate you."

"I'm not worried about it." A half-truth. She didn't need everyone to like her. Laura Lynn and Marcus were enough. "Besides, he's in as much trouble as I am. He's going to get even more detention when they find out he's spreading the rumors."

"How *was* detention today?"

Mandy shrugged. "Got all my homework done. Even with Pete shooting spitballs at me every time Mrs. Turner looked away."

Laura Lynn opened her mouth to say something else when she closed her eyes and groaned. Mandy didn't think it was possible, but she turned even whiter than before. Laura Lynn shot to her feet, and then just stood there. She looked torn between running out of the room and just collapsing on the spot.

"I don't feel good."

Mandy didn't have time to ask her what was going on before Laura Lynn rushed to the bathroom and hunched over the toilet. She didn't even bother closing the door. Next came the sound of heaving. Mandy rushed over and pulled Laura Lynn's hair away from her face. She wasn't sure what else to do.

After a few minutes, Laura Lynn slid away from the toilet and laid her head on the cool tile floor. If it wasn't for her heavy breathing, Mandy might've thought she was dead. She reached down and checked Laura Lynn's pulse. It was racing, and her wrist was slick with sweat.

"I'm going to get your mom."

Laura Lynn groaned. Mandy thought she heard the world *no* somewhere in there.

Mandy hesitated. She didn't want to get Laura Lynn in trouble, but she was worried about her friend. Maybe if she just drank more water and threw up a few more times, she could get it out of her system. But when Mandy turned to leave and grab her glass, she caught sight of the toilet, and her stomach clenched at the amount of blood.

13

When the doorbell rang, Bear intended to chase off whichever news reporter or nosy neighbor had been bold enough to see if they could get some answers out of him. His mood had soured to the point of active hostility. Part of him was glad Mandy wasn't home to see him brooding, but the other part knew he would've kept it together better if she were here.

When he opened the door, he found himself face to face with McKinnon. He wasn't sure if she was a welcome distraction, or if she'd end up making his evening worse. It depended on whether she came bearing bad news or good.

"Evening, Sheriff." He didn't bother reining in the gruff of his voice. "What's up?"

"I've got some additional information on the girl. Thought you might like to hear it."

Bear studied her face. It didn't seem likely she had ventured to his neck of the woods to keep the homeowner informed—she wasn't required to do that. It appeared as though she had invited herself over to see if she could shake any information loose. After yesterday's events, he could see why. If her theory was correct and the conspiracy was as big as she thought, she could trust few people. Normally, you wouldn't lean on the new guy in town, but he might be her only ally.

"Yeah, come in." He stepped to the side, then shut the door and led her to the kitchen. "Tonight's drink is vodka. You in?"

She tipped her head to the side in contemplation. "Yeah, I'll have one." She took it with a nod of thanks. "Rough day?"

"Assume you've seen the news?"

"Yeah. Sorry about that. We tried to keep it quiet, but people talk. Small town and all." She sipped at her drink, then made a face. "Strong."

"Puts hair on your chest." Bear slammed his drink back and poured another. "I went to the store earlier and came back to a guy on my front lawn, snapping pictures like he works for *Better Homes & Gardens*."

"Get a good look at him?"

"Not really. Tall, skinny. Dark hair. Fast."

"Could be anyone." McKinnon pointed at a kitchen chair, and when Bear nodded, she pulled it out and sat. "If they give you too much grief, call me. I can assign one of my guys to watch your house."

Bear scoffed. He had to work his face back to a neutral position. "Appreciate the offer, but there's nothing they can do that I can't."

"Legally?"

He shrugged. It was a slow, arrogant motion. "They won't find any evidence. There's nothing *to* find."

"They don't know that."

"It's more a pain in my elbow than anything. But I appreciate the offer." Bear took a sip of his drink, topped it off, then sat down across from her. "What kind of information did you dig up?"

"Finding that piece of hair was a huge break. We're very lucky it stayed preserved. Wouldn't know half of what we do without it." She let that sink in for a moment. "Her name was Katie Lamoureux. She was twelve years old. Almost thirteen."

"Christ." Bear tipped his drink back but stopped short of finishing it in one go. He knew she was young, but putting a number to it made it ten times worse. "She one of the missing persons?"

McKinnon nodded. "Went missing a couple days before her thirteenth birthday. Her parents said she wasn't the kind of kid to wander off, but her best friend at the time said they had been planning to run away. Police looked for a bit. They figured that's what happened when she didn't show up. The best friend maintained Katie wouldn't have run off without her."

"Any connection between the Lamoureux family and the guy who owned this place—Olson?"

"Other than the fact that they both worked at HealTek, no. They were in different departments. Were they friends? Did they hang out? Grab lunch together? There's no way of knowing, really. It was almost fifteen years ago now."

"How'd she die?"

McKinnon pulled a piece of paper out of her pocket. "That's where it gets interesting." She unfolded it and spread it out between them. "She was poisoned."

Bear leaned forward, trying to read the toxicology report. "There are worse ways to go."

"I'm not so sure." She pointed to the page. "Hypernatremia. She was dehydrated. Hyperkalemia. Too much potassium. Hyperglycemia. Too much blood sugar. The list goes on."

"So, she was either a very sick kid, or—"

"She was poisoned." McKinnon shook her head. "Her friend, Eileen, had stated she was having cramps and throwing up before she disappeared. The police didn't think much of it since they determined way too soon she ran away."

"Frequent vomiting explains the dehydration."

"Hyperglycemia can cause vomiting. Too much potassium can make you weak."

"I doubt she fell into that tank on her own," Bear said. "Maybe someone poisoned her so she wouldn't put up a fight?"

"She was a tiny kid." McKinnon shook her head. "And from what I've read, pretty quiet. Kept to herself. Did well in school. Never got in trouble. I don't think an adult would have to do much to overpower her or convince her to come with them."

"So, intentional poisoning then."

"The problem is, we don't recognize what it is." McKinnon folded up the paper and stuffed it back in her pocket. "I had my guys go through it three times. They matched these issues with the other trace elements in her system. Nothing adds up to any common poisons."

"What about the uncommon ones?"

"Some of them almost fit the criteria, but there's nothing that's a perfect match."

"Something new?"

"New fifteen years ago," McKinnon said. "You'd think we'd be aware of it by now."

"You'd think."

There was a beat of silence. Both took a sip of their drinks and stared off into the distance.

"There's another problem," McKinnon added.

"I think we have enough to worry about at the moment."

McKinnon didn't laugh. She didn't even crack a smile. "The reason I left the other day is because my neighbor's daughter was just diagnosed with cancer. Inoperable. Untreatable. She's going to die within the next six months to a year. She's fifteen."

Bear finished his drink. He didn't know what to say.

"I think she was poisoned." McKinnon met his gaze with watery eyes.

"Poisoned?" Bear failed to keep the disbelief out of his voice. "With cancer?"

"She was fine six months ago. Not a care in the world. Bubbly, outgoing. Good kid." McKinnon rolled her glass between her hands, watching as the liquid sloshed up the sides. "Then she started getting sick. Slowly. Weakness, nausea, vomiting. Muscle cramps. She started wasting away. Getting paler and thinner. She had no interest in anything anymore. Quit sports. Quit doing art. She loves horseback riding. One day, she just decided she didn't want to do it anymore. Couldn't. It was too painful to ride.

"They took her to the doctor." It didn't take a genius to see what came next. "And found cancer."

"She had a tumor the size of a softball in her stomach. And smaller tumors throughout her body." McKinnon looked up at him. "She will die, no matter what they do. She won't see sixteen. And if she does, won't be nothing sweet about it."

Bear considered pouring himself another drink, but he knew it would only make him feel worse in the long run. "The cancer caused all that?"

"Some of it. That's the problem. They couldn't explain all the symptoms."

"Which is why you think she was poisoned."

"It's just a working theory." McKinnon sat back and blew out a breath of air. It ruffled the hair around her face. "But Katie Lamoureux's symptoms wouldn't have looked dissimilar. Maybe she had cancer, too, but we couldn't detect anything from the sample we had."

"Someone buried Katie. Which meant they thought someone would figure out it wasn't a natural death."

"But why would someone want a twelve-year-old dead?"

Bear opened his mouth to spout a couple of possible reasons when the vibration of his phone interrupted them. He reached deep into his pocket and pulled it out. "It's Mandy." He hit answer and held the device to his ear. "Hey, kid. What's up?"

"Can you come pick me up?" Her voice was muffled, like she didn't want anyone to hear her. "Like, right now?"

Bear sat up straight. Alarm bells went off in his head. All the alcohol drained from his system, and his mind felt sharp and clear. "What's wrong?"

"Laura Lynn keeps throwing up. I saw blood and told her mom and she's freaking out. I just want to come home." There was a desperation in Mandy's voice that he rarely heard. "Please."

Bear locked eyes with McKinnon, who looked as on edge as he felt. "I'm on my way."

14

BEAR THREW THE TRUCK INTO PARK, JUMPED OUT, AND SPRINTED UP THE driveway. He heard McKinnon call after him, but the world was a blur of sights and sounds. He considered the consequences of bursting through the front door of Laura Lynn's house versus knocking and waiting for someone to answer. Mandy saved him the hassle by opening it first.

He came to a halt, sweat-drenched and panting. Not from exertion, but anxiety. It took him a moment to comprehend Mandy standing in front of him. She was safe. He knelt in front of her. "You okay?"

"I'm fine." She almost sounded annoyed. "It's Laura Lynn..."

"But you're fine? You don't feel sick?" For all Bear wasn't sure about McKinnon's theory, he wasn't about to put Mandy's life on the line to test it. "Do you have any symptoms?"

"Symptoms of what?" Mandy looked over his shoulder at the approaching sheriff. "What's going on?"

McKinnon put a hand on Bear's shoulder. "We should talk to her. Both of them."

Bear's first instinct was to get as far from this as possible, but when he looked into Mandy's eyes, he knew that wasn't an option. They'd only been here for a month, and Laura Lynn was the first and only friend Mandy had made around her age. The rest had been agents and killers and mercenaries. Bear owed it to her to find out what was going on.

"Are they still inside?"

Mandy nodded and led the two of them through the entrance and into the living room, where Laura Lynn lay groaning on the couch. Her mother was preparing something in the kitchen, and they could hear her speaking in low murmurs, as though she were on the phone but didn't want anyone to hear.

McKinnon approached the couch and knelt next to Laura Lynn while Bear and Mandy hung back. "Hey," she whispered. "My name is Josie. You're Laura Lynn, right?"

The girl nodded. Even from a distance, Bear could tell she looked pale and tiny, like she hadn't been eating. She was too weak to pick up her head, but she pointed her finger to the glass of water sitting on the table next to her. The sheriff picked it up and let Laura Lynn take a tiny sip. A bit of water dribbled down her chin.

Setting the glass back on the table, McKinnon wiped away the droplet of water with the cuff of her sleeve. She smiled down at the girl. "What's been going on? You're not feeling well?"

Laura Lynn shook her head. "My stomach hurts." Her voice was so weak, Bear had to take a step forward to hear her. "I threw up."

"I'm sorry to hear that." McKinnon wrapped two fingers around the girl's wrist to take her pulse. "Do you know why? Was it something you ate?" When Laura Lynn shook her head, McKinnon smiled gently. "That's okay. We're gonna figure it out, okay?"

As Laura Lynn closed her eyes, her mother walked back into the room with some soup. She noticed Bear first and startled, almost dropping the bowl. Then her gaze slid over to her daughter, and to the sheriff, who was now standing next to her. "What's going on?"

The Sheriff stepped forward. "Mrs. Weinberger?"

"Cynthia."

"Cynthia. I'm sorry to barge in on you like this. Mandy let us in."

Bear offered his hand, which Cynthia took gingerly. "My name is

Riley. I'm Mandy's father. She was worried about her friend. Your daughter seems pretty sick."

"It's nice to meet you." The woman didn't look like she meant it, but decorum forced her to repeat the words anyway. She put the bowl of soup down on the table next to the water. "Laura Lynn is fine. It's a little cold."

"She threw up blood." Mandy's voice was even, but Bear could sense her frustration. "I don't think it's just a cold, Mrs. Weinberger."

"I've been sick, too. So has my husband. It's nothing." As if on cue, the woman's chest heaved, and she went into a coughing fit. She pulled a tissue from her pocket and covered her mouth. When it passed, she stuffed the tissue back in her pocket, but not before Bear saw a drop of blood on it. "It'll pass."

"I don't think you're—" Bear started, but McKinnon held up a hand to cut him off.

"This is not the first time I've seen this sickness," McKinnon said. "It's imperative you get your entire family to the doctor before it gets worse."

"My husband, he—" She cut herself off, embarrassed.

Bear knew what that look meant. "What doesn't he want you to say to us?"

When the woman shook her head, McKinnon took a gentler approach. "That's fine. But I need you to tell me if you've eaten anything or drank anything that could've done this. Taken any pills? Any drugs? Something your daughter could've gotten into?"

"No, nothing." Mrs. Weinberger looked scared now. "We haven't eaten anything out of the ordinary. We don't have any drugs in the house. Not even prescription."

"When did the symptoms start?" McKinnon asked. "Yours? Your husband's?"

The woman opened her mouth to answer, but the front door flew open and a man in a dark suit rushed into the room. He was short and fat, with a balding head. He ripped his jacket off, revealing the sweat stains under his arms. "What's going on here? Who the hell are you?" He glared at his wife. "*What* did you tell them?"

Bear put himself between the man and the other women. He held up his hands in peace. "Whoa, there. Calm down."

"Don't you dare tell me to calm down in my own home!" Mr. Weinberger only came up to Bear's shoulder, but he didn't look afraid of the stranger in his house. "Get out! All of you. You don't have permission to be here. Especially you, Sheriff."

McKinnon took a step forward. "Your daughter is very sick—"

"That's for me and my wife to deal with." He pointed to the door, and Bear got a whiff of the body odor emanating off him. He smelled like salami. "Get out."

Bear pushed Mandy toward the door and waited for McKinnon to follow. He let the two of them out first and then turned to face Weinberger. He brought himself up to his full height and then stepped forward. "Take care of it." Bear glanced over at Laura Lynn. "Or I will."

Weinberger didn't have a chance to reply before Bear turned on his heel and stormed down the driveway. A second later, the door slammed, and they could hear muffled fighting from inside. It was mostly Weinberger's voice, punctuated by screaming sobs from his wife.

Bear started to go back inside, but Sheriff McKinnon put her hand on his arm. "You'll just make it worse. I'm calling an ambulance." She held the phone up to her ear. "Mrs. Weinberger won't turn them away."

Bear growled in defeat and slid behind the wheel of the truck. The Sheriff took the front passenger side, while Mandy buckled herself into the back. "None of them looked good. Did you see how much he was sweating? That's either fear or he's just as sick as they are."

"Her heart was racing. It—" She broke off. "Yes, this is Sheriff McKinnon. I'm requesting paramedics to…"

Bear ignored the rest of her words as he twisted around in his seat to catch a glimpse of Mandy. Her eyes were still wide and shining. "It's going to be okay. We'll make sure she gets to the hospital."

Mandy's voice was tiny. "Is *she* going to be okay?"

"I'm not sure." It was as close to the truth as he could get, especially after learning about what had happened to McKinnon's neighbors. "But we'll make sure someone looks at her. Best we can do right now, kid."

Mandy nodded and broke eye contact. She looked out the window and angrily wiped away a tear. Bear turned back around and gripped the steering wheel with both hands. He wanted to storm back inside and shake that man until he came to his senses. What was pride or fear when it came to your kid? You were supposed to do everything you could to protect them. What could be bigger than that?

Bear shifted the truck into reverse and turned out of the driveway before he did something he'd regret. McKinnon was still on the phone with the hospital, giving them as much information as she could. When she hung up, she dialed one of her deputies and filled them in on what had just transpired.

Bear was so focused on his thoughts he didn't even see the minivan driving on the wrong side of the road creep up alongside him. Just as he caught sight of the vehicle out of the corner of his eye, it slammed into them. The sound of vehicles colliding rivaled that of a bomb. The impact jolted everyone. Bear smacked his head against the window.

He kept his hands on the wheel, trying to keep the truck steady, but the minivan weighed more. It slammed into them again. The sheriff dropped her phone and cursed. She leaned forward, looking past him, trying to see who was driving. It was all Bear could do to keep an eye on the road ahead.

The street curved to the left. Bear punched the gas, racing to get ahead of the van. But the driver must've anticipated the move because he stayed neck-and-neck with the truck. He kept his vehicle straight right until the road turned, then he swerved to the left and back to the right, slamming into the side of the truck one more time.

Bear grunted as his head hit the window for a second time. The truck hit the shoulder, and the gravel twisted the wheels out from under him. It lurched one more time to the right, down a small hill, and over a bump in the grass that lifted him straight out of his seat. The top of his head slammed into the roof. A large oak filled his view. He used all his strength to crank the wheel to the left and then slam on the brakes. The tree clipped his right-side mirror, but the vehicle came to a stop without any major damage.

But the truck didn't matter. Mandy did. Twisting around, he looked to the backseat, where Mandy appeared shaken but whole. No blood or tears. She nodded silently, and Bear let out the breath he didn't know he was holding. When he twisted back, he caught sight of the van speeding off down the road through the haze of dust and dirt he'd kicked up on his way over the embankment.

"Everyone okay?" McKinnon shouted.

"We're good." Bear turned to her. "You okay?"

"No." McKinnon hunched over and scooped up her phone, which was still on the call with her deputy. "I'm pissed."

15

MANDY SAT ON MARCUS' BED AND LET HER LEGS SWING BACK AND FORTH, bumping off his bed frame in a rhythmic *thump, thump, thump.* His room was exactly how she had pictured it in her mind—covered in posters of sci-fi movies, cluttered with gadgets and gizmos, and smelling vaguely of nachos.

But it was clean. No dust—not on the blades of the ceiling fan or behind the TV or under the bed (she'd checked when he ran downstairs to get them a couple Cokes)—and no dirty clothes piled on the floor or shoved into the closet at the last minute. Even the controlled chaos of his tech toys made sense to her uneducated eyes. There was a place for everything, even if *everything* was all over his room.

"Here you go." Marcus handed her the soda. "What do you think?"

"Of what?"

"My room!" He beamed. "Isn't it awesome? My mom doesn't care what I do up here, as long as I keep it clean."

"That's awesome." She was happy for him. "I need some posters for my room."

"I have some extras, if you want."

"Maybe some other time."

Mandy tried to ignore the way his face fell. How could she tell him she didn't know how long she'd be living in her house? Decorating her room seemed pointless if they were only days away from moving again. Bear hadn't said as much, but she knew him better than he thought she did. He wanted to get as far away from all this as possible.

She raised her Coke to her lips to avoid the awkward silence but winced when she moved her shoulder wrong. Marcus didn't catch it, and she forced her face into a neutral expression before he could take another glance. No one had been seriously injured yesterday, but she had a couple bruises from bouncing off the door while they slid down the hill. Bear had a couple lumps on his head from when he hit it against the window and roof, but he said it didn't hurt much. She wasn't sure she believed him, but they hadn't had much time to talk. He made her go to bed as soon as they got home while he stayed up talking on the phone with the sheriff. When she woke up the next morning, she had already formed her plan to visit Marcus. Bear hadn't hesitated. It felt like he wanted her somewhere far away from the house.

"See this PC?" Marcus asked, drawing Mandy's attention back to the present. "I'm mining Ether on it."

"What's Ether?"

"It's a cryptocurrency. It's how I'm going to make my first million. And then I'm going to create the *next* big thing."

"What's the next big thing?"

"Well, I don't know yet." He frowned, but another grin quickly replaced it. "But I'll know it when I see it." He pointed to a drone. "Maybe a flying car. Have you ever seen that old movie *The Fifth Element?*"

"No." Mandy hadn't seen a lot of things. "What's it about?"

Marcus thought for a moment. "A supreme being comes to Earth to save it from an evil corporation and a violent race of aliens, but she gets sad because we're not taking care of the planet and we're always fighting with each other. So, a taxi driver has to convince her we're worth saving, and he does it through the power of love."

"Wow." Mandy thought that sounded cheesy. "That's... weird."

"Super weird." Marcus grinned. "But I love it. Anyway, they have flying cars, and I think it would be cool to be the first person to build one and make them available to everybody."

Mandy thought about the accident she had yesterday and wasn't sure she was keen to get into a car that could fly. That sounded a lot more dangerous. She pointed to a laptop hidden under a pile of books. "What's that one for?"

Marcus was an innocent-looking kid with a baby face, but when he looked where she was pointing and grinned, Mandy couldn't help but think he looked a lot more like a movie villain. "That's my hacking computer."

"Really?" Mandy's heart was racing. This was why she wanted to talk to Marcus. She knew he'd be able to help her, but she'd never imagined a scenario this perfect. "What kind of places can you hack into?"

"Pretty much anywhere." His chest puffed out. "Last month, I hacked into my church's website and changed the copyright line at the bottom to *Jesus Christ*." He was shaking with laughter. "I'm still waiting for someone to notice."

"That's pretty funny." Mandy laughed, but her mind was working overtime. "Where else can you hack into?"

Marcus didn't miss the urgency in her voice. "Why?"

She shrugged. "Just wondering."

He put his hands on his hips. "If you need me to hack into something for you, I will. But you can't keep me in the dark. That would be dangerous to both of us."

Mandy sighed. He had a point. "Laura Lynn is sick. Like, really sick. She was throwing up blood yesterday."

Marcus paled. His arms dropped to his side. "Really? Is she gonna be okay?"

"Don't know," she said. "Something weird is going on. Her dad seemed more concerned about no one finding out she was sick than doing something about it. The sheriff called an ambulance for her, and I guess her mom let them in. I wanted to check up on her. See if there's anything in her charts or something." Mandy wasn't one hundred percent sure how it all worked, but if she could get into the system, she'd figure it out. "I want to make sure she's okay. I think my dad is keeping something from me."

Marcus sat down at his desk and pulled his laptop out from under a stack of books. He opened it and looked over his shoulder. She turned around so he could put in his password, and only turned back when he told her it was okay. He typed in an address at the top of the screen, but his finger hovered over the enter key before he pressed it down.

"Is this why you wanted to hang out with me today?" He looked up at her. "Just to check on Laura Lynn?"

Mandy hesitated. She thought he'd respect her honesty but lying would be the easier route. She went for a blend of both. "Yes and no. I'm worried about Laura Lynn, and I knew you could probably help me. But I wanted to hang out. You're weird, but in a cool way."

Marcus pondered that for a moment, then shrugged a shoulder and turned back to his computer. "Works for me."

Marcus' fingers were a blur of motion over the keyboard. They moved so fast, Mandy couldn't keep up. Before she knew it, they were staring at an administrator's login screen. With the click of a button, Marcus could look up any patient and see their personal information.

"Whoa." It wasn't lost on Mandy how illegal this was. "How did you do that so fast?"

"It's not like it is in the movies. That was my first lesson." He laughed, then pushed the glasses up on his face. "The most important part is hiding your location. In this case, I made my computer look like it was at Dr. Sing's house."

"Is that the login you're using?"

"Yep. She's a friend of my mom's. She keeps a sticky note of her password on her desk in her home office. I saw it when we were invited over for dinner a couple months ago." He shook his head. "Someone needs to teach her about proper cyber security."

"She isn't going to think a kid would be able to log into her account and get away with it."

"True." He grinned, and Mandy grinned right back. "Innocence is on our side."

"You know this isn't exactly hacking, right?"

He shrugged. "Maybe not. More luck than anything else, but I would've been able to figure it out. I could've hacked into her email and probably gotten her password that way. But you have to be careful about logging in on different devices and deleting the security warnings to cover your tracks."

Mandy wanted to pretend she cared about those kinds of details, but she'd be lying. Every minute that passed felt like Laura Lynn was getting farther away from her. She pointed to the search bar. "Put her name in there."

Marcus did as he was told, and a few keystrokes later, they were looking at a complete list of Laura Lynn's symptoms, as well as her prognosis. Neither of them dared to breathe. Marcus hit a button, and the printer came to life, whirring and clicking and spitting paper out onto the floor. Neither reached for the information, for fear that it would make it true.

Instead, they turned to each other, a mirror image of fear and panic. Mandy couldn't even think of two words to say as her heart leapt into her throat.

16

BEAR PACED THE LENGTH OF THE HOUSE, HIS MIND IN OVERDRIVE. HE'D sent Mandy to hang out with the kid who was good with computers. There was a risk with her out of his sight. He needed her safe and somewhere away from all of this. Plus, he needed space to think. The body, the reporters, the questions from the sheriff. He could handle all of that. But someone had tried to run them off the road. With Mandy in the car.

His rage level had passed ten out of ten hours ago.

It was only mid-morning, but Bear had been up for hours. His sleep had been restless. He knew he had to up his game. Finding that body had shaken something loose. Perhaps the van had only been a warning. He had to prepare for whatever came next.

His phone vibrated. He had it to his ear before the second ring. "Yeah?"

"It's McKinnon." Her voice was steady but tense. "I've got some info."

Bear stepped up to the blinds in the living room and parted them with his fingers. The activity had become his favorite pastime. "Hit me with it."

"I ran the partial plate I got last night along with the make and model of that van."

"Tell me it's good news."

"Could be worse. The partial plate matches with about twenty different vans. All the same make and model."

Bear let the blinds drop closed. "That seems abnormal. Who do they belong to?"

"Bowser Freight. It's a shipping company. They've got a couple different locations in a few states, and there's a facility halfway between here and Rochester."

"Sounds like a plan."

"Hang on, cowboy." It sounded like McKinnon shifted her phone from one ear to the other. "I want to know what we're dealing with before we go in there, guns blazing. And if they've got damage to a van, I want to prove it's the one that hit us."

"You want to go back to the scene of the crime?"

"You in?"

Bear was itching to get answers, even if it meant throwing a few punches. *Especially* if it meant throwing some punches. But McKinnon was right. They'd be better off going into this place with as much evidence as they could gather. It'd be worth the trouble if it meant pinning down whoever did this.

The truck was in a body shop. They had to replace the driver's side door, fix the front bumper, and put on a new passenger side mirror. Money wasn't the issue. Time was. It'd be a couple of days before he'd have his vehicle back. Bear already felt locked in. McKinnon had offered to drive him around, and although riding in the front seat of the sheriff's cruiser wasn't exactly lying low, going to Rochester to rent a car for two days didn't seem worth it.

Besides, they had work to do. Riding together saved time. They could discuss the specifics, ideas, and hunches.

Within half an hour, Bear and McKinnon were standing on the side of the road where they'd found out how well the truck would handle an off-road experience. Looking at the terrain in the daylight made Bear realize how lucky they had been. If they had hit that tree, one of them would've been seriously injured. What if it had been Mandy?

He had to shake his body to get away from the thought.

McKinnon handed him a plastic Ziploc bag and a pair of gloves.

"Pick up anything that looks like it came from that van. Even if you're not sure, toss it in there."

Bear squeezed on the gloves. They cut into his wrists. "What are these, extra small?"

"Mediums. It's all we had."

"Remind me again why we're out here?" Bear asked, even though he'd agreed to it. The sun was scorching, and the heat made him angry. "Isn't this what deputies are for?"

"I wanted to look myself." McKinnon took out her phone and snapped a pic of the tread marks. Bear was sure they were from his truck, but he didn't bother saying anything. Better to have it all accounted for. "Not really sure who I can trust anymore."

"So, you brought me, the guy you hardly know?"

She shrugged. "You seem all right to me."

"Now you sound like me." He chuckled. "You worried about your own people?"

"I'm worried about everyone."

"Even me?"

"Especially you." McKinnon glanced back at him and smiled. "But not about this. You've got something to hide, but I don't think it has anything to do with why we got run off the road."

"Not this again." Bear had no intention of dumping his stuff on her, no matter how many times she asked.

"In all seriousness," she said, grunting as she stood up while putting a piece of orange plastic in her bag, "yeah, I am worried. If what happened to the girl in the tank, Katie, is happening to Laura Lynn and my neighbor's kid, then the police knew about it. Or if they didn't, they knew not to ask questions about it. Luckily, I'm not that smart."

"You're plenty smart, Sheriff." Bear meant it. "But that doesn't mean you're not up to your eyeballs in it."

"Tell me about it."

They worked in silence for a few minutes. Bear found some pieces of plastic here and there, a few months-old cigarette butts, and a crumpled-up napkin. He could feel the sweat running down his back. "In my experience, if someone's trying to kill you, you're on the right track."

"Not exactly the welcome wagon you want, though."

"You got any enemies?" Bear found some fiberglass from a fender and stuck it in his bag. "Could this be something unrelated to Katie and your conspiracy theory?"

"Old Man Jones thinks I cheat at chess. Could be him. Heard he's got ties to the mafia." McKinnon grinned when Bear looked up at her with a scowl. "I should ask you the same thing. You seem like the kind of guy who's been in a fight or two. Got any enemies?"

"Not in this zip code." Then, under his breath, "That I know of."

The pair of them made their way down the side of the road and searched through the tall grass. Bear found some shattered glass that he was sure was from his truck, but he put it in his bag, anyway. It was harder finding anything here, and after another half hour, they leaned up against the tree, both sweating and out of breath.

"I'll show you mine if you show me yours." Bear held up his bag.

McKinnon raised hers, too. It was about twenty percent fuller than his, not least because of a partial headlight she'd picked up on the shoulder. "The van took some damage. There'll be no hiding this. It'll have to go in for repairs, same as your truck."

Bear pushed off the tree and ripped the sweat-stained gloves from his hands. He ran his palms down his shirt. "What do we know about this Bowser company?"

"Seemed normal to me. Like I said, they do a lot of shipping. Started off as a moving company in the fifties, then got some bigger clients. Started doing freight instead. The original company was founded just outside Rochester, but they've got some facilities in New Jersey and Pennsylvania. They seem like a legitimate company. At least on paper."

"They usually do. But it only takes one person. If someone's using their vans to go on joyrides, the company won't be happy about it. Let's hope that makes them more willing to hand the person over."

McKinnon began the trek back to her cruiser. "Only one way to find out."

17

As they pulled into Bowser Freight's parking lot, Bear leaned forward to decrease the glare from the cruiser's hood and take it all in. The building had all the hallmarks of a family-owned business with a modicum of success. Half the building looked old and well-worn, while the addition had clearly been built a decade or more later.

The old half of the warehouse held the entrance and a main office, as well as two loading docks. Four more had been added later, with the last two allowing for a semi-truck to fully pull into the building.

Bear whistled. "Seems like they're doing good for themselves."

"Must be," McKinnon said. "But it makes me wonder if they've got any side hustles."

Bear looked around the lot. "Don't see any vans."

"Let's go ask them about it."

McKinnon got out and crossed the parking lot with Bear in tow. Her stride was casual, but he caught her taking in the entire building, the gears working in her head. What would they do if they found a damaged van on the property? What would they do if they didn't? And more importantly, what would happen if they couldn't get inside to begin with?

Bear cracked his knuckles in anticipation. McKinnon gave him a sharp look. He feigned innocence, but he was ready for whatever might happen.

A stocky man stood outside the entrance and lit a cigarette. He sucked in a deep breath and blew it out, the white smoke obscuring his face for a few seconds. But Bear could tell he never took his eyes off them. His upper lip twitched as they approached.

"Good morning." McKinnon's voice was cheery and nonchalant. There was no way the two of them wouldn't look like a threat to someone who had something to hide. "Can I get your name, sir?"

The man peered at them. Bear wondered if he'd refuse. But after a beat, he said, "Howie."

"Got a last name, Howie?"

He pointed at the sign above him that read "Bowser" in big red letters.

"You're the owner?" McKinnon asked.

"Co-owner. With my brother." Howie took another drag and looked Bear up and down. "What can I do for you?"

"We had a report of a van driving someone off the road last night. Make and model matches the kind your company drives."

"It's a common van." Howie looked off to his right as he exhaled smoke. His voice hadn't changed, but Bear saw him stand up a little straighter. Was it guilt or fear? "Lots of shipping companies use them."

"We also had a partial plate." McKinnon frowned, as though she were sad to relay this information to him. "Matches a few at this site."

Another drag. Another few seconds that Howie kept his facial expression hidden. He met McKinnon's stare. "What are you implying?"

Bear didn't wait for McKinnon to answer. "Think it's obvious. We want to know if it was one of your vehicles."

"Was anyone hurt?"

That threw Bear off. People who had something to hide rarely cared about that. He relented. "No."

After another beat, the man said, "We didn't have any van drivers out last night. And I didn't see any come in with damage."

McKinnon gestured to the front door. "Mind if we look around?"

"Don't you need a warrant for that?"

McKinnon's face stretched into a wide grin. "Only if you have something to hide."

The man knew what McKinnon meant. But he wouldn't make it easy on them. "Got a badge?"

Bear scoffed. He pointed to McKinnon's sheriff uniform, then gestured to the cruiser behind them. "Really?"

Howie shrugged. It was lazy. No heat behind it. "Can't be too careful."

McKinnon pulled out her badge and held it up to him.

He leaned forward and read it for a good ten seconds. "All right." He dropped his cigarette and stubbed it out with his toe. "Vans are 'round back."

Howie walked them along the side of the building to a parking lot they hadn't noticed on the way in. More than a dozen vans were lined up in perfect rows, waiting to be loaded and driven to their destinations.

Bear counted them in his head. "You got more than just these?"

"A handful are out today." Howie pointed to the immaculate side of the closest van. "But we wouldn't let them drive off if there was even a scratch on 'em. Got a reputation, you know."

"Mind if we walk around?" McKinnon asked.

"Knock yourselves out."

McKinnon and Bear approached the first van in silence. Bear took in every inch of the vehicle. The panel doors, the bumpers, the fenders, the headlights, the side-view mirrors. He even leaned his forehead up against the glass and cupped his hands around his eyes, trying to see if there was anything in the center console that screamed, *I recently tried to kill three people.*

They did this with every van. Sixteen in total. They were spotless. Half the vehicles were at least five years old, but there wasn't a scratch on them. Not a spot of rust. Bear would've thought it was strange if there'd only been one or two in perfect condition, as though they'd recently been given a makeover, but a fleet of this size meant Howie and his brother took pride in their stock. Nothing criminal about that.

When they reached the final van in the last row, McKinnon blew a lock of hair out of her face. She turned to Bear. "You see anything?"

"Nothing. No dents or dings. No scratches. Not even anything that looks like it's been recently repaired." He could feel his temper flaring again. "You sure the van came from here?"

"No, I'm not sure." McKinnon was having trouble holding back her frustration, too. "Just seemed most likely. Without the full license plate, we're just taking an educated guess."

Bear scuffed the pavement with his boot. Loose rocks went skittering into the closest tire. "No glass or anything lying around either. Even if that van belongs to the company, I don't think the driver brought it back here. Could be anywhere at this point."

McKinnon made her way back to Howie, who stood at the back entrance smoking another cigarette. "How many vans did you say were out on the road today?"

"Four. We have a fleet of twenty here." Howie blew out a breath of smoke, angling it up and away from them. "But like I said, if one was banged up, we wouldn't have let it off the lot."

Bear hooked a thumb over his shoulder. "Those are some good-looking vans."

"Thank you." Howie dropped the cigarette. "We take pride in what we do. Wouldn't have gotten this far if we didn't."

"You have a place you take your vans if they get damaged?"

"Nah, just take them to the cheapest place. Nowhere in particular."

Just then, the back door opened and a skinny man in his twenties popped his head out. He took in the Sheriff and Bear with wide eyes, then turned to Howie. "Chief, we need you back inside for a sec."

"Be right in, Charlie. Thanks." When the kid shut the door behind him, Howie held out his hand to McKinnon and Bear in turn. "Sorry I couldn't be more help. If there's anything else I can do, just holler. You can call the main office and tell Marie to transfer you."

"Thanks for your time." McKinnon waited until Howie disappeared into the building before trekking back to the car. "Well, that was a bust."

"Seems strange not to have a go-to guy for vehicle work, don't you think?" Bear was grasping at straws, but something didn't feel right.

"Especially with that many vans. Not even a mechanic on site? Just go to the cheapest place?"

McKinnon shrugged, then slid into the front seat of the car. "Maybe that's how they save money."

Bear squeezed himself in beside her.

She turned the key in the ignition and the vehicle roared back to life. "Look, if he was hiding something, he deserves an Oscar. He was cool as a cucumber. Didn't resist. Didn't try to slow us down."

Bear didn't know what to say. She was right, of course, but saying it out loud was admitting that they'd hit a dead end. He hated dead ends. With the van out of action and nowhere to be found, there was only so much they could do to dig it up again. You couldn't follow a trail that had gone cold.

18

Every cell in Mandy's body buzzed with energy as she walked home from Marcus' house. She was supposed to stay there until dinnertime, when Bear would pick her up, but as soon as she saw what was in Laura Lynn's file, she couldn't wait. She tried calling, but Bear wasn't picking up. And she needed to move. Be active. *Do something.*

Sitting still with this kind of info led her mind down the obsessive path. Since leaving Europe, those types of thoughts had subsided. Even thinking about them got her a little upset.

So, she said goodbye to Marcus and slipped out the back, where his mother wouldn't see her. She'd probably get a lecture from Bear. Whatever. It'd be worth it to bring him this information. The papers in her backpack felt like they were on fire, radiating a heat that soaked through her clothes, into her skin, and buried itself in every muscle of her body.

The walk from Marcus' house to her own would only take her about fifteen minutes. A single country road skirted the center of town and acted as a straight shot between the two houses. Every time a car passed, it kicked up dirt and gravel, making Mandy cough and choke and spit. She had the urge to flip them off every time someone new drove by, but she resisted. She had more important things to focus on. If only the people in this town knew what she knew.

Mandy was still processing. When they'd logged into the hospital's portal, she wasn't sure what she was looking for. She just wanted answers—answers that adults wouldn't volunteer. If Bear was hellbent on keeping her out of his investigation with the sheriff, then she'd form her own hypothesis and conduct her own experiments.

When they'd looked at Laura Lynn's file, the answers had jumped off the page. The doctors didn't know what was wrong with her, but they were treating her like she'd been poisoned. Laura Lynn's bloodwork showed not enough of some chemicals and too many of others. Mandy couldn't pronounce half the words. The doctors' notes showed they didn't know why. But something was wrong. And it'd been wrong for weeks.

The first culprits that came to mind were Laura Lynn's parents. Mandy had dismissed that idea as soon as she'd thought of it. Mrs. Weinberger had said they'd all been feeling sick. What was the point in slowly poisoning your daughter if you were going to eat the same food or drink the same drink?

No, someone else was doing this to them.

But *why*? Laura Lynn was fourteen years old. She didn't have any enemies. She was the sweetest girl Mandy had ever met. Her family was targeted at random, or her parents were. Mrs. Weinberger was a kind, soft-spoken woman. A bit too much of a doormat. Unless that was a cover Mandy couldn't see through, then the reason they were on someone's radar was likely Mr. Weinberger's fault. He seemed like a guy who pissed people off regularly.

Mandy had no idea what he could've done. Laura Lynn didn't enjoy talking about her father much. She didn't even know what his job was, nor what kind of extracurricular activities he was involved in.

So, they were back to the drawing board. It had taken Marcus a minute to find the right keywords, but he searched the hospital's database for similar symptoms. More than a handful of cases came up. Was the hospital aware they were all related? Did they have any clue they had an epidemic on their hands?

Mandy wasn't sure that was the correct word for this situation, but it *felt* right.

Her ears perked up at another car coming up behind her. She moved over to the side of the road, along the tree line, and got ready to hold her breath. The amount of dust directly correlated with the speed at which the car would be moving. Her brain tried to come up with a formula, but it sputtered and stalled. She liked math, liked the order of it, but it didn't always come easily.

The car slowed. That was unusual. Mandy looked over her shoulder and saw a white panel van, like the one that had tried to run her, Bear, and the sheriff off the road yesterday. Her neck and shoulders tingled. Goosebumps erupted all over her body. Half of her brain told her to run, but the other half told her to hold her ground lest she trigger a predator's hunting instinct.

She kept walking with her eyes forward, watching the van approach from her peripherals.

It pulled up next to her.

Mandy stopped and turned to the driver, squaring off with the van and staying on the balls of her feet. She looked the man in the eyes, absorbing every feature of his face. Taking in as much detail as her brain could process.

He had dark hair and tanned skin. It wasn't wrinkled like he was old, but like life's lessons had worn him down. Although something about his expression told her he hadn't learned very many of them. He had a tattoo on his neck, and although she could see splotches of color, she couldn't make out any shapes. When he hung an arm out of the vehicle, there was a shiny gold watch on his wrist. She vaguely wondered how much it was worth. When the man opened his mouth to speak, she saw he was missing a tooth along the top left-hand side of his mouth.

"Do you need a ride?"

"No, thank you."

The last thing Mandy wanted to do was be polite to a creep like this, but she was hedging her bets. Firm answers, direct eye contact, and no fear. Maybe he would move on. She wouldn't be an easy target, despite her size and age, and she wanted to let him know that up front.

"Are you sure?" His brow furrowed in mock concern. "Your back-pack looks heavy."

"*No, thank you.*"

"Come on, it's hot out. You'll get home way faster."

"I'm not going home." She hoped he didn't know where she lived.

He smirked, and she realized they both knew that was a lie. "Mandy." His voice was firm now. Deeper. Scarier. There was a dark glint in his eyes that sent another wave of goosebumps skittering over the surface of her body. "Get in the van."

Mandy took off running like her life depended on it—and it probably did. Whether or not this was the same guy who ran them off the road, he was definitely working for the same people. This wasn't the first time someone had attempted to get to Bear through her. Bear had trained her for this. She was ready for this. Every fiber of her being focused on one thing.

Staying alive.

As she sprinted away, she almost relished the burning of her muscles. This was doing something. She had gathered more evidence as soon as the van had pulled up next to her. She hadn't caught a glimpse of the license plate, but she knew what the driver looked like. And he was easy to identify.

Mandy heard a curse and the van door popping open behind her. Then the crunch of gravel underfoot. She didn't dare look back. She kept her eyes forward, pumping her arms in rhythm and pushing off the ground with all her might. She was the fastest in her grade, even among the boys, and she was nearing top speed.

Her feet left the ground. Something had caught hold of her backpack and yanked her to a halt, sending her sprawling onto her back like she was awkwardly sliding into home plate. Gravel cut into her elbows as she landed, and dust replaced the air in her lungs. She tried to cough, but she could only manage to wheeze.

"Why are you running, huh?"

The man was hovering over her now. His face a sneer, even less inviting than before. Up close, she saw his cheeks and forehead were pockmarked. And though the tattoo was hidden by his collar, she saw hints of red and blue. Was it the American flag?

Mandy didn't have any more time to cement the man's image in her head. When he reached down to grab her by the shoulders, she slammed her foot into his crotch.

He grunted and fell to his knees just as she rolled out of the way.

In seconds, she was back on her feet. Before she could run away again, his hand clamped around her wrist like a vice. Pain shot up her arm, and she couldn't help the cry that escaped her mouth.

He yanked her closer. "You're going to regret that."

"Doubt it." Though she was scared, something in her had awoken. No matter how much she had complained to Bear about all her boring and repetitive lessons, she was once again reminded of how important they'd been. Everything came second nature. She didn't even have to think.

Instinct.

She dragged her fingernails down the man's face. She could've punched him in the nose, but despite being strong for her age, she was still small. And this would leave a mark. He howled in pain, and she took advantage of his distraction to peel back his thumb and release her wrist from his grip.

Mandy hopped back two steps, distancing herself. She saw him in a new light now. He was skinny, but he had muscle. That meant he was fast. The man was also tall, and his arms had a long reach. That would be to her disadvantage, too. He had caught up to her so fast, and because of her backpack, he'd had something easy to grab onto to slow her down.

Her brain yelled at her to ditch the bag. The burning-hot papers stuffed into the main pocket were enough for her to dismiss the idea. She'd never be able to remember everything on Laura Lynn's charts without them, and she needed to show Bear what she'd found.

But when the man whipped out a knife, everything around her came to a halt. She and Bear had trained with weapons before, carefully at first and then increasing in speed and intensity over the years. He'd never gone full tilt at her before, not like this guy would. She knew the basics. She only had to keep it simple.

Mandy slung off her backpack and used it as a shield. When the driver lunged, she spun out of the way and deflected with her bag. The knife caught and ripped open the front. The backpack's contents spilled out onto the road, whipping about in the wind.

He saw her eyes get wide. His narrowed into another sneer. "Worried about your homework?"

She didn't bother responding. The fight was taking all of her concentration. Maybe when she was older, more experienced, she could throw in a few comeback lines, like Bear did. As it was, she needed to focus. Now was the time to decide—grab what she could, or run?

The man lunged again, and Mandy spun out of the way a second time. But he was ready. With his other arm, he grabbed her around the neck and pulled her in close. She had a feeling he didn't want to kill her —just take her hostage—which meant he was also at a disadvantage. She was fighting for her life, and she'd do whatever it took to survive. No matter the consequences.

The driver had underestimated her. She might not have been as strong as him, but she was just as fast. As she aligned her body to his, she stomped down on his foot with all her might. It did nothing. Steel-toed boots.

Changing tactics, she swung her arm down. For the second time in as many minutes, she hit him as hard as she could in the crotch. He bowed. She dropped the backpack and made to swing a second time. His hands were rushing to protect himself, and Mandy used the momentum to push his wrist down at an angle and drive the knife into his leg. It didn't sink all the way to the hilt, but it would need immediate medical attention.

The man was distracted by the pain in the lower half of his body. His bloodied hands slipped off the knife's handle.

Mandy reared back and flipped her hips to ramp up the torque as she drove forward and slammed the heel of her hand into the guy's face, breaking his nose. His head tipped back, and blood spurted from his nostrils. She curled her fingers into a fist, pulled back, and with all her might, punched him in the throat.

The man went down, gasping for air. But Mandy didn't stick around to gloat. He'd already proven he was fast on his feet and could recover quickly. She spun around and sprinted into the woods, using the trees to cover her path. If she could stay off the road, she'd have a chance. He might know where she was going, but he wouldn't dare attack the house with Bear at home. She just had to hope her dad wasn't out with the sheriff.

As Mandy pumped all her remaining energy into her legs, her final thoughts lay with the answers covering the road behind her. She let out a few creative curses—the kind she'd heard Bear speak on more than one occasion—and then moved on.

It was a loss, but she was determined to recover, one way or another.

19

BEAR HAD ONLY BEEN HOME FOR FIVE MINUTES. IN THAT TIME, HE'D checked the entire house for any disturbances, circled the backyard to see if anyone had been poking around, and cracked open a beer. He'd drained half of it in one gulp when the front door crashed open.

He was through the kitchen and into the living room with a butcher knife in hand within a matter of seconds. He had the weapon clutched in an attack position. Who the hell had been so bold as to attack him through his front door? He lowered the knife when he realized that the figure hurtling toward him was a dusty and dirty Mandy.

As she launched herself into his arms, he dropped the knife and scooped her off the ground. She wasn't crying, but he could feel her ragged breaths against his neck, and the shaking of her limbs told him she'd sprinted home.

He kicked the door closed and locked it with his free hand, then placed Mandy on the couch. She didn't let go. He had to pry her hands from around his neck. When she looked up at him, he noticed a scrape along her face that had beaded with blood. Her hair was a tangle of knots, and dirt had clung to the sweat on her arms.

"What happened?" Bear knelt in front of her. "Are you okay? Hurt?"

She shook her head. Her eyes were still a little wild. "Not hurt. I'm okay." She swallowed. Caught her breath, then inhaled deeply and calmed herself further. "Someone attacked me."

His attention went to the front door. "Did they follow you here?"

"I don't think so."

"I'm going to go check, okay? You stay here. I'll be back in sixty seconds. Tops."

Mandy looked like she wanted to protest, like she wanted him to stay and hug her and tell her everything was going to be okay. But she swallowed her fear and nodded, folding herself into the couch, closing her eyes, and continuing to take deep breaths.

Bear snatched the knife off the floor and parted the blinds. The front yard seemed clear. He slipped out the door and walked down the driveway to the sidewalk and peered up and down the road. No cars. No pedestrians. It was relatively quiet for a Saturday afternoon.

Once he was satisfied, he checked the perimeter, peering into the woods to see if any figures were darting through the trees. A branch popped to his left, but the squirrel scurrying away told him it wasn't the quarry he was hunting.

Inside, Bear poured a large glass of water and gave it to Mandy, who gulped it down. Her gasping breath when she finally lowered the glass indicated she had spent a fair amount of energy.

He waited until she stopped drinking and faced him before he spoke. "What happened? Tell me everything, step by step."

"I was at Marcus' house. We found something about Laura Lynn. He hacked into the hospital and found her file."

"He what?"

She ignored the interruption. "The doctors think she was poisoned." She paused here, waiting for a reaction, but Bear kept his face neutral. "There are other patients with the same signs and symptoms. We printed off the information. I wanted to show you." She looked down, momentarily embarrassed. Her voice, already straining past the dirt in her throat, got quiet. "I called you, but you didn't answer."

Now it was Bear's turn to look away. He pulled out his phone and saw one missed call. He cursed. "I'm sorry." He met her eyes. "With everything going on, I got distracted. It won't happen again."

"It's okay." Mandy sounded cavalier, but he could tell she was hurt. "I decided to walk home. I know I shouldn't have." She rushed on, "But this feels big, Bear. Something is going on."

"I know. We're working on it." He stopped himself from chastising her for ignoring the rules and walking home by herself. Something told him she had learned a lesson today. "What happened when you walked home?"

"A van pulled up behind me. Another panel van, like the one from yesterday. And the driver stopped and leaned out the window. He asked me if I wanted a ride home. I said no. He didn't like that. He knew my name. So I ran. But he caught me and we fought." She gasped around a sob, her bottom lip quivering. Bear pulled her into a hug, but after a few seconds, she pushed him away with a gentle hand and finished her water. She sounded stronger now. "He had a knife, and I stabbed him in the leg with it. Then I broke his nose and punched him in the throat." She grinned now, proud. But it only lasted a few seconds. "But I lost my backpack. The papers. I just ran. I ran all the way here."

"You were smart to leave them behind." He ducked his head to meet her downturned gaze. "Hey, you did good, kid. You did the right thing. I'm proud of you, okay?" He waited until she nodded before he continued. "Was it the same van that hit us?"

"I don't think so. I mean, there was no damage. It looked perfect. Could they have fixed it that fast?"

Bear thought of his own truck, which would be in the shop for the next couple of days. "I doubt it. What about the guy? What do you remember about him?"

"Tall and skinny. Brown hair, cut short. He was white. Had a tan. A missing tooth. Here." She pointed to her own mouth. "And he had a neck tattoo. Blue and red. I couldn't see what it was, though."

"Do you think you'd recognize him if you saw him again?"

Mandy steeled her gaze. "Definitely. I scratched his face. There'll be a mark."

He patted her on the head. "That's my girl."

She grinned up at him, all the fear drained from her face.

"Now do you understand why I don't want you walking alone?"

Mandy looked away. "I know, I know." She sobered. "Bear?"

"Yeah?"

"What's going on?"

Bear took a deep breath and held it, then blew it out through his mouth, flapping his lips. Sounded like an eighteen-wheeler with a flat tire. "Honestly? I'm not sure." He stood and parted the blinds again. Clear. He paced the living room. "But someone doesn't want us poking around."

"Did you figure out who tried to hit us yesterday? Do you think it was the same guy?"

"Not sure. The van belongs to a shipping company outside town. Or at least we thought it did. They have an entire fleet. But they were all in perfect condition. All accounted for. Except a few on the road today." Bear took out his phone and sent a quick description of the man who attacked Mandy to the sheriff. "Maybe Sheriff McKinnon can match the driver to the company's employee list."

"What about the records?" Mandy asked. "People being poisoned?"

"We're working on it, kid." When her face fell, his heart stuttered. "Do you remember anything on the papers? Any names of chemicals in their system?"

Mandy looked down at her feet. "No. I could barely pronounce any of them."

Bear didn't know whether to reassure her or continue to keep her as far away from this as possible. Before he could decide, there was a deafening banging on the front door. Mandy leapt up and sprinted across the room, hovering in the doorway to the kitchen, ready to run if Bear told her to.

Bear grabbed the knife a second time and parted the blinds. The front yard remained still. He wrenched open the door, but no one was there. It took him a few seconds to notice the envelope on the ground. He scooped it up, checked his surroundings one more time, then slammed the door shut behind him.

"What's that?" Mandy asked.

Bear didn't relinquish his grip on the knife as he opened the letter and took it all in. It was printed on blank paper and typed in capital letters. His eyes skimmed the words once, twice, three times before he made sense of it.

STOP. YOU'RE MAKING IT WORSE.

YOU DON'T KNOW WHAT YOU'RE GETTING INTO.

THEY'LL NEVER STOP CHASING YOU. LEAVE NOW WHILE YOU STILL CAN.

20

BEAR'S MIND WAS WORKING OVERTIME AS HE MADE HIS WAY AROUND HIS room and started pulling clothes from his dresser and weapons from his various hiding spots. Mandy was talking, but he couldn't hear what she was saying. The blood pumping from his racing heart drowned everything else out.

After receiving the letter, Bear had catapulted himself through the front door and back out to the street. He looked up and down the sidewalk, but there was nobody near his house. He figured it'd been a full minute between the knock and him going back outside.

Had someone sped off in a car or a van? Possibly. He'd never know. He went into the backyard and spent at least ten minutes peering into the woods. Was someone out there watching them? Had they thrown themselves behind a tree, hoping Bear would give up the search so they could vanish?

He wasn't sure what he'd do to the person who left the letter, but he knew he'd demand some answers. It had been more of a warning than a threat, but the message was clear: You're in over your head. Bear would've probably ignored the sentiment. Perhaps it was some good Samaritan who didn't know what Bear was capable of.

But it happened moments after someone had gone after Mandy. Had it been by chance that they'd found her walking back from Marcus' house? Or had they been watching her? Stalking her? Were they waiting to see if she'd leave, or had they planned to attack the house and steal Mandy no matter what?

Bear's vision turned red. Soon, fear mixed with the anger. If it had been just him, he would've gone on a rampage. Tracked down the guy who had run him off the road. Find whoever had left the letter and demand some answers. Go all the way to the top until he figured out what the hell was going on. Then dismantle it all piece by piece.

But it wasn't just him. He had Mandy, and smart and strong as she was, she wasn't a match for what they were up against. She'd been lucky today. Mandy needed to learn what it was like to be a normal girl in a normal town leading a normal life. Not dealing with this mess.

Instead, her best friend was in the hospital, she was fighting off assailants on her own, and a boy who liked her was hacking into hospital databases so they could conduct their own investigation. It was all too much, and Bear knew there was only one solution.

Run.

It was never his first choice, but sometimes you had to swallow your pride to protect the ones you loved. Clive had gone above and beyond by erasing their records and setting up this house for Bear. The universe had a sick sense of humor. It had placed them in the middle of a conspiracy. Bear was uninterested in solving the mystery. He was done with that life.

After seeing no one in the woods, Bear pushed his way through the door and launched himself toward his room. He heard Mandy shouting behind him, but he ignored her. Nothing she could say would change his mind. They were leaving. He'd find a car and get them out of there. Then he'd find a new town. A new house. A new life. Things would be normal. So normal, they'd be boring. He could do with a little boring.

"Bear!" Mandy's voice finally cut through his thoughts as she tugged on his arm. "What's going on?"

He turned to find fear and anger and anxiety shining in her eyes. He softened, but he didn't stop packing his duffle bag. Hers would be next. "We have to go. Now."

"Why?"

He tossed her the letter. "Can't afford to be on someone's radar. It's not good. For either of us."

"So, what? We're just going to abandon everyone?" Mandy's voice wavered. "We're just running away?"

He took her by the shoulders and made her look into his eyes. "Sometimes you have to run. No shame in it. It's saved my life more than once. We're not here to be heroes, Mandy."

"But they need our help." She waved the letter in front of him. "We're only making things worse because we're close to figuring out what's going on around here."

"The sheriff can take care of herself." Bear snatched the letter out of her hand and folded it into his pocket. "We don't owe anyone anything."

"Laura Lynn can't take care of herself."

"She's got parents. She's not my responsibility."

"Her parents are useless." Mandy threw her hands in the air and grunted in frustration. "Her mom has no idea what's happening, and her dad only cares about himself."

"Not my problem."

"Well, it's my problem!" Mandy's voice had ratcheted up higher. She tugged on his arm so hard that it spun him around to face her. "And I'm your problem. She's my best friend, Bear. My *only* friend. I can't leave her."

Bear shook his head. "What about the other kid? Marcus. Laura Lynn isn't your only friend."

Mandy jabbed a finger at him. "Use your brain. If they saw me coming from Marcus' house, they could find him next." Her eyes widened, like she just realized the implication of what she'd just said. She pulled out her phone and sent a text message. "We can't leave them to defend themselves."

"They've got the sheriff." Bear zipped the duffle and made for Mandy's room. "She knows what she's getting into. She can handle it."

"What if she can't?" Mandy ran ahead of Bear and threw her arm across the entrance to her room, barring his entry. He could've easily picked her up and moved her out of the way, but the look on her face told him it wouldn't be worth the trouble. "What if we leave and they all die?"

"She can handle it," Bear said again, his voice a little less gruff.

"What if she can't?" Mandy dropped her arm and looked up at him with tears sparkling in her eyes. "Bear, what if more kids get sick?"

He looked away from her pleading eyes.

Mandy waited a beat while the tears spilled over her eyelids and down her cheeks. "What would Sasha say if she saw you running again?"

An invisible hand wrapped around his heart. He could've convinced himself that McKinnon could do this herself because her dogged determination would lead her to answers. But the kids? They didn't deserve this. And if what McKinnon thought was true, they weren't just getting sick. They were dying.

And Mandy was right. Sasha wouldn't respect him if she could see him now.

Bear searched for the words to convince himself it was worth leaving, but he came up blank. He'd be protecting himself and Mandy, but people would suffer. That seemed to be a theme with him. He got people hurt. Like Sasha.

He'd made a lot of mistakes in his life. Had a lot of regrets. But one thing Bear prided himself on was giving more good to the world than he took from it. If heaven was real, he wasn't sure he'd earn a spot, but he didn't think hell was a destination he was headed for either. He'd helped a lot of people along the way. Why was this town any different?

It's not. He scratched at his beard. *But I am.*

It was fear, plain and simple. He couldn't give a crap about his life and where he ended up. He probably deserved whatever he had coming to him. But he cared about Mandy. What she'd gone through until now was tragic, but it could be fixed. See a shrink. Get it off your chest. Do better.

Easy.

But what she learned now, as a teenager, when she had more control over her life than she ever had before—that would stick with her. The lessons Bear gave her were for her own survival, but he owed it to her to make sure she turned out a good person. The stuff she'd seen was enough to corrupt anyone. But Mandy was good. Selfless. Heroic. That was the fire he wanted to stoke in her.

And what kind of example would he be setting if he dowsed the flames? That people weren't worth saving? He didn't want her to grow up in the world believing that, even if he sometimes thought it.

Before Bear could find an excuse, his phone chirped. He pulled it out and looked at its screen. McKinnon had texted him. *No word on the driver yet, but found the van,* she said. *In a body shop outside town. You coming?*

It was a simple question. In or out?

But the answer could lead him to consequences he wasn't willing to pay.

21

BEAR SAT IN THE FRONT SEAT OF MCKINNON'S POLICE CRUISER, questioning whether he'd made the right decision. Mandy's eyes had lit up when he suggested she go to the hospital with Marcus and his family to visit Laura Lynn. He hadn't made any promises that they'd stick around for longer than the day. This way, he could investigate the body shop with the sheriff, and Mandy and her friends would be safe.

McKinnon held the letter open in front of her. She'd been staring at it for a good sixty seconds. "And you have no idea who dropped this off?"

"If I did, they'd be in the backseat of your car."

"It's a warning," she said, "but it sounds like they're trying to help. That's hopeful."

"They want us out of town. They want us to stop looking into this. That's not hope. They don't want to hurt us, but they're still part of the problem if they're not willing to help."

"Oh, so there *is* an us now?" The look on McKinnon's face was difficult to read. "Interesting."

Bear crossed his arms over his chest. "Look, I want to figure out who the van driver is. Plain and simple. The rest of it is TBD."

"Sure it is." McKinnon grinned. "Something tells me if you really wanted to go, you would have gone by now."

"Any luck finding the guy who attacked Mandy?" The change in subject wasn't subtle.

McKinnon sobered. "No. Went back to where it happened. Zero evidence. Mandy's backpack and medical papers were gone."

Bear nodded. He stifled a growl from overtaking his words. "We'll find him. Only a matter of time."

"I'm gonna pretend that didn't sound ominous and move on." She handed the paper back to him. "Ready to go in there?"

Bear looked at the body shop across the street. It was a mid-sized building with three bays. Two of them were full. One of the vehicles matched the description of the van. "What're we up against?"

"Just a small-town business. Handful of employees. None of them have any records, and the shop hasn't been in any trouble in the past. For all intents and purposes—"

"Looks good on paper." He shrugged. "Heard that before."

"Let's see what they have to say." McKinnon hooked her fingers around the doorhandle and pushed. "Then we can jump to conclusions."

"Yay for clichés." Bear followed her across the street and to the open bay with the van. Two guys were taking a coffee break. They stared at the sheriff when they saw her uniform.

"Morning, fellas." Just like at Bowser Freight, McKinnon kept her voice upbeat and even. "How you guys doin' today?"

"Not bad, Sheriff. What's going on?"

Bear eyed the guy who spoke first. He was tall and well-built, but still a size or so smaller than him. His skin was pale, and he was blonde with blue eyes. No tattoos. The man standing next to him looked like he could be his brother. He had a couple tattoos, all black and white. None on his neck. A bust for the guy who had attacked Mandy.

McKinnon pointed to the van. "I was wondering if you could tell me what's going on with this vehicle."

The first guy set his coffee down. Bear caught a nametag on his uniform. Ralph. "Any particular reason?"

"We think it could've been involved in a hit-and-run last night."

The other guy grinned. "Did the deer file a complaint?" He and his buddy laughed.

Bear and McKinnon exchanged a look of confusion. Ralph waved them around to the front. Bear inspected every detail of the vehicle on his way over. There should've been damage to the door and the front fender. Even the side mirror. He saw none. Everything looked perfect, like it had never even winked at a guardrail wrong.

Bear joined McKinnon at the grill. Sure enough, there was blood and fur sticking out of the grate. It was fresh, too. A clump of fur had fallen on the floor. Bear picked it up. It was coarse and damp. Real. He tossed it back down.

"When did the van come in?" McKinnon asked.

"This morning. Figure the deer hit was last night." Ralph looked at the other guy, who nodded.

"You get a lot of vans in like this?" Bear asked. His questions sounded more aggressive than McKinnon's. He didn't bother reining it in. It'd worked the better part of two-and-a-half decades. Why stop now?

"Panel vans?" Ralph shrugged. "Yeah, I guess. They're not uncommon. We got a couple shipping companies around these parts that use them. A few cleaning companies, as well."

"Do you do business with Bowser Freight?"

Ralph didn't skip a beat. "Yeah, sometimes."

"Ever find anything strange about their vans?"

"Other than Howie Bowser is a neat freak?" Ralph laughed, and the other guy joined in. "If I'm being honest, man, I don't really like working for them. We do a good job here, but that guy is nuts. Everything's gotta be perfect. Dude's got OCD or something."

"Do the vans come in with a lot of damage?" Bear asked, ignoring the anecdote. "Do the drivers seem aggressive or out of place?"

"Not really." Ralph frowned. "Is Howie in some kind of trouble?" His eyes widened and he looked fearful, as though he had implicated Howie. "Look, I was just joking. He's a good guy. Just finnicky is all."

"We're not implying otherwise." McKinnon's voice was soothing. "Just looking to figure out where the van came from and who was driving it, is all."

"Well, this one's not one of Howie's," the other guy said. "It was some Mexican guy. I think he's a handyman. He's got a whole bunch of tools in the back."

"Mind if we take a look?" Bear asked.

The two exchanged a look. Ralph was the one brave enough to speak. "Look, man. I don't want to get anyone in trouble. This isn't our property, so we can't do that."

"We understand." McKinnon's smile was bright. She handed him a card. "If you see a van like this come in with some damage to the passenger side, give me a call, all right? I'd appreciate it."

"Sure thing, ma'am." Ralph took the card and put it in his breast pocket. "Will do."

Bear and McKinnon retreated to her car. They stood on opposite sides of the hood, staring back at the body shop. Bear gathered the hair off his collar and let the cool afternoon breeze dry the sweat that had formed on the back of his neck.

"Another dead end." Bear didn't keep the bitterness out of his mouth.

"You know that quote about Thomas Edison?"

"We're not trying to invent the light bulb."

"No, but we are failing closer to success. Every dead end narrows the playing field."

"Has anyone ever told you you're annoyingly optimistic?"

McKinnon grinned. "I tell myself that every day."

"Plates were different," Bear said. "Definitely hit a deer. That's hard to fake in such a short amount of time. Driver description was different from the guy who tried to hurt Mandy." His fist curled just thinking about it. "Don't you think it's weird that every answer is perfect?"

"What do you mean?"

He turned to look at her. "Between Howie and these guys, we've got nothing. Every situation has an explanation. That's not normal."

"It is if they have nothing to hide."

"Everyone has something to hide."

McKinnon shrugged. "I don't disagree, but that doesn't mean they're hiding something that has to do with Katie, Laura Lynn, or the rest of it."

"I don't buy it."

"Is that your instincts talking?" McKinnon asked. "Or are you just looking for a fight and not getting one?" Bear went to answer, but her phone rang. She held up a finger and put the device to her ear. "Hello?"

McKinnon's eyes shifted to Bear's, and he knew something was wrong. His mind went to Mandy. He pulled his phone out of his pocket to check if he had any missed calls. None. When he looked back up at the sheriff, she was already halfway inside the car.

"No, no. Stay there. Hide." She shoved the key in the ignition and turned it. Bear hardly had the door closed before she peeled out. "I'm on my way."

22

McKinnon raced to the other side of town with the lights on and sirens wailing. What should've been about a ten-minute trip took less than five. Bear tried to ask her what was going on several times. She ignored him. She focused on getting to whoever had been on that other line.

As they pulled up a long gravel driveway, McKinnon unfastened her seatbelt to launch herself out of the car. They were halfway to the two-story log house when she spoke for the first time. "Stay here."

"What am I, a dog?"

"I mean it."

"Like hell."

"I'm serious—"

"I can handle myself. You don't have backup."

"If you get hurt—"

"I won't sue you."

She cut him a glance but didn't say anything.

"What's the situation?" Bear asked.

"Sixty-five-year-old white male in distress. His name is Carl Donovan. Called to tell me there was an intruder. He's in his bedroom with the door locked, hiding. Said he could hold out for a few minutes. Sounded like the intruder had a weapon."

"Gun?"

"Don't think so, but I can't be sure."

McKinnon slammed on her brakes and cut the engine. Before the two of them were out of the car, a figure emerged from the back of the house and sprinted into the woods.

Bear took off, calling over his shoulder. "I got this. You make sure Donovan is okay."

"Bear!" she shouted. "Riley, no!"

Bear ignored her, pumping all his rage into his legs and sprinting at max speed. He was a big guy. Most people underestimated how fast he was.

As Bear tore through the woods, he kept an eye on the figure in front of him. The man was tall and skinny and moved like a bullet through the trees. He kept trying to throw Bear off by weaving in and out of the bigger trunks, but Bear kept his trajectory straight. He was gaining on the intruder.

The man's breathing was ragged. Bear had an advantage there, too. He was fresh. And it had been a while since he'd gotten a chance to chase someone down like this. Whatever the other guy had been doing in the house, he'd already spent some of his energy. Bear just hoped Donovan was still alive to tell the tale.

As they neared the edge of the woods, Bear took a chance and launched himself forward, tackling the man and sending them both sprawling to the ground. Bits of roots and branches tore into his skin. The adrenaline pumping through Bear's veins meant he barely felt it.

The other guy grunted as he hit the ground. He was quick to recover, kicking out and pushing Bear off him. For a beanpole of a man, he was strong. And he was also fast. He was up on his feet before Bear made it to a knee. That's when Bear noticed the other man was holding a branch. He swung it at Bear's head with lightning speed. Bear blocked it with his arm. Pain shot up to his shoulder. It was enough to send him back a few steps. The other man darted away.

Bear took off toward the road fifty yards ahead. The assailant had put enough space between them that Bear only caught a glimpse here or there as they both dodged and weaved through the trees. If this ended up a footrace to the finish, Bear was confident he'd catch up. But if there was a car waiting for the man, Bear's chances would dwindle to nothing.

Closing the distance, Bear risked picking up a heavy branch and launching it at the man's back like a javelin. It hit him between the shoulders and sent him stumbling. It couldn't have hurt that much because he popped right back up and kept running. But it was enough for Bear to gain a few feet. And that was all he needed.

Through the trees, Bear spotted another white panel van. He couldn't tell if it was idling because of the wind rushing past his ears. If this guy was smart, he'd be ready to take off as soon as he jumped inside. Bear pushed the last bit of energy into his legs. He had to give everything now. Or he'd return with nothing.

With a guttural grunt of effort, Bear lunged again. Instead of going down, he hoisted the guy off his feet and slammed him against the back of the van, making sure his face collided with the door. Bear wrenched the guy's arm up until the man cried out. Then he pressed his forearm across the back of his neck, pinning him to the van.

"Nice try," Bear growled in the man's ear in between heavy breaths, "but I win."

The man only wheezed in response. Whether it was from their race or the way he'd hit the van, Bear wasn't sure. Nor did he care.

"Who the hell are you?" Bear kicked out the man's knees, sending him to the ground, then grabbed a fistful of hair and wrenched his head back. "What are you doing here?"

The man just glared at him. Bear took in the details of his features for the first time. Dark hair. Tanned face with a couple scratches down the side. His grimace revealed a missing tooth. A splash of color drew attention. Red and blue. A tattoo. Up close, Bear saw it was an American eagle. This was the guy who had attacked Mandy.

"You son of a bitch."

The man grinned up at him like he knew what he was thinking. There was no fear in his sharp, beady eyes. "How's the kid? She make it home okay? Let her know I've got her homework if she wants it back."

Bear didn't bother responding. He reared back and slammed his knuckles into the bridge of the other guy's nose. Blood started gushing, but the guy just laughed. Bear pulled back to do it again, when a flash of black out of the corner of his eye caught his attention.

He looked up just in time to see another figure rounding the van. The new guy scooped up the branch. Before Bear could let go of the tattooed man and defend himself, the second guy swung, connecting with the side of Bear's skull.

His vision went black around the edges. He dropped to a knee. Another flash of pain spread through his head, neck, and shoulders, and he fell to the side.

Bear was on the ground with the two figures standing over him. He tried to get up, but the branch was already swinging toward his head for a third time. He deflected the blow, leaving his stomach wide open for the tattooed guy to kick him in the gut. Bear grunted as all the air left his lungs. Before he could recover, the second guy brought the branch back down on his skull one final time.

23

BEAR SHOOK OFF THE COBWEBS AND SAW THE MEN RACING AWAY IN THE van. Dirt and bits of gravel pelted his face. He ignored the painful throbbing in his head to peer through the cloud of dust. He couldn't make out the license plate. He cursed and spat out mud, then clambered to his feet. He regained his balance in a few seconds. He touched his fingertips to his head. They came back bloody. Not enough to make him worry.

By the time Bear made it back through the woods, McKinnon was halfway across the yard. She jogged to catch up to him. She stopped a few feet short. "What the hell happened to you?"

"Pinned him down on the other side," Bear said. "But there was a second guy. He jumped me and they sped off."

"In a panel van?"

"How'd you guess?" Bear followed her back to the house. "And before you ask, didn't get a license plate." He scowled. "The guy who went after Donovan was the same guy who tried to kidnap Mandy. Matches the description perfectly."

"Did you get a glimpse of the second one?"

Bear shook his head and winced at the way it throbbed. "No. Similar build and features but didn't get a good look at him before he knocked me out."

"You gonna be okay?"

"Trust me, I've had worse." Bear pointed at the house. "Everything all right in there?"

"Yeah. He's a little shaken up. Not hurt, though." She opened the front door and made her way through the entrance. "Let me make some introductions. Got a feeling you'll be interested in what he has to say."

Bear followed her up the stairs and down a short hallway. The house had that feeling of having been lived in for decades. It was full of pictures on the walls. Knick-knacks and souvenirs on tables. A lot of stories were wrapped up in a home like this, and even though it had a woman's touch, there was something dusty and forgotten about it.

McKinnon knocked on a door at the end of the hallway. It was splintered along the middle but hadn't cracked all the way. "Carl, it's me. I've got Riley with me."

The man's response was muffled. "Did you tell him yet?"

"No. I think it'd be better if he heard it from you."

A few seconds of silence passed before Bear felt the floorboards creak and the door swung open to reveal an older man in a sweater and a pair of slacks. McKinnon had said he was sixty-five, but he looked younger. His eyes were sharp and bright, and his skin had only a few age spots around his brow. He looked strong, but clearly smart enough not to fight a man half his age.

Bear didn't bother to beat around the bush. "Tell me what?"

The old man retreated into the room and sat down on the bed. Bear caught a sense of wariness on his face, but he didn't look scared. "My name is Carl Donovan."

"I've heard." Bear regretted his tone as soon as the words were out of his mouth. He cleared his throat and tried again. "Are you okay? Did they get you?"

"I'm fine. Saw them coming. Don't think they were expecting me to move as fast as I did. Made it upstairs and locked myself in before they could do anything." He shifted his focus behind them to the door. "Gonna have to replace that, though."

"I'll get Joe to swing by," McKinnon said. "He'll do it for the cost of the door."

Bear didn't know who Joe was, and he didn't care. "You called the Sheriff directly. No 911." He waited for the old man to refute it. When he didn't, Bear turned to McKinnon. "And you're keeping something from me. Thought we were in this together?"

"We are—"

"Don't blame her, son." Donovan stood up. He was a full head shorter than Bear. "I told her to keep my name out of it. Obviously, things didn't go according to plan."

Bear crossed the room and peered out the window at the driveway. The cruiser was sitting there, its lights still flashing and the passenger side door still open. He turned back to the others. "Now seems like a good time to fill me in."

Donovan made eye contact with the sheriff, who nodded her head in approval. He took a deep breath and shoved one of his hands in his pocket. He held Bear's gaze. "I called Sheriff McKinnon two days ago with some information about the girl you found. Katie. I remember when she went missing. It was a tragic story. There was a lot of back-and-forth back then about what might've happened to her. Most people thought she ran away. But another little girl, Katie's best friend, said she never would've done that. Something bothered me about the whole affair. I knew her father. We worked at HealTek together. We weren't friends. He wasn't the nicest guy. We'd say hello in the morning, you know? You form a connection with someone just by seeing them every day."

Bear nodded his head and remained quiet.

"Walter wouldn't answer any of my questions. Completely shut down. And not like a father who was grieving. Like a father who was afraid." Donovan swallowed, and his voice trembled. "I started asking around. At first, I just wanted to see if there was anything I could do to help, you know? Start a collection or sign a card or something. But no one would talk about it. Eventually, one of the higher-ups came down to talk to me. Said I was endangering company morale. Can you believe that?"

"Sounds like a company line," Bear said.

"After that, I stopped asking about it. Kept to myself. Had a few people distance themselves from me. I was up for a promotion, too. I had as much of a chance as anyone, but they gave it to my subordinate. He jumped three levels in a day. He's one of the top earners at the company now."

"The people at HealTek didn't want you asking questions about this girl's disappearance." Bear shook his head to clear away the thousand and one questions he had. "This is the same company that eighty percent of this town works for?"

"The very same."

McKinnon stepped forward. "Tell him about this morning."

Donovan looked away now. "I sent you that letter."

Bear blanched. Then he turned to McKinnon. "Did you know?"

"I didn't." She held up her hands when he squinted at her. "I swear."

He turned back to the old man. "Why'd you do that?" After a beat, "*How'd* you do that?"

"I paid a kid a hundred bucks to deliver it. Told him to drop it off, bang on the door, then run away. If he could do it without you seeing him, I'd give him another hundred."

"He earned that two hundred." Bear tipped his head back and blew out a breath. Another bout of dizziness snaked through him. "Why give me a warning at all?"

He shrugged. "I thought I was being smart. Didn't think it'd get back to me."

"Still. You didn't have to do that. You said we were making it worse. Why?"

Donovan sat back down on the bed. He looked ten years older. "I have many friends who still work at the company. It's a family business in a way. Fathers and mothers and then sons and daughters. If you're not working at HealTek, then you know a dozen people who are."

"Someone approached you."

"Several someones." Donovan squeaked out a sad laugh. "I don't think any of them know what's going on. Just like I didn't really know what was going on back then. But you can tell when people are on edge. It kicks your survival instincts into overdrive."

"Why you?" Bear asked. "I assume you're retired."

"Barely, but yeah. As for why me?" He paused for a moment. "I guess I stirred the pot once. They thought I might do it again."

"Why now?"

McKinnon answered for him. "Carl and I have a mutual friend. My neighbors." She looked sad at the mention of them. "When their daughter fell ill, it reminded Carl of—" She broke off, looking at him.

"My wife," he said. "She died from the same symptoms a while back. Now I can see it for what it was. A warning. But back then? I was too absorbed in my own grief to notice anything else. I kept my head down and out of trouble because it was the only way I could get through life without her."

Bear paced the room. There were too many puzzle pieces on the table. "So, Katie goes missing, and her friend says she was sick. Your neighbor's kid gets sick, and so does my daughter's best friend. All have the same symptoms. All three families had people who worked at Heal-Tek, including yourself. We know the company didn't want people asking questions. We get run off the road. Mandy almost gets kidnapped. People pressure you to keep your head out of the game. All signs point in one direction."

"What about Bowser Freight?" McKinnon asked. "We couldn't place the van at their company."

"They do medical shipments for HealTek." Donovan looked sick to his stomach. "They don't advertise it, but they do. Have been for decades."

Bear turned to McKinnon with fire in his eyes.

She held up her hand to stop him. "We don't have any evidence. Nothing tangible. We don't know whether it's the whole company or just one person. And we can't take on HealTek without knowing exactly what we're up against. It'd be a suicide mission. For all of us."

Bear threw up his hands. "Then where do we get some evidence?"

"Eileen Mayberry." Donovan looked at Sheriff McKinnon. "Katie's friend. I haven't talked to her in years, but I know she's never forgotten what happened back then. She spent half her teens protesting the company. Everyone thought she was a nut job. She eventually got run out of town. It wouldn't surprise me if she was still obsessed with Katie's case."

Bear stepped forward. "Can you tell us where she lives?"

"No, but I can tell you how to find out." He shifted his gaze to McKinnon. "On one condition."

"Which is?"

"You send me somewhere HealTek will never find me."

24

Mandy tucked the blanket around Laura Lynn's arm and smoothed a piece of hair away from her face. The other girl had just fallen asleep again. Mandy felt better when she could talk to her best friend and gauge the level of pain she was in. However, the doctors had said getting as much rest as possible would help Laura Lynn feel better.

That morning, Bear and the sheriff had dropped Mandy off at Marcus' house so she could go with them to the hospital. Marcus' mom was consoling Mrs. Weinberger outside the room, talking in hushed voices like they didn't want to let the kids know how serious the situation was.

Ironically, Mandy was pretty sure she was the only one out of all three kids and both adults who had any inkling of what was going on here.

When Mandy returned to the chair next to Marcus, he looked up.

"So, are you going to tell me what happened?"

Mandy had hinted that something went down after she left his house earlier in the day, but his mom had ushered them into the car, and there had been no time to speak privately until now. Mandy was bursting at the seams with information. "Some guy tried to kidnap me," she said.

Marcus' eyes widened and then shot to the door, like he was half a second from sprinting across the room and getting his mom. "Are you joking?"

"No." Mandy scooted closer to him. "I was walking back from your house. This guy pulls up next to me in a van. He offered to give me a lift to my house. Like that would work now? Maybe back in the fifties."

Marcus looked like he wanted to join in the on the joke, but fear prevented him. He leaned in closer. "How did you get away?"

"I can take care of myself." Mandy flexed an arm, then giggled at Marcus' unchanging expression. "Seriously, dude, lighten up. I'm *fine*."

"But weren't you scared?"

Mandy thought about lying to him, but when she remembered her relief upon seeing Bear at home, she almost teared up again. "Yeah, I was scared." Her voice was quieter now. "Terrified. Everything sort of happened in a blur. I got a couple good shots in. My dad taught me how to fight. But I was lucky. As soon as I had a chance, I just ran away. And all the information we printed off is gone."

"That's why you wanted me to bring my laptop today." Marcus tapped his bag.

She nodded. "I'm sorry. I really tried to save it. But my bag ripped, and—"

Marcus placed a hand on her shoulder. The look on his face was so sincere, she really did tear up this time.

"It's okay. I'm just glad you're safe. That paperwork isn't worth your life." He let his hand drop. "What's going on, Mandy? Your dad finds a body in the back yard from, like, fifteen years ago. Laura Lynn and a bunch of other people get sick. And you almost get kidnapped. Even in a movie, this wouldn't make sense."

"We also almost got run off the road last night," she added. "By another van. I don't know if it was the same guy. I'm gonna be jumping every time I see a van for the next few years."

"Are they after you?" he asked.

"I think they're after my dad. They want him to stop looking into all this."

Marcus looked sheepish, like he was ashamed that he was afraid. "Maybe you should. I mean, is it worth it? Putting your life in danger?"

Mandy felt her anger spike, but she cooled it by looking over at Laura Lynn. Marcus was a nice guy—he was sweet and smart and funny and weird. She liked him a lot, but he was sheltered. He hadn't seen what Mandy had seen growing up. She tried not to blame him for thinking the best thing to do was keep your head down when you were afraid.

"It is worth it." She turned back to him. "And when my dad figures all this out and saves everyone, you'll see I was right."

Something changed in Marcus' expression. He wasn't any less scared, but there was a determined set to his jaw now. "Okay. Let's do this." He pulled out his laptop. "I can bring up the information again, but I'm not sure how we'll print it off. I might just have to email it to you."

She'd set up an email for school. It wasn't ideal. She was afraid someone would be able to trace the information, but she needed those hospital records. "That works, I guess."

Marcus' fingers flew over the keyboard. When he dramatically hit enter, his mouth turned down. "That's weird."

"What's wrong?"

"I think I might've put the password in wrong. Hang on." He tried again. When he looked up at her, she knew they were in trouble. "It's not working. Someone must've figured out what we were doing."

"Now what?"

Marcus leaned over to check that his mom was still out in the hallway. "I'm not sure, but whatever we do, we have to do it fast. They're not going to leave us alone for much longer."

"You won't be able to get back into the system?"

He shrugged. "I mean, I can. Eventually. It'll take some time to do it so we don't get caught."

"And I guess we'd give ourselves away using a hospital computer."

"Just a little bit."

Mandy sat up straight. "Actually—"

"No." Marcus leaned closer, his voice coming out as a hiss. "That's really dangerous, Mandy. What if you're caught?"

"What are they going to do? I'm fourteen. They won't throw me in juvie. At worst, I'll get a stern talking to." She put her hands on her hips while making a serious adult face.

"You don't know that." Marcus looked worried. "Someone tried to kidnap you *just a few hours ago.* Are you crazy?"

"Only a little bit." She grinned and got to her feet. "I'm going to pretend to go to the bathroom. Then I'm going to see if I can find Dr. Sing's office. Maybe I can find her new password or get on her computer. There's gotta be something useful in there."

Marcus threw up his hands. "There is so much that could go wrong with this plan. What if she's in there? What if someone sees you? What if there's nothing to find?"

"Then I'll wing it."

As Marcus' jaw dropped in disbelief, Mandy skipped across the room and into the hallway. The adults stopped talking as soon as they saw her. "I just have to pee," Mandy said in her sweetest voice.

Marcus' mom smiled down at her, and Mandy headed toward the sign for the bathroom. She turned back to the two women before she entered. They were engrossed in their conversation once again. She figured she'd have at least twenty minutes before they started to wonder where she was. Maybe another five or so before one of them tried to find her in the bathroom. It should be more than enough time.

Mandy continued down the hallway and around the corner. No one paid her much attention. She held herself like she knew where she was going. When she reached the elevators, she looked at the directory. Dr. Sing's office was two floors above her. She was off to a good start.

She decided to take the stairs to get a peek at what the floor looked like. From her vantage point in the stairwell, this one seemed busier than the last. But luck was on her side. Dr. Sing's office was right across the hall.

Mandy waited until the hallway was empty before launching herself from the stairwell into the corridor. She was light on her feet, just like Bear had taught her. She leaned her ear against the door to the office and waited for three beats to see if she could hear anything. All was silent. She tried the handle. Locked.

She had expected this. It had been one of the first lessons Bear had ever taught her. Mandy pulled a bobby pin from her hair and stuck it in the lock. Thank God she hadn't needed to steal a keycard.

The lock popped. Mandy had to resist the urge to cheer. She slipped inside, shut the door with a tiny *click*, and locked it behind her. The lack of windows left the room pitch black. She switched on her phone's flashlight.

Aside from the desk and a couple chairs, metal containers filled the entire room. Filing cabinets. They weren't even all the same size or color, like Dr. Sing had collected them over the years as her client list expanded. Some of them looked rather beat up and old, but a few were brand new and still shiny.

The first thing Mandy tried was the computer. It was old and took a few minutes to boot up. When it did, it prompted her for a password. She looked around the desk to see if Dr. Sing had been stupid enough to keep a sticky note with the information here, too. She cursed when she came up with nothing. She shut the computer back down so it wouldn't look like anyone had tampered with it.

Most of the doctor's desk drawers were filled with office supplies, like pens and pads of paper. There were some latex gloves and sample boxes of medications, but Mandy didn't recognize any of the names. There was a drawer that was locked. After a few seconds, she picked that one, too. She wouldn't be able to close it again without the key, but that was a risk she was willing to take.

Inside, there were several mid-sized journals. Mandy peeled one open and saw notes in tiny handwriting filled them. It was cursive, and she could barely read it. There were names and dates and some drawings along the margins. They looked like patient notes, but if Dr. Sing had a method for how they were organized, it was a code Mandy couldn't crack. She decided to leave the journals for now. Maybe something else would prove more useful.

Mandy bumped the drawer closed with her hip and made her way around the desk. There were at least half a dozen filing cabinets to choose from. She went with the oldest looking one first. It pulled open with a squeak and was heavier than she expected. It was full of files labeled last name first. She didn't recognize any of the names from the list she had pulled earlier, and their charts were full of information she didn't know how to read.

Closing the drawer, Mandy blew out a breath of air before opening another. She had been so hellbent on getting answers she hadn't stopped to wonder what she should be looking for. It's not like there'd be a folder labeled WHY PEOPLE ARE GETTING POISONED. She wasn't even sure if she was looking in the right place. Dr. Sing was only one of the many doctors in the hospital. It was a good place to start, but who was to say she was involved at all?

Mandy closed the second drawer and opened another. She did this a dozen more times until she had gone through every filing cabinet. She was painfully aware that her twenty minutes were almost up. If she didn't get back from the bathroom soon, Marcus' mom would start to worry, and then the whole hospital would be looking for her. The last thing she needed was to be caught in here red-handed.

Not that she'd found anything important.

Mandy closed the last drawer and slumped against the wall. She thumped her head back in frustration, not caring how much it hurt. But the wall gave a little, and the sound was more hollow than solid. Turning, she inspected it more closely.

It was a brown panel wall from the seventies. She didn't know how old the hospital was, but on her way in, she'd noticed one wing looked newer than the other, like they had added on instead of overhauling the whole thing.

Mandy pressed her hands against the wall and pushed. A section gave way and clicked open. The seams were hard to spot amongst the panels, but now that she knew it was there, she could see them easily enough. Dr. Sing had built a small hidden compartment in the wall and had partially hidden it with one of the filing cabinets.

Mandy slid the panel over on its track and used her phone to look inside the cubbyhole. It was small, maybe the size of a safe, but full of files and notebooks, similar to the ones she'd found in the desk. But these were hidden for a reason.

There was a small switch on the back of the wall inside the compartment. Trying to resist the urge to flip it was futile, so she did. When she pushed the little nob up, the panel slid back into place, nearly invisible to the naked eye. Pressing on the piece of wall again clicked it open, the nob turned down once more.

A simple contraption, and one that would hide whatever Dr. Sing didn't want others to see.

With little time to spare, Mandy moved fast. She pulled out the first folder and skimmed the pages. They were shipping orders for antivenom from all kinds of snakes and ordered in huge quantities. At least a thousand at a time. Mandy looked up at the wall, lost in thought. Most hospitals kept antivenom on hand, but not in this quantity. She knew the stuff was expensive and in low supply due to the complexity of making it. Why would Dr. Sing need so much?

After snapping a photo of a few of the shipping orders, she replaced the file and grabbed another. More shipping orders. This one was for a drug she couldn't even begin to pronounce. She had no idea what it was for, but she took a picture anyway. Maybe Bear would know.

Mandy grabbed a notebook and opened it to a random page. The doctor's same small handwriting was squeezed into the page. It was dated from last year, and when she skimmed the words, she caught a few she could read. *Trial. Prognosis. Side effects. More time. Larger subject pool.*

From what Mandy gathered, it sounded like Dr. Sing was conducting some sort of experiment, like a clinical trial. But what did that have to do with antivenom? And why would she keep it a secret? And where could she conduct something like this without people noticing? Surely the hospital would notice her ordering so much.

Mandy heard the squeak of shoes outside the office door, followed by a muffled voice speaking on the phone. She snapped a picture of the notebook and shoved it back into the compartment, then froze, holding her breath. How long had it been? Well past twenty minutes. Was Dr. Sing returning to her office?

Her worst fears were confirmed when she heard a key inserted into the door. Mandy flipped the switch inside the compartment in a flash and turned off the flashlight on her phone. Shoving the device into her sock, she leapt across the room, away from the secret panel. The best she could do was hide behind the door and hope the doctor wouldn't notice her.

But it was no good. As soon as Dr. Sing flipped on the lights, she swung the door closed so she could hang up her jacket on a hook on the other side. When she caught sight of Mandy, she dropped her phone and let out a startled scream.

Busted.

25

MCKINNON PARKED THE CAR AROUND THE CORNER FROM THE BOOKSHOP where they were meeting Eileen Mayberry. Bear peered through the window and checked the street. It was bustling with people. Wasn't much of a surprise for a Saturday afternoon in the fall.

"Busy," McKinnon remarked.

Bear grunted in response. He wasn't sure how he felt about their current situation. The old man they'd rescued earlier in the day had called Eileen on his phone. She was quick to answer him but clammed up as soon as she realized he wasn't alone. Donovan had no idea where she lived, and she wasn't giving up that information. After explaining the situation and vouching for Bear and McKinnon three times, the old man had convinced her to meet them.

That's how they'd ended up outside the Book Emporium about an hour north of town. Eileen had instructed them to meet her in a back room. It was smart, Bear realized, for both parties. Public enough that the situation was unlikely to go sideways, and private enough that they could talk uninterrupted.

McKinnon popped open her door, and Bear followed her inside the shop. The woman behind the counter greeted them with a smile that fell from her face as soon as she saw the sheriff's uniform. That thing was like a beacon of distrust.

And people rarely had nothing to hide.

"We're here to meet Eileen?" McKinnon asked.

"She's in the back already," the woman said. She looked Bear up and down, and the crease between her eyebrows deepened into a ravine.

"Thanks." He smiled in the hopes of putting her at ease. But the crease didn't disappear.

The two of them made their way between packed bookcases. Bear knocked over a handful of stacked books and couldn't manage to bend over to pick them up. McKinnon shot him a look like he'd done it on purpose. He shrugged in response.

The back room was cordoned off with a heavy sheet of plastic that McKinnon pushed to the side. There was a short hallway that opened into a break room. It had a single table, a couple chairs, and a refrigerator. Bear was disappointed to see there wasn't a coffeemaker.

In the center of the room, a young woman sat with her hands folded in front of her. She looked at war with herself—should she run, or stay and get answers? Should she help, or continue her investigation on her own? Was this a mistake, or would it finally put her best friend's case, and soul, to rest?

McKinnon spoke first. "Eileen?"

"Yes."

The sheriff held her hand out. "You can call me Josie."

Eileen shook her hand, then turned to Bear. He cleared his throat. "Riley." He extended his own hand, which engulfed hers. "Appreciate you meeting with us."

The young woman nodded. Her dark bangs fell into her eyes. She wore heavy makeup and all-black clothes. There were half a dozen shiny silver rings on her finger, and a handful of necklaces circled her neck. Everything had been selected to look casual and thrown together.

"Thank you for finally taking this seriously." There was a bite to her words. "Only took fifteen years."

"I'm sorry about that." McKinnon pulled out a chair and sat down.

Bear followed suit. "I haven't been the sheriff for long, and I didn't know anything strange was going on until we found Katie's body."

Eileen shifted her gaze to Bear. "You're the one who found her."

"I am."

Her features softened. "Can you ell me about it?"

"I was digging out my garden when I found a septic tank." Bear had relayed the story many times, but it felt different sitting across from Eileen. "When I opened it, I knew the bones were human. There was a clump of hair stuck in the lid. That helped them identify her."

"You know, it's funny. Back when I still believed in something, I'd pray every night that we'd find her. Even if it was a body. By that time, I knew she wasn't coming back. I just wanted closure." Eileen picked at her cuticles. "And now that I have it, I don't feel any different. Nothing's changed."

"I'm sorry," Bear said, and he hoped the young woman believed him.

"Do you know how she died?"

"Not exactly," McKinnon said. "Evidence points to her having been poisoned. She was sick. But we can't know if she'd been strangled or drowned or any number of other possibilities."

"Sounds like you know more than me," Eileen said. "Not sure how I can help."

"What were her parents like?" McKinnon asked. "We're having trouble tracking them down."

"Her mom was an addict and pretty negligent." Some of the edge was back in Eileen's voice now. "Her father was a dick. He yelled a lot. Pretty sure he hit her mom."

"Do you know where they are?"

"Last I heard they moved across the country. Washington State, maybe? That was years ago."

"What about Jeremy Olsen?"

Eileen's eyebrows knit together. "Jeremy? What does he have to do with this?"

"He was the previous owner of the house before I moved in there," Bear explained. "We're wondering if he could've had something to do with Katie's disappearance."

After Olsen's name had surfaced, McKinnon had tried to locate him, to no avail. It was a good line of questioning. Perhaps Eileen knew him and had kept in touch.

Eileen paled. "Jeremy was a friend of Katie's dad. I never knew how they knew each other. Mr. Lamoureux worked at HealTek, but I don't think Jeremy did. He was always hanging around, doing odd jobs for the family, and for other people, too."

"What kind of jobs?"

"Picking stuff up. Dropping stuff off. Fixing this and that." She leveled them with a look. "For a while there, I thought he was a good person. I always saw him mediating fights between people. I'd hear him say he'd go talk to this person or that person. Now, I realized he was probably the muscle."

"For who?"

Eileen shrugged. "Mr. Lamoureux? Someone else? HealTek in general? I'm not sure."

McKinnon leaned forward on the table. "You seemed pretty scared when you heard his name."

"He was nice to me when Katie and I were kids. He was in his early twenties at the time. We both had a crush on him, you know. He was in shape. Good looking. And he paid attention to us. Made us feel good about ourselves."

"Did anything ever happen between you two?"

Eileen looked away. "Not until later. I wouldn't drop the Katie thing. He kept coming around, trying to convince me to just let it go. That it wasn't worth it. We hooked up a few times. I'll admit," her voice bitter now, "he kept me distracted for a while."

"But not forever?"

"I've thought of Katie every day for the past fifteen years. I needed answers. I needed someone to be responsible. I thought Jeremy was helping me cope. But he was just trying to make me forget."

"What else happened?"

"We had a fight. Everything blew up that night. He threatened me in a parking lot." She looked away and clenched her fist as though she hadn't moved past this. "Mr. Donovan was actually the one to break it up. He's the only one I trust from back home. He told me to get out. I didn't want to at first. When Jeremy came back later that night, I ran. Didn't have a dollar to my name. But I ran."

"You made the right choice." McKinnon took out her notepad and jotted down a few words. "Do you have any idea where Jeremy Olsen is now?"

"No clue. We didn't exactly stay in touch."

Bear shifted in his seat, drawing the young girl's attention. "Does the last name Weinberger mean anything to you?"

"Yeah, I know the Weinberger's. Well, not personally. That whole family worked at HealTek when I lived back home. The father—dead now—was high up in the company. Right there with Katie's dad. And his eldest son took over his role when he retired. I never liked any of them. You could tell they didn't care about what the company was doing. All they cared about was money."

"In all these years," McKinnon started, "did you ever find anything on Mr. Lamoureux or HealTek or Jeremy?"

Eileen took a deep breath and blew it out, her bangs fluttering in the disturbance. "Let's just say that Mr. Lamoureux was nothing like his father. He was a terrible worker who always did the bare minimum to get by. He was given a C-level position in the company, but he cared more about the title than the actual work. Liked to flaunt it in other people's faces without actually contributing to HealTek's agenda."

"Which was what?" Bear asked.

She shrugged. "Hell if I know. Most of that was confidential. But this was a post-9/11 world. There were rumors about biological weapons and super soldier serums." She waved her hand. "Crazy stuff. But Katie's dad liked to run his mouth."

"He got in trouble," McKinnon said. "A warning?"

"A few, from what I heard. Not many people liked him." She picked at her cuticles again. "I think Katie was his final warning. He packed up his wife and they hightailed it out of there within a few months. I think they knew she was dead. Even without a body. Everyone did. And I think we all knew who did it, even if we didn't say it out loud. The police didn't even bother chasing them when they moved out of state."

Bear's phone vibrated in his pocket. He thought about ignoring it, not wanting to disrupt the flow of Eileen's story, but then he remembered what was happening to Mandy the last time she tried to call him. He stepped away to answer it.

"Bear?" Mandy's voice was small on the other line.

"What's wrong?"

"Nothing, I'm okay." Her words were fast, and he could tell she was holding something back. "But I need you to pick me up from the hospital. And, uh, Sheriff needs to come back, too."

"What happened?" Bear hated the way his brain sifted through a thousand scenarios in a matter of seconds. "Are you hurt?"

"Not hurt," Mandy said. Her voice was strained. "Just in trouble. Big trouble."

26

Bear hadn't looked Mandy in the eye since they'd picked her up from the hospital. The doctor who'd caught Mandy breaking and entering, Dr. Sing, had left the hospital without instructions for what to do with Mandy. When Sheriff McKinnon showed up, security handed the girl over.

Mandy sat in the back of the police cruiser. Bear stared straight out the windshield, gathering his thoughts. McKinnon looked like she wanted to say something, maybe even tell Bear not to go too hard on Mandy, but she didn't dare.

After a short period, Bear found some words. "You shouldn't have done that, Mandy."

"Break into the office?" Mandy asked. "Or get caught?"

Smart ass. "You know what I mean." Bear kept his voice even, but as he twisted around in his seat to look at her, he felt his temperature rise. The least she could do was look remorseful. "That was stupid, Mandy. And you know it. You could be in serious trouble right now."

"I know, and I'm sorry. Really. I shouldn't have done that." A little smile formed on her lips. "And I definitely shouldn't have gotten caught."

Bear ignored the joke. "What were you thinking? I know you want to help. You can't do it like this. We—the two adults in the car—had it handled."

"I don't agree." Mandy stared him in the eyes. "And if you did, how would I know that? *You don't tell me anything.*"

"You're fourteen. You're a kid. You don't get to know everything."

"That's ridiculous." Now Mandy was the one with some growl in her voice. "You want to keep me safe? Then keep me informed. I can't be smart when I'm in the dark."

"I'm supposed to be smart for you. You're supposed to listen to me."

"You told me a long time ago not to rely on anyone but myself. You trained me to keep myself safe. I understand you don't want me in the middle of this—and hey, it's not like I have a death wish or something— but I *can* help you. Laura Lynn is my friend. I have to *do* something."

McKinnon turned to Bear, wearing her neutral cop expression. "She has a point."

Bear turned away. He cracked his window to let some cool air in. "So now you condone this behavior?"

"Absolutely not." McKinnon turned to face Mandy. "That was dumb, Mandy. You shouldn't have done it, and you definitely shouldn't have gotten caught." Mandy giggled, but when Bear twisted around to glare at her, she had already wiped the grin clear and tried to appear innocent. Wide eyes and all. "You could be in serious trouble right now, but you're lucky Dr. Sing isn't looking to teach you a lesson."

"I know." Mandy sounded like she was getting the message. "I'm really, really sorry." She looked down at her knees, then back up. "But don't you want to know what I found?"

Curiosity rose in Bear. He tried to squash it back down. It was no use. He had to know. "All right, I'll bite."

Mandy had the good sense not to sound too smug. "Dr. Sing has a hidden compartment in her office!" The words rushed out as one long blurred sound, leaving her breathless, like she'd been dying to tell them. "On the far side, kind of behind one of the filing cabinets, you could press the wall in, and a little panel would pop open. Inside, there was paperwork she obviously didn't want anyone else to see."

"Why her?" McKinnon asked. "How did you know to go to her office?"

"I didn't." Mandy looked away. Bear knew she was hiding something. "It was a lucky guess. My friend Marcus' mom is friends with Dr. Sing. I figured I'd see if she was hiding anything."

"What was in the compartment?" Bear asked. He didn't approve, but he didn't want Mandy to get into any more trouble. And he definitely didn't want to drag Marcus or his family into it.

"All these shipping orders for antivenom. Like, thousands of vials of it."

"Antivenom? For snakes?"

She nodded. "I thought that was weird, too. It was too much for this hospital. I mean, I don't think I've seen a single snake since we moved here. Why would she need that much?"

"No idea." Bear wracked his brain. It was such a random and specific thing. There had to be a purpose for it. "Anything else?"

"I found journals in there. I couldn't read her handwriting, but it sounded like they were testing something. She had written out a bunch of results for a clinical trial. I wasn't sure what it all meant, but it's pretty weird that she was hiding it, right?"

"Yeah," McKinnon said, her voice faraway. "Pretty weird."

"Did you tell the Sheriff what I found earlier?" Mandy's voice was hesitant, like she was worried about getting into more trouble. "On the computer?"

"No, but you might as well."

"I, uh, came across some information," Mandy began.

"Came across some information?" McKinnon asked.

Bear waved a hand half-heartedly. "It's better if you don't ask."

"Okay." McKinnon looked skeptical for a moment, but when she turned to Mandy, she'd smoothed her face. "Go on."

"I saw Laura Lynn's charts. Information about her in the hospital's computer system." Mandy flushed, but she hurried on. "She's really sick. Like she's been poisoned. I wasn't sure what all the chemicals meant or all the words, but it's obvious something's been building in her system. Then we searched for her same symptoms in the system."

McKinnon raised an eyebrow. "We?"

"Me." Mandy flushed deeper. "I searched for her symptoms. There are a lot of people who've been sick lately. They show the same symptoms at first, but it ends up being different diseases. Some recover. Some don't. A lot don't. But it usually runs in families."

"What do you mean?" McKinnon was wading into the deep end.

"The people who are sick, it's usually the whole family. Like Laura Lynn and her parents. People who share the same last name. So, I presume they live in the same household."

"You presume, huh?" McKinnon looked like she was caught between being amused and being impressed. "Why would that be important?"

"Because that can help us figure out how people are getting sick. Or at least narrow it down. Like food poisoning. If there's bad food, the entire family is gonna get sick. Whoever is doing this isn't trying to target one person. Or, if they are, they don't care if there's collateral damage. And it always seems like the kids get it worse."

"Collateral damage?" She turned to Bear. "Who is this kid?"

Bear shrugged.

"The kids' immune systems probably aren't as strong," McKinnon said. "And they're smaller, so they'll get sick faster."

"Exactly." Mandy was on a roll now. "So, maybe if we figure out the method, we can work backwards and figure out what's going on."

"Could be food," Bear said. "But how would they guarantee the family eats it? What if they decide to make meatloaf instead of spaghetti and tomatoes from the neighbor's garden?"

"What about in the air?" Mandy said. "Could it be something they pump into the house?"

"Unlikely." Bear's mind was racing now. "That's a lot harder to control. And whoever is doing this would have to be careful to avoid it themselves."

"If we think HealTek is involved," McKinnon began, "maybe it's something the employees are bringing home with them."

"You think HealTek is involved?" Mandy sat forward. "Since when?"

"Since this afternoon." Bear's voice indicated she shouldn't expect any further explanation. "But if it is something from the company, then what? Meds? Can't guarantee everyone will take them. Food? It'd be kind of obvious that some people were eating it and others weren't. And again, can't guarantee it gets eaten when it comes home."

There was silence in the car as everyone wracked their brains.

Bear broke it. "If we put pressure on Dr. Sing, she might talk."

"I'm going to pretend your intent isn't as ominous as it sounds," McKinnon said. "But if she's got HealTek behind her, she's probably smart enough to keep her trap shut."

"Any chance we can get a warrant?" he asked.

"Not without proof."

"About that." Mandy pulled her phone out and handed it to Bear. "Will this help?"

Bear looked down at the phone and swiped through the pictures Mandy had taken in Dr. Sing's office. The shipping orders were more significant than she'd realized, and Bear was able to paint a mental picture. Not only was Dr. Sing ordering vast quantities of drugs, but also altering the original order in the hospital's records, replacing the name for the antivenom with a name for a common drug. Dr. Sing was falsifying evidence.

27

Three hours later, McKinnon had a warrant. She and Bear put together their plan of attack in the hospital parking lot.

"What'd you end up doing with Mandy?" McKinnon asked.

"I tried to get Marcus' mother to take her again, but she refused."

"Mandy did almost get her son arrested."

Bear waved away the comment. "They seem like a family with a good lawyer."

"You have a point there." She chuckled. "So, where is she now?"

"Movie night at the library."

"Oh, I'm sure she loves that."

It was Bear's turn to chuckle. "It was ten and under, too. We had to tell them she was big for her age. She's not going to forget this one. Might not forgive, either."

"It's for her own good," McKinnon said. "She understands that, even if she doesn't like it."

He nodded. "The library has plenty of places to hide. Several exits. She's smart. And that's only if these guys are dumb enough to attack a bunch of kids in public. They may have half the town working for them, but that's a little bold, even for them."

"We can only hope. Still not sure how they have gotten away with everything."

"Money. Manipulation. A charming personality, you would think. That's always benefited me."

McKinnon laughed and said nothing.

Bear pointed to the paper she'd just pulled out of her pocket. "How was getting the warrant?"

"Smooth enough. A little push back. The falsified records made the difference."

"Did they ask where you got the pictures from?"

"Oh yeah. Told them it was an anonymous informant. Needed to remain that way until after their testimony. We need to protect the sanctity of the investigation."

"And they bought that?"

She shrugged. "More or less." McKinnon took a deep breath, held it, then blew it out. "You ready for this?"

"Always."

"Come on." As they made their way across the parking lot, McKinnon cleared her throat. "By the way, we may need to rely on *your* charming personality."

"Oh?"

"There's a security guard at the hospital who doesn't like me very much, and I'm pretty sure he's on duty."

"What'd you do to him?"

"I arrested him for a DUI a couple of years back. His name's Billy Stewart. He was a cop, and he asked me to drop the charges in the name of *'solidarity amongst officers.'* I didn't. He got fired. Now he works in security."

"And he's been your arch nemesis ever since."

"Pretty much." McKinnon pulled the door open for Bear, and the two of them made their way back to the security desk. A short, muscular man with a week's worth of stubble sat behind the desk, playing on his phone. "Hey, Billy."

He looked up, his face falling as he took in the pair of them. He placed his phone on his desk, face down. "It's Security Officer Stewart."

"Billy." Bear leaned on the counter. "We're gonna need you to unlock Dr. Sing's office. Sheriff here has some official police business to conduct."

Billy sized up Bear. Apparently didn't like what he found because he ignored him and turned to McKinnon. "If you want to get into the doctor's office, you either need her direct permission or a warrant to—"

McKinnon slid the piece of paper across the desk. "Right there."

Billy took his sweet time picking up the warrant and reading every word. As the seconds ticked by, Bear felt his patience wearing thinner. His hand curled into a fist, and McKinnon shot him a look. It wouldn't be good for their investigation if he caused a scene here. Bear was sure it'd make him feel better briefly.

"This says you're allowed to explore anything within the confines of Dr. Sing's office, including her computer and physical files."

McKinnon stared him down. "I'm aware. I requested the warrant."

"Just making sure we're all following the rules here."

"I hear you're a rule-breaker yourself." Bear didn't hide his smirk.

"I don't think I like your attitude." Billy's eyes narrowed as he looked up at Bear.

McKinnon huffed. "I don't really care what you think, Security Officer Stewart. That's a warrant. You're obligated by law to take us to Dr. Sing's office. If you don't, I'll have you arrested. You might lose this job, too." She leaned closer. "And we'll still get into her office. I'll kick down the door and put it on your tab. How about that?"

Billy's face turned beet red, but Bear couldn't tell if it was from anger or embarrassment. Either way, he kept his mouth shut as he grabbed a keyring off the wall and led them up to the office. When he unlocked it, McKinnon snatched the warrant from his hand, gestured for Bear to enter the room, then slammed the door in Billy's face.

"Prick," McKinnon said under her breath.

"It's always the short ones," Bear said.

"Height or length?" McKinnon laughed when Bear's mouth dropped open.

"Sheriff, you do have a sense of humor hidden in there."

"Must mean I like you."

"I'm flattered," he deadpanned. "Really, I am."

McKinnon's face dropped as she glanced around the room. "You see anything wrong?"

Bear looked for himself. The room felt small for a doctor's office, and he wondered if Dr. Sing saw any patients in here or if she just used it for paperwork. What had probably been an organized office earlier in the day was now in mild disarray. A handful of filing cabinet drawers were hanging open, as was a drawer in the doctor's desk. A cup of pens had been knocked over and abandoned.

"Looks like she left in a hurry," he said.

McKinnon snapped on a pair of gloves and handed some to Bear. She walked over to the wall Mandy had described with the hidden compartment. When she laid a hand on the panel and pushed inward, the door slid open. She made a sound of approval followed by a discontented click of her tongue.

"What's wrong?" Bear asked.

McKinnon stepped to the side. "Empty."

Bear peeked inside. The compartment no longer held any of the shipping orders or journals Mandy had taken pictures of earlier. The only thing left inside was the switch to close the door. Bear cursed.

"She knew we were coming," he said. "Dr. Sing wasn't taking any chances. She either figured Mandy had found the compartment or was worried we would on our search."

"She's one step ahead of us right now, and I don't like it." McKinnon peered into a few of the open filing cabinets. "There are files missing here. Mandy said they were all full. Half of these are empty."

Bear sat down at the desk and pressed the button to turn on the computer's monitor. When it came to life, Bear cursed again. He read the dialog from the pop-up window. "Your system has been returned to factory settings."

McKinnon looked at the computer over his shoulder. Her breath was hot against his neck and ear. "No way."

Bear pulled open the desk's drawers. He found sample medications and a bunch of rubber bands, but the journals Mandy had described here were missing. "What's our next step?"

"Dr. Sing is scared." McKinnon stood up straight. "She's running. If we catch up to her, we might get her to confess once we tell her we're more interested in whoever she's working for."

"*Are* we more interested?"

McKinnon scoffed. "Hell no. If that page in her journal is any sign of what the hell she's been up to, she's going to be far worse off than just losing her license."

"Do you know where she lives?" Bear asked.

A smile crept onto McKinnon's. "I do."

28

BEAR AND MCKINNON HAD DEBATED WAITING TO GET A WARRANT FOR DR. Sing's house. McKinnon didn't think the judge would grant one, and they were low on time. If the doctor knew they were closing in on her, she'd do everything in her power to get out of dodge. They wanted to catch her before she could disappear.

"Whatever she was doing had to be big," Bear said. "She had a career, a good job. A husband and kids, too, right? She either thought this was worth it, or she had to believe she'd never get caught."

"Maybe both." McKinnon took a corner sharp and hit the curb. "Either way, we have a chance of getting her to talk. If she's this scared, she knows we're close. She'll want to save her own skin."

"And she'll be more prone to turn on whoever she's working for." Bear cracked his window and let the air ruffle his hair. They were going at least eighty. "Hey, maybe I can use my charming personality on her, too. I think Billy really took to me."

"Oh, yeah." McKinnon chuckled. "He's your number one fan now."

The conversation died as they got closer to Dr. Sing's house. When they turned into the driveway, Bear whistled at the sight of the three-story Victorian and its well kempt garden featuring life-sized concrete lions perched on the front steps.

"The more she's got to lose," McKinnon said, "the more likely she'll talk."

They were cautious as they parked the car and approached the house. Bear wasn't expecting a physical altercation, but he didn't love the idea of being unarmed. He figured McKinnon would frown upon him carrying, even if he was licensed in New York. It'd be her badge for inviting him along if things went sideways.

McKinnon knocked on the door, and they both listened for sounds of activity. Dusk had fallen. The crickets were out in droves. Their sounds filled the cool night air. Goosebumps crawled along Bear's skin with every gust of wind. Winter was approaching. In hindsight, Upstate New York might not have been the best place to settle down, though it looked like the universe had known that before he did. Was there any way he'd be able to stay after this was all over? Even if he wanted to?

After a minute, Bear circled the front of the house, trying his best not to tramp through the garden. When he peered through the front window into what looked like an office, his blood ran cold. Every gust of wind chilled him to the bone.

He took a moment to confirm what he was seeing. There was blood spatter and brain matter on the window. "Sheriff, we've got a body."

McKinnon didn't waste any time unholstering her gun. Bear joined her at the front door. The itch to have his own weapon in hand returned. The sheriff looked back at him like she knew what he was thinking. Her eyes were full of apologies, no solutions. He'd have to stay outside or go in unarmed.

She tried the door. The knob turned, the latch clicked, and it swung open on silent hinges. The house was quiet. All the lights were off. A prickle of anxiety slithered across the back of Bear's neck. At least one person was inside, dead. Through the window, he couldn't confirm the identity, but placing a bet on Dr. Sing felt like a safe gamble. The question was whether she was alone. Where was her family? Where was the killer?

McKinnon made her way through the foyer and into the next room. Dr. Sing's office was filled with ornate mahogany furniture and surrounded by shelves filled with medical textbooks. It would've been beautiful if not for the doctor's stiff body slumped over the desk. Her head was turned to the side. Her eyes wide with shock.

"Stay here," McKinnon said. "I'm going to clear the house."

Bear didn't argue.

She made her way through the foyer and the next room, calling for backup over the radio. He waited to hear any shouts of surprise or gunshots. Everything remained dead silent. He turned back to the body.

Dr. Sing sat in her office chair, her head on her desk and her arms dangling by her side. As he made his way toward the window, he noticed a 9mm pistol on the ground and side-stepped to avoid it. At first glance, this looked like a textbook suicide.

But it didn't sit right. Why not just run? She had enough money to leave. And what about her family? Maybe she didn't want to leave them behind, but wasn't killing herself worse? And why go to the trouble of clearing out your office if you were just going to come home and put a bullet in your brain?

Something must've happened between then and now.

McKinnon returned to the room, holstering her weapon. "House is clear. The department is on its way." She looked pale. "Three bodies upstairs. The husband and two boys. All point-blank range. No sign of a struggle." She glanced at the body in the room. "Murder-suicide?"

"You think?" Bear didn't hide the skepticism in his voice.

"No, but that's what it looks like. You find anything?"

"Murder weapon." He looked to the gun on the floor. "And look at her computer screen. It has the same message as the one in her office."

"All the files erased." She shook her head. "Subtlety is not a strong point here."

"They didn't have a lot of time to work." Bear looked around the desk and noticed the trashcan was stuffed full. "Look at this. Shredded papers. If they'd have been smart, they would've taken everything with them." He stepped over to the window and rapped his knuckles on the glass. "I think we're being watched. They had to have been here when we arrived. Otherwise, why not make the scene look perfect?"

"They wanted it to look like a suicide." McKinnon paced from door to desk, desk to window. "They want it to look like she was hiding something. Something she'd die for. I bet if we put those shredded pages together, they'll point a finger at Dr. Sing. And only Dr. Sing."

Bear shook his head. "Her entire family is dead. Are we supposed to believe a doctor would kill her family and then herself?"

McKinnon shrugged. "People do it all the time. And what do the neighbors say? 'They were always so nice. I'm so shocked.'"

Bear had nothing to offer other than a shrug.

"If she was conducting illegal clinical trials, it wouldn't come across as strange." She pretended to read a newspaper headline. "Rogue Doctor Implicated in Human Experimentation, Kills Family, Then Self."

Bear didn't like how this sat with him. The evidence Mandy had gathered wouldn't be enough to tie anything to HealTek. They still didn't understand the full scope of what was happening in this town. The evidence was not enough to flush someone out.

McKinnon circled the room, observing the pristine bookshelves and checking corners for hidden evidence. Bear pulled out his phone and sent a check-in message to Mandy. She responded with an emoji rolling its eyes, which he took to mean she was bored out of her mind but safe. He sent back a bee emoji for the hell of it.

"Bear." McKinnon's voice was sharp. He looked up. She held a cell phone in her gloved hand. "Look at this."

"That Dr. Sing's?"

"Might be. Won't be able to get in with a passcode, but if it's new enough..." McKinnon walked over to the body and held the phone to the dead woman's face. A screen full of apps appeared. "For once, technology is on our side."

Bear decided not to bring up the fact that he had only recently learned phones could do that. He'd spent way too long on the run with simple burners. He missed the days of Motorola T720s. Greatest flip-phone ever made. He'd have to get used to this new world if he wanted to survive in it. Maybe he'd get Mandy to teach him a few things.

He leaned over McKinnon's shoulder. "Anything good?"

She swiped a few times and went to the Messages app. Dr. Sing had recently spoken to her husband and one of her kids, as well as another doctor and her mother. But at the top of the list was a number without a name attached to it. McKinnon pressed on the message.

She read the message aloud. "Can't do this anymore. I'm out. Find someone else."

Bear read the next line, the one from the unknown number. "Sorry to hear that." He stood up and glanced around the room. "Pretty sloppy, leaving the phone behind. Must've been in a hurry."

"Look at the time stamp," McKinnon said. "She sent that after they caught Mandy. She knew we were onto her."

"The response came about an hour ago. When we were at her office. You know what that means?"

"What?"

"We're making them nervous."

29

McKinnon's deputies showed up to catalog the crime scene and take the bodies away. She relegated Bear to the foyer. They hadn't allowed him to look through the house by himself with everyone else there. It was for the best. He'd get in the way or raise suspicions if he found something.

He spent the time observing McKinnon in her element and came away impressed with how she commanded her team.

Most of them gave her begrudging respect, only two older guys resisting. She handled it well. She'd listen to their suggestions, and if they had a better way of doing something, she'd give them the green light. If she thought her way was better, she'd explain why and give them no room to argue. They didn't always like it, but they got the job done.

Bear wondered how many of them had ties to HealTek. How many could be playing spy?

McKinnon was in a tough spot. She had to do her job as sheriff and open the murder investigation. However, it provided another avenue for HealTek to get a peek into how far they'd come. She didn't give away any other information they'd gathered so far. It was all business as she took care of the Sing case.

After another hour—and another moody check-in from Mandy to which Bear followed up with a turtle emoji—McKinnon and Bear went back to her office, leaving a couple deputies to monitor the crime scene overnight. They'd have a full day of interviews in the morning. No one was looking forward to breaking the news to the town.

"Lots of people liked her." McKinnon sat in her office chair. She cradled a whiskey in one hand. "She was a good doctor. Did a lot of volunteer work. Made an incredible pot roast. Seriously, I don't know how she did it. Tried to get the recipe from her once and you'd think I had asked for her first born." McKinnon looked like she regretted the words as soon as they came out of her mouth. Dr. Sing's firstborn was dead, too. She took a healthy swig of her whiskey and bared her teeth as it burned her throat.

Bear took a sip from his glass. "She was either good at hiding who she really was, or she had some crazy blackmail against her."

McKinnon drained her glass and got up to pour another. She twisted the lid off the decanter and paused. When she turned to Bear, her eyes were wide. "Seriously, what the hell is going on here?"

"I don't know. It started with Katie. Maybe if we figure out what happened to her, we'll blow this whole thing wide open."

"But everyone who knew Katie when she was a kid is gone. Her parents, neighbors, Eileen. No one else has come forward."

"They might be too scared."

"I would be, too. But with the kids getting sick? Why won't anyone offer information to put an end to this? Especially Laura Lynn's father. He's gotta know something."

"Remember what Carl Donovan said?" Bear put his glass down on the table and leaned forward. "He said he never knew what HealTek was up to. They kept enough pressure on him to keep his mouth shut. Maybe Mr. Weinberger is hoping HealTek can reverse whatever is going on with his daughter if he remains quiet."

"How does that help us?" McKinnon splashed whiskey into her glass and sat back down. "We have to find someone willing to talk. Someone who knows something that'll help us. We need to figure out if this is one person or the whole board."

Bear opened his mouth to make a sarcastic comment when he heard a sharp rap on the door. McKinnon sat up and threw Bear a puzzled look, but he just shrugged as if to say, *it's your office.* She grunted and got up to answer.

"Sheriff McKinnon, it's nice to see you again. My name is Henry Richter, I serve on the city council. We met last year at the Christmas party."

"Of course." McKinnon sounded relaxed but Bear noticed the tension rising in the room. "This is my friend, Riley Logan."

Bear stood to shake the man's hand. He was tall, probably in his late thirties, and fit. He looked comfortable in his three-piece suit, like he'd been wearing it since the day he was born. His jacket was draped over his arm, and he held a hat in the opposite hand. Bear didn't bother being gentle when he introduced himself.

"Quite a grip." Richter looked up at him with beady, snake-like eyes. His charm was disarming, but Bear saw its danger. Richter was coiled, ready to strike. "Do you mind if I come in?"

"We were actually just wrapping up," Bear said. McKinnon shot him a look, but he ignored it. "It's been a long day. Have you heard?"

"About Dr. Sing? Yes, of course. What a tragedy. My family has known hers for years." Richter looked like he meant it, but there was something practiced about his words. Didn't all politicians sound that way, though? "Still can't believe she'd kill herself."

"Neither can we," Bear said with zero inflection.

McKinnon cleared her throat. "I don't think you're here for condolences, Mr. Richter. What can I do for you?"

"I'm here on behalf of the city council to ask that you close Dr. Sing's case as quickly as possible. She was a pillar of this community, as you well know, and we'd hate to see an investigation into her death drawn out. The people of this town deserve to mourn quickly and quietly. Everyone will feel better once it's been taken care of."

Bear straightened and spread his shoulders. "That sounds an awful lot like sweeping it under the rug, councilman."

"What I think Riley means," McKinnon said, "is that we would love to wrap this up sooner than later. *However,* my number one priority for this case is justice."

"Justice?" The man laughed and looked between them like he was missing something. "She killed herself. It's not like you can hold her responsible for that. I think she's already paid the price."

"My job is to explore all the options," McKinnon asserted.

Richter smiled and pulled out his phone. "Of course, of course. I understand." He hit a few keys and looked up again. "I've been instructed to offer you monetary compensation for your work. We want to make sure you have enough resources to get the job done as soon as possible."

"Sounds a lot like a bribe," Bear said.

McKinnon didn't correct him this time. "I can't accept whatever you want to give me." She paused a beat to let it set in. "No matter how generous. It's against the law."

"Nonsense." Richter waved away the comment. "Your predecessor did it all the time. It's not illegal if you're enforcing the rules, right?"

McKinnon stiffened. "Councilman Richter, it's time for you to leave. Thank you for the offer. I decline."

Richter's expression changed, and for the first time, Bear thought he saw the man's true nature. "Please don't do that, Sheriff McKinnon. This really is in your best interests."

"I'm sure it is," she said. "But my answer still stands."

Richter looked like he wanted to argue, but McKinnon's jaw was set in stone. The councilman nodded his head at both, tucked his phone away, and turned to leave. He paused halfway down the hall as though he wanted to try again but thought better of it and turned the corner.

Bear was grateful he was gone, but his gut was telling him this had been their last chance. They had just crossed the point of no return. HealTek would no longer play nice.

30

M<small>ANDY WAS HALFWAY THROUGH SECOND PERIOD ON</small> M<small>ONDAY MORNING</small> before she realized half the school was avoiding her and the other half was talking about her. If Laura Lynn had been with her, she would've already gotten the scoop.

But Laura Lynn was fighting for her life in the hospital.

At first, that's what Mandy thought they were all talking about. By now, the whole town knew that Laura Lynn was sick. No one mentioned it except in hushed whispers. Mandy hated that. Laura Lynn's situation was already bad enough, she didn't need people warping it into gossip.

Last night, Marcus had called Mandy to give her an update. Laura Lynn was stabilizing, but they were having trouble keeping her hydrated. It didn't help that she couldn't really eat on her own either, so they needed to find ways to give her enough nutrients. Marcus said his mom was confident they'd figure out how to make her better. Mandy had her doubts. Marcus' mom didn't know everything, and her line sounded like what you told your kid to make them stop worrying so much.

The school wasn't talking about Laura Lynn. Or if they were, they weren't shooting Mandy dirty looks because of her. By fifth period,

Mandy knew something was wrong. Kids would move away from her in class, purposefully turn their backs on her. It's not like she was friends with any of them to begin with, but the majority had always been at least neutral toward her.

In English, she asked Jessica Danvers for a pencil, and you would've thought Mandy had kicked her puppy. The other girl made a sound that could only have meant *you disgust me*, and it took all of Mandy's willpower not to stick a piece of gum in her hair.

When lunch finally rolled around, she looked forward to sitting at a table in the corner, away from everyone else. She never had any interest in joining other people to eat, but today she was grateful not to have to interact with them.

A tickle of anxiety crawled up her neck like a spider at the thought of Marcus. She normally saw him in the hallway between classes. He'd been absent today.

A spike of fear rode in on the back of her anxiety. Was it possible he had gotten sick, too? She'd just talked to him last night. He had shown no signs. The thought calmed her down before she realized the tattooed man had followed her from Marcus' house. They hadn't been able to get a hold of Mandy. What about Marcus and his family? She doubted Marcus' parents could protect him the way Bear protected her.

Mandy was so sick to her stomach with worry that she couldn't eat her lunch. Normally, Marcus would've arrived by now, plopping his tray down next to her and regaling her with some weird sci-fi movie fact or an update on one of his many projects. She didn't always understand what he was saying, but she liked he took the time to explain it to her. He never got mad at her questions, no matter how many she asked.

Halfway through lunch, Mandy started scanning the lunchroom in case she'd missed him walking in. Her heart sank. On the other side of the cafeteria, Marcus sat with two of his science club friends. She'd seen them around school before. They seemed nice enough. Laura Lynn was friends with them too, but they rarely hung out outside of class.

Mandy's anxiety turned to confusion. Had he not seen her? Or maybe they were working on a project together that she didn't know about. The three of them had their heads bent over something in the middle of the table. It looked like they were studying it intently. Every once in a while, Marcus would bring up his hand and do something, then they'd go back to staring at it.

Deciding she would not finish lunch, Mandy stood up and tossed her food in the garbage. She made her way over to Marcus' table. When her shadow fell across the three boys, they looked up in unison. That's when Mandy saw what they were staring at.

A phone.

"Hey." Mandy's voice was quiet and unsure. "I thought we were going to have lunch together today." She didn't add *you know, like we do every day*, even though she wanted to.

He looked away from her. "I had lunch with my friends instead."

That was a strange way to put it. Marcus' response didn't leave room for questions, but Mandy had never been very good at keeping them to herself. "What are you looking at?"

"You mean you don't already know?" Marcus asked. "That's surprising."

Mandy took a step back. His voice had never been so cold before. "What are you talking about? Know what?"

"Your Instagram." He met her gaze now with steeled eyes. "Someone found it. Now everyone knows what you've been saying about them this whole time. You're not a good person, Mandy."

"I don't have an Instagram." Mandy hated that she sounded choked up. But she was shocked and hurt and frustrated. "I haven't said anything about anyone."

"I don't want to sit with you today." There was a finality in Marcus' voice. "Or any day. I don't want to be friends with you anymore. Not if that's how you think of me. Not after everything I've done for you."

Mandy didn't know what to say. Tears threatened to spill over. The last thing she wanted was for Marcus and his friends to see her cry. Without another word, she turned on her heel and sped out of the cafeteria. The other kids were a blur as she raced down the hallway and into the bathroom. She went into one of the stalls a split second before the tears spilled down her cheeks.

There had been another girl washing her hands when Mandy had entered, so she kept her crying silent. She tried to take deep breaths to calm her breathing and her heart rate, but the tears never stopped flowing. She had to find something else to focus on to distract her from her feelings.

Mandy dumped her backpack on the ground and pulled out her phone. The school had instructions to always keep them in their lockers, but she liked to check it occasionally, in case something had happened and Bear needed her. They'd never know she kept it in there unless she gave a teacher a reason to go through her bag.

After downloading Instagram to her phone, Mandy made up a username and logged in. Then she searched for her own name. It wasn't a very good secret account because the first result was exactly what she was looking for. There was a candid picture of her, grainy and a little blurry, as though they had taken it from a distance, maybe down the hallway. The bio read, "Mandy Logan. Unfiltered. Every day I'll post a new description of my classmates." The account had six followers, and it wasn't following anyone in return.

The tears flowing down Mandy's cheeks were now ones of anger. How could Marcus believe she'd do this? They hadn't known each other for long, but she thought he understood her. She really thought they were friends.

Mandy scrolled down the page and clicked the first image. It was a rainbow background with text over the top that read, "Jessica Danvers is a fat pig. Someone should put her out of her misery. Oink, oink." The caption had a little pig emoji, like one of the stupid ones Bear would send her when he couldn't think of a witty reply. Or he thought he was being witty. *Whatever.*

Mandy wiped away her tears, now more in shock than anything. No wonder Jessica hadn't wanted to give her a pencil this morning. The next post was about a person named Jordan Cox. The caption wasn't clever. It infuriated her that anyone would think she couldn't come up with a better line than that. Besides, she didn't even know who Jordan was.

The third post made Mandy's heart come to a shuddering stop. "Marcus Allman has such a big crush on me, and it's so annoying. He's such a pathetic little dweeb. How could he think I'd ever be interested in him? I'm just using him to pass math class, hahahaha." There were two emojis in the caption, the smiley face with the nerd glasses, and the one where the hand was sticking up its middle finger.

But the next post made her want to throw her phone at the wall. "Laura Lynn Weinberger deserves to die." Several skull emojis followed it.

Mandy's sob surprised her. The sound reverberated around the bathroom, and she held her breath, trying to be as quiet as possible. Had the other girl left yet? Had anyone else come in? She didn't hear anyone make a noise.

The phone felt like hot metal in her hands. She backed out of the Instagram app and then held her finger down on the little icon. Deleting it would be the only way to purify her phone after that, and she didn't hesitate. She had no interest in reading the rest of the posts. That would make things worse.

Mandy sat down on the lid of the toilet with a huff. The pain in Marcus' eyes made sense now. Part of her wanted to run back into the cafeteria and convince him she had nothing to do with this. But she knew it wouldn't make a difference. He was too hurt right now, and he wouldn't listen to anything she said. Especially if his friends were there telling him to just ignore her.

The bell rang. Mandy jumped. She could hear kids scuffing their feet outside the bathroom door. It opened a couple of times as girls came in and went out again, trying her stall to see if it was occupied. She just stayed silent, waiting for them all to leave. The bell rang again.

She'd be late for her next class. Did she care? No. She wouldn't go back out there with tears in her eyes. She'd hold her head high and pretend it didn't bother her, even if it killed her inside. It was bad enough Laura Lynn was sick and couldn't come to school. Mandy had lost Marcus, too.

For the first time in a month, she felt completely and utterly alone.

31

BEAR HAD NEVER BEEN SO GRATEFUL TO A TRUCK. HE HAD PICKED IT UP from the shop as soon as they opened, barely reading over the bill before he signed it and handed over his credit card. He snatched his keys from the kid in the front office, headed outside, and jumped behind the wheel. It smelled like maple syrup. Bear couldn't think of anything but pancakes.

Georgie's Diner was packed. Business was booming. He'd hadn't been in since finding Katie's body. The rumors had spread fast. Bear wasn't what you'd call a social butterfly. The only real conversations he'd had besides with Mandy had been with McKinnon. Everyone else wanted to talk about him, not with him.

When Bear sat himself in a corner booth, a hush fell over the diner. Then the whispers grew louder. Normally, it wouldn't have bothered him much—he was used to sticking out in a crowd—but it made him antsy.

A line from Carl Donovan's letter played over and over in his head: *You're making it worse.*

Caroline brought Bear his usual cup of coffee, but it wasn't accompanied by her trademarked smile today. "The usual?"

Bear thought she sounded off. He didn't make a big deal out of it.

Maybe the diner's other patrons had him on edge. "Pancakes and double bacon, with scrambled eggs and wheat toast." He smiled up at her. "Thanks, Miss Caroline."

She nodded and returned to the back. Bear could see her chatting with George, who looked at him with tight lips and narrowed eyes. He nodded his head once, and Caroline left the back, walking around the counter and heading to her other tables. Several people avoided eye contact with Bear as he looked around the diner.

The chatter eventually picked up again. It felt normal, except for the occasional death glare. Bear was used to them by now and it wouldn't put him off his breakfast. In fact, he held the gaze of anyone who tried to stare him down. They weren't gonna win that contest.

Besides, what did they have to be so mad about? Even if he was making their lives more difficult, wasn't it for the right reasons? He wanted to know what had happened to a girl who had died fifteen years ago. He wanted to figure out why another girl was sick. He could understand why they wanted to stay out of the situation, but at what expense? Where was the line?

Apparently, the situation hadn't warranted them crossing it yet.

A few minutes later, Caroline returned with a plateful of food. She topped off his coffee and walked away without another word. When Bear pulled the plate closer, he found a piece of paper wrinkled underneath. He grabbed it and unfolded it.

Stay sharp.

The handwriting was sloppy, like they had written it in a rush. Bear looked up and saw Georgie staring at him. The other man watched Bear for a moment, then looked away. The look in George's eyes told Bear everything he needed to know.

The town was turning against him. They didn't like Bear sticking his nose where it didn't belong. George liked Bear and was giving him a warning. But George wouldn't get in the middle of the situation. Neither would Caroline. Whether they agreed with Bear's actions, he wasn't sure, but this was as much of a head's up as he was gonna get.

Two men stood from their table and approached Bear. They looked like brothers, both with sandy brown hair and pale blue eyes. They had patchwork beards and crooked teeth. Their jeans and flannels were dirty and worn. He couldn't remember their names, but George had pointed them out when Bear had first arrived.

Not a single brain cell between two of them, he'd said. *But you'd be an idiot to pick a fight.*

Bear had taken that as a challenge. The juvenile side of him had wanted to know if he could go toe to toe with the Meathead Brothers. But the other half knew it wasn't such a good idea. Even if nobody liked these guys, the town would take the brothers' side over Bear's. Familiarity bred some loyalty.

Bear picked up a piece of bacon and shoved it into his mouth. "Can I help you, fellas? Last I saw, Scarecrow was heading south."

Meathead One screwed up his face. "We don't need no scarecrows."

Bear washed his bacon down with some coffee. "It's a *Wizard of Oz* reference, pal. Come on." He batted his gaze between the two of them. "Don't tell me you've never seen it? It's a classic."

"We're not your pal," Meathead Two said. "We want you to leave."

"Look, I'm just trying to eat my breakfast in peace. I'll go when I finish. Scout's honor."

"We want you to leave now," one said.

"I want you to listen to what I'm saying. I'll go slower this time: When I'm done, I'm gone."

"You're done when we say you're done."

"That's not how that works." Bear cut off a neat piece of his pancake and popped it into his mouth. "What exactly is the problem here?"

"You're sticking your nose where it doesn't belong."

"What's it to you?" He wanted an actual answer. "It's no skin off your nut sack."

"Don't matter," Two said. "We ask you to do something, you do it."

"Yeah, that's not gonna work here, fellas." Bear sized them up, knowing he was taller, even if they were wider. He'd be faster, too, but the curve of their noses told him they'd taken a few punches. "I don't like being told what to do."

"Too bad."

Bear lifted his coffee to his lips. He wouldn't satisfy them with any further conversation, and it seemed like they picked up on the hint.

Meathead One smacked the mug out of his hands, sending hot coffee and ceramic shards all over the floor. The noise in the diner vanished.

Before Bear could exit the booth, Caroline was between them, pushing the brothers away and smacking them with a towel. They immediately backed up, flinching every time she whipped them in the face.

"You two leave him alone, or so help me, I will call your mother right now." She was red in the face. "Don't think you're too old to get a beating from her. If you don't sit back down right now—"

Bear tried to stifle a laugh.

After Caroline drove the two men back to their seat, she returned to Bear. Her voice was quiet, but it cut like a knife. "And you."

"Me?"

She shook her head and knelt, gathering the bigger chunks of his mug in her skirt. "*You.* I know you think you're trying to help, but you're just stirring the pot. It's not doing anyone any good. Least of all, us."

"I'm not the one—"

"You knew what you were doing coming in here." She stood up and tossed the shards into the garbage. When she turned back to him, the color had drained from her face. "You're a good man." She was even quieter now. Her voice wobbled. "George and I hold nothing against you. But you gotta understand that the people in this town stick together. They don't always see reason. Don't always see the bigger picture. They're more concerned about the here and now than the future."

"I never intended to cause trouble, Miss Caroline." The heat had left his voice. "Not for you and George."

"I know." Caroline stepped closer to the table. "But people are afraid for their livelihoods. Everyone's made a deal with the devil here. You can't blame them for being afraid of seeing everything they've worked for go down the drain."

She had a point. The town had slipped into bed with HealTek a long time ago. Parents passed the deed onto their children. If Bear upset the balance by taking the company on, who knew what would happen to the town.

"I can't blame them," Bear said. "But I can't agree with them either."

"I know."

"And I'm not one to back down from a fight."

"I know." She sounded sad this time. "Your meal's on the house. Finish up. Maybe when this is over, we'll see you again."

Bear nodded his thanks. He finished every bite of his meal. After throwing a wad of bills on the table, he walked through the diner and gave the room a wave before exiting and getting into his truck.

At this point, it was the only place in town where he was welcome.

32

Bear beat the bus home by twenty minutes. Enough time for him to grab his gloves and start working on the front garden. It felt like months had passed since Mandy had come bounding up the driveway, a smile on her face. Just an hour before he found Katie's body.

Right before everything went downhill.

He drove those thoughts out of his mind. Today was cooler than it had been in weeks, and for once, he didn't have rivers of sweat rolling down his back. Manual labor felt good. His muscles pushed and pulled. Every time he reached his limit, he felt stronger. Gardening wasn't as flashy as a weight rack, but it kept him loose.

The squeal of brakes told him it was just past three o'clock in the afternoon. He smacked the dirt from his gloves and wiped the sweat from his brow. Mandy stomped down the school bus steps and up their driveway. He raised a hand in greeting, like he had just a few days ago, but there was no laughter or rolling of her eyes or even use of her new favorite word, *lame*.

Mandy marched right by him, through the front door. She slammed it shut behind her.

Bear had dealt with plenty of Mandy's tantrums over the years, but this had *teenager* written all over it. Despite his bad day, he had no problem shrugging off dirty looks and ill tempers. But Mandy was still sensitive, as much as she didn't want to admit it to him. And he wondered what happened at school to elicit this behavior.

He gave her a solid five minutes to cool down before he went inside. He washed up, then climbed the stairs to her bedroom. The door was shut halfway. He knocked before pushing it open. Mandy was grabbing clothes out of her dresser and shoving them into a duffel bag.

"Whoa, whoa." Bear stepped into the room. "What's going on here?"

"You were right." Mandy was full of emotion. "We should leave. Is there any point in staying here?"

"What happened?"

"What do you mean, what happened? Haven't you been paying attention?" Her voice was sharp, but there was pain, not anger, behind it. "You found a dead body. Laura Lynn is sick. Everything is falling apart. Everyone hates me."

"Everyone doesn't hate you."

"Yes, they do."

Bear walked up to her and gently took a shirt out of her hands and set it on the bed. Tears streamed down her face. "I don't hate you. So, technically, everyone doesn't hate you."

Mandy shook her head. "You don't count."

He put a hand over his heart. "That hurts."

She tried to push him away, but he didn't budge. "You know what I mean."

Bear tilted her face so she'd look at him and see how much he wanted to help. "Who hates you?"

"Everyone." Her voice was quiet. "Marcus."

Bear tried to control the ripple of anger that coursed through him. The kid was only fourteen years old, but Bear swore to God, if that pipsqueak hurt her, there'd be hell to pay. "What happened?"

"It's not important."

"It's important to me."

"Why can't we just leave?"

"For the same reason you told me we couldn't. There are a lot of people in this town affected by what's going on, not the least of which are a bunch of kids." He softened his voice. "Including Laura Lynn."

Mandy huffed and collapsed onto her bed in a heap. She buried her face in her pillows. Bear still caught what she said. "This isn't fair."

"Are you going to tell me what happened?"

Mandy rolled over onto her back and stared straight up at the ceiling, avoiding eye contact. Her words came out in a rush. "Everyone was talking behind my back today, and normally I don't care because, whatever. But Laura Lynn isn't there, and it's harder to ignore them. And I didn't see Marcus all day until lunch, and he didn't sit with me, and when I went over to his table, he was mean." She blinked away some tears. "He was looking at his phone and said he didn't want to be friends with me anymore because of something I posted on Instagram."

"You don't even have an Instagram." Bear froze. "Do you?"

"No!" She threw her arms up in the air and let them crash back down again. "I had to make one just to see what he was talking about. Someone was pretending to post as me, saying awful things about people in my grade. They said Laura Lynn deserves to die, and they said Marcus liked me and he was pathetic and that I was using him to pass math class."

"I can see why he was upset." Bear placed a comforting hand on her shoulder. "Kids can be mean. But there must be a way—" A banging from downstairs interrupted them. It was a knock on the door, but it made Bear's heart race all the same. "Stay here."

He made his way down the stairs and positioned himself along the wall so he could peer through the blinds and see who was on the other side of the door. The knocking came again, but this time it was less sure. The person on the other side moved a little to their right, and Bear caught sight of his face.

Bear opened the door. He towered over the kid. "What do you want?"

"Oh, hi, Mr. Logan. Um." Marcus looked down at his shoes. "I was wondering if Mandy's home?"

"I don't think she wants to talk to you right now."

He sighed. "Yeah, I kind of figured that. Could you—"

"I don't want to talk to you right now."

"I understand." He stepped back, stopped, and looked Bear in the eye. "Give her a message for me?"

Bear let the silence hang in the air for a minute. He tried not to enjoy the way the kid squirmed on his doorstep. "What?"

"Can you just tell her I'm sorry I ever believed she wrote that stuff?" Marcus looked down again. "That was stupid. I should've known better. I should've, I dunno, asked her about it first instead of getting all butthurt."

Bear opened his mouth, but Mandy beat him to it. He hadn't even heard her come down the stairs. She was getting better at remaining invisible.

"What made you change your mind?" She squeezed past Bear. She still sounded hurt, but there was genuine interest in her voice.

"I, uh, found a way into the account."

"Found a way, huh?" Bear chuckled. This kid was going to end up on a watch list or recruited by the government by the time he turned eighteen. Perhaps both.

"Yes, sir." He gulped and looked beyond Bear to Mandy. "It's Pete. He used his own email address to make the account. He was the one who posted all that stuff."

"Didn't really take a genius to figure that out," Mandy said.

"Look, I'm sorry. It's just—" Marcus' gaze flickered to Bear and back to Mandy. He didn't want to say whatever it was in front of her dad, but Bear wasn't going anywhere. Let the kid suffer a little longer for making his daughter cry. "It hurt my feelings, okay? I really thought we were friends. Like real friends. And then I read that—"

"We *are* friends." Mandy took a step forward, pushing Bear a little to the side. "I would never say that about you."

Marcus smiled, and Mandy returned the gesture, even if she still had a few tears in her eyes. "Do you maybe want to hang out?" The boy's eyes darted to Bear and back. "I did kind of ride my bike here, though. My mom thinks I stayed late after school."

A buzzing in Bear's pocket caught his attention. He pulled his phone out. McKinnon. "You." He pointed to Marcus. "Come inside and sit on the couch. Call your mother. She needs to know where you are." He aimed his finger at Mandy. "You. Make a snack or something. Stay out of trouble. And no eavesdropping."

Mandy scowled, but when Bear raised his eyebrows at her, she scampered off into the kitchen. Then he put the phone to his ear, narrowly missing the call altogether. "What's up? Any news?"

There was a cough and a wheeze on the other line. "Something's wrong."

"McKinnon?" Bear didn't bother keeping the panic out of his voice. "What's wrong?"

"I don't feel good." Another cough. Something brushed against the phone. When the sheriff spoke again, her voice was muffled, like she'd dropped her cell and couldn't reach it. "I need help."

33

BEAR MADE IT OUT THE DOOR IN UNDER SIXTY SECONDS. HE SHOVED Marcus' bike in the back of his truck while the kids climbed in. The boy's mother had made it clear she wasn't comfortable with Mandy hanging out at their house anymore. According to Marcus, she wouldn't be home for another couple hours. It'd be a surprise for the woman. Bear had instructed Marcus to tell her they didn't have any other choice.

Mandy wanted to come along to McKinnon's. Bear refused to allow her. He didn't know what he was walking into. She'd said she didn't feel good. He presumed that meant she was sick and not injured. Considering they had a poison epidemic on their hands, he had an idea of what was happening. Her symptoms had come on at once, though. Not gradually like Laura Lynn's. That meant it was something different. Potentially deadlier.

Bear came to a screeching halt outside Marcus' house, not even bothering to turn into the driveway. He twisted around in his seat and looked Mandy in the eye. "Grab the bike, go inside, lock every door and window. If anyone other than me or his mother comes to that door, you don't answer it. I don't care if it's a cop or a neighbor or his favorite uncle, you hear me?"

Mandy nodded and said, "Yes, sir."

"Good. If someone breaks in, what do you do?"

"Run or hide."

He turned to Marcus. "If anything happens, stick with Mandy. Listen to her. She'll protect you."

If this teenage boy had any qualms about a girl protecting him, he didn't show it. He just nodded his head, tears in his eyes. "What's going on?"

"Not sure yet. But I'm gonna figure it out." Bear turned back to Mandy. "I'll send you a text once I know what's going on with the sheriff, okay? Check in with me in an hour."

"I love you." Mandy's voice cracked. "Be careful."

"I love you, too," Bear said. "Always am."

He waited for them to grab the bike and shut the door behind them before he took off down the road, tires squealing. It was drizzling now. The dark sky cast the world around him into shadow. Bear operated on autopilot while his brain worked through various scenarios. He had to be prepared for anything. Luckily, he had tossed his Glock in the glove compartment as soon as he got his truck back from the car dealership.

The sheriff lived a couple minutes outside town. Bear made it in less than ten. He pulled into the driveway and skidded to a stop behind the sheriff's cruiser. The front of the house looked normal. The door was closed, the blinds open. He grabbed his gun anyway.

Bear dropped from the truck and left the door open. He allowed himself five full seconds to stop and listen. The only sounds he heard were the distant passing cars and chirping birds. He approached the house. Leaned his ear close to the door. All he heard was silence.

Bear tested the doorknob. Unlocked. He swung the door wide and pressed his back to it as he turned to clear the room.

As he climbed the stairs, he thought he heard a soft moan. Bear quickened his pace. Kept his feet light. At the landing, he headed left and cleared each room. Nothing. Another groan, this time louder and more drawn out. Bear stalked down the hallway in the other direction.

In the first room he came to, Bear saw McKinnon on the floor next to her bed. Her cell phone was inches away from her outstretched hand.

Bear moved on. It killed him, but he had to clear the other rooms. A spare bedroom. A bathroom. A closet. He had to be sure they were alone and that no one would jump him.

After inspecting the final room, Bear sprinted back to McKinnon's side. He knelt beside her and checked her pulse. She stirred but didn't open her eyes. He felt the blood pumping through her veins. Her heartbeat was erratic and slow. Her breathing was shallow.

"McKinnon?" Bear peeled one of her eyes open. "Josie? Can you hear me?"

Another soft moan escaped her mouth, but otherwise, she didn't move. Her eyes were unresponsive, like she saw right through him. Bear ran his hands down her arms and legs and neck, feeling for any breaks or injuries. He detected none. His worry deepened. How did they get to her? Out of everyone, she was the hardest to target.

Those questions would have to wait. Bear snatched her cell phone, then stuck one arm under her neck and one under her legs. He groaned as he lifted her. Her slender body was dense with muscle. By the time he reached the truck, Bear was out of breath. He had to remind himself he was still recovering from surgery.

Bear placed the sheriff in the passenger seat and buckled her in. When her head rolled to the side, he lowered the back of the seat until she was almost flat. He had no way of telling if she was comfortable. He'd need to drive slowly and take the corners easily.

After slamming the door shut, Bear sprinted back to the house. Part of him wanted to go upstairs and see if he could find anything. A pill. A needle. A weapon. Anything that might be out of place. But time was of the essence.

He closed and locked the front door. Ran back to the truck and hopped in. The sheriff stirred. Bear threw the truck in reverse and headed back the way he had come. The hospital was ten minutes away.

Bear pulled up the number on his way. Someone answered after a half a dozen rings. He didn't bother hearing what the woman on the other line had to say. "I'll be arriving in about ten minutes. I've got Sheriff McKinnon with me. She's sick."

"Injured?" The woman's voice was sharper now. "How?"

"Not injured. Sick. I don't know how."

"Sir, call 911. She needs an ambulance."

"I'm already on my way," he roared. "She might've been poisoned. Her pulse is erratic. She's having trouble breathing. She's unconscious, but moving and groaning occasionally, like she's in pain."

"Did she take anything?" The woman asked, sounding like she wasn't sure what he expected from her. "Eat anything?"

"I don't know. Didn't see anything around her in her bedroom. She called me twenty minutes ago, and then I assume she collapsed."

"I'll prep a room. What's your ETA?"

Bear looked at the clock again. "Eight minutes. Maybe less." It's not like he was abiding by the rules of the road. He saw a light turn yellow up ahead and slammed down on the gas. "Definitely less."

"Keep her talking. See if she can give you any information."

Bear put the phone on speaker and then stuck it in his cupholder. He placed a hand on the Sheriff's shoulder and jostled her slightly. "Josie? Can you wake up? I need you to talk to me."

She groaned again. Her eyes fluttered, then closed. Her mouth opened like she was gasping for air.

"She can't breathe. I'm two minutes away."

"Bring her in through the back entrance. It's closer."

That's all Bear needed to hear. He pulled into the parking lot, swung around, and parked at the rear entrance. A couple of cars honked at him. Bear ignored them. He put his truck in park and jumped out without cutting the engine.

McKinnon groaned again as he hoisted her into his arms. She looked pale. Sweat gathered on her brow.

"Hang tight," he said. "Almost there."

They were halfway to the entrance. A pair of nurses burst out of the sliding doors, pushing a gurney. Bear didn't ask questions. He placed McKinnon on the bed.

Bear made it to the first set of double doors before one of the nurses detached herself from the group and held up a hand. "You can't go back there." She sounded like the woman on the phone. "Wait here. We'll give you any updates as we can."

"I want to stay with her."

"You can't." Her tone made it final. "Either stay here or give me your number. I'll keep you informed."

He thought about pushing past the nurse and through the doors. That would bring more attention to his situation. And he had enough problems already.

34

B<small>EAR TRIED SITTING IN THE WAITING ROOM, BUT THAT LASTED ALL OF FIVE</small>
minutes before he stood up and started pacing. The nurses gave him a
wide berth. Someone awaiting news about a loved one was common in
their world.

He sat down again, bouncing his leg to expel the energy coursing
through his body. He felt like he could fight an entire army. Part of him
thought that was a good idea. He could always go knocking on Heal-
Tek's door if he wanted some trouble. He doubted McKinnon would
approve, though.

Although Bear hadn't known the woman for very long, he'd come to
respect her. She was a kind, caring person who helped people. He'd run
into enough corrupt cops and officials over the years. They were easy to
spot. McKinnon was as advertised. His time here could've been far
worse without her.

The elevator opened with a *ding*. Bear craned his neck in search of a
momentary distraction. He found something much better. Laura Lynn's
father stepped into the waiting room. He looked pale and haggard. The
girl was upstairs fighting for her life. Bear couldn't feel bad for the guy.
He was hiding something.

He was on his feet before his brain told him *don't do it*. Weinberger was distracted, trying to pull his car keys out of his pocket. He stumbled through the sliding doors as though he hadn't slept in a week. Bear followed. He waited for the man to get close enough to reach for the handle of his car before spinning him around and pinning him against the door. Weinberger grunted. Then his eyes went wide with recognition.

"You?"

"Me."

"What… what do you want?" He struggled to wiggle free. Bear leaned in harder. "You better back off, or I'm calling the cops."

"Which one? Don't expect the sheriff to come to your defense. *Your* people put her in the hospital."

Weinberger froze. "What are you talking about?" His eyes flickered to the hospital. "Sheriff McKinnon is—"

"Poisoned." Bear applied more pressure. "And you know more than you're letting on."

"I don't." Weinberger struggled to get the words out. Bear was like a concrete slab pressing down on him. "Come on, man. I don't know anything. Seriously!"

"How am I supposed to believe you? Your kid's sick, and you didn't even want to call an ambulance."

Weinberger closed his eyes. When he opened them again, Bear saw fear. Fear of losing something precious to you. "I know." His voice was low. Strained. "I know. I messed up."

"You did more than mess up."

"Don't you think I know that!" Weinberger pushed back. He was weak. Couldn't have moved Bear if he put everything he had into it. Bear relented and took a step back. "I thought things would be different. I thought they would fix this before it got to that point."

"Tell me what's going on. I can fix this."

"You can't—"

"You don't know what I'm capable of."

Weinberger tipped his head back and laughed. He looked insane. "You don't know what *they're* capable of."

"Then tell me."

"I know nothing." Weinberger was calm now. Rational. "I'm just a warehouse manager."

Bear lifted an eyebrow. "You're a manager and you don't know anything?"

"They make me leave the room."

"Why?"

Weinberger's shoulders slumped as he exhaled in Bear's face. The man's breath smelled like coffee. The guy looked around to make sure no one would overhear them. "I really don't know anything, okay? We get in shipments every day from around the country. Pills and supplies and compounds. I'm in charge of making sure everything gets to where it's going. Most of the time."

"Most of the time?"

"On certain days at certain times, I'm encouraged to step out of the room for an hour. That's when the special deliveries come in."

"What's in the special deliveries?"

Weinberger scrutinized him, and a little bit of the man Bear had met the other day returned. "You think I know that? They make me step out for a reason, man."

Bear backed up another foot. Weinberger didn't look like he wanted to run. Bear needed the space to think. "Do you have any idea why they make you do that? You've never gotten curious? Tried to stick around?"

"Nah, man." Weinberger pulled a crumpled cigarette out from his pocket and stuck it between his lips and lit it. Didn't even offer Bear one. Not that Bear would've taken it. "They watch everything we do when we're on the clock. They count our keystrokes. They see everything."

"If you had to guess, what would your first thought be?"

Weinberger stared him down. Bear could see the wheels turning. Weinberger might not want to admit it, but he'd thought about this before. "Some sort of chemical compound. Something we're not supposed to have. Something they keep off the books."

"Why?"

"I don't know, man. I really don't. They don't pay me enough to know. That's for the bigwigs."

"Who are the bigwigs?"

"Anderson. Caplan. Johnson. Olsen."

Bear snapped to attention. "Olsen? Jeremy Olsen?"

Weinberger nodded. "And half a dozen more. They're on the website. It's not like they're hiding. They're on the board."

"Why do you keep working for them? After what they did to your daughter?"

"We don't know for sure—"

Bear laughed. "Why are you in denial? How is that helping your daughter?"

Weinberger couldn't find an answer.

Bear stepped forward. He was in the man's face again. "Why are you protecting them? Why are you letting them do this?"

"I'm not letting them." Weinberger sounded defeated.

"You're not stopping them either."

"How? This company is my only source of income. My dad worked there before I did. I'm a legacy employee. They pay me just enough to cover my bills, but not enough to pack up and move. My family needs me to keep this job. And you don't know what it's like in there. If you're part of the group, you're golden. Free ride. Easy job. But the second you ask questions, everything falls apart."

"Is that what happened with Laura Lynn? Is that why she got sick? You started asking questions?"

"I got curious about the deliveries." Weinberger wouldn't meet Bear's eyes. "It'd been happening for years. I finally broke. I wanted to know. But I didn't find anything."

"Give me something that can help me." Bear pushed all his anger to the side. "Please."

Weinberger tipped his head back and stared at the sky. The drizzle from earlier had dissipated. "I know to step out of the room when certain lot numbers appear on the schedule. Seventy-two, thirteen, a hundred and six, and ninety-seven. Those show up most often."

"How is that supposed to help me?" Bear asked. "You gonna let me into the warehouse?"

Weinberger shook his head. "It'd be impossible to sneak you in.

There's an easier way." He swallowed, like he was pushing past a lump in his throat. "Bowser Freight delivers the packages. You'll have an easier time getting into their system."

Bear cursed. He knew Bowser had been involved, even if they couldn't find any evidence. How had they been so close without a single clue to back up their hunches? Then Bear remembered they'd been doing this for decades. They'd had a lot of time to perfect their con.

"Don't go anywhere," Bear said. "I may need you again."

"Are you really going to do this?" Weinberger asked. "It's a suicide mission."

"I've got nothing to lose. Sometimes you gotta bite the hand that feeds you. And if you're too much of a coward to do it," he said, "then I guess I will."

35

Bear waited until dusk. It wasn't easy. He wanted to crash through the door and take the entire building single handedly. That would do no one any favors. Stealth would be key here. Despite his size, he had experience slipping in and out of the shadows undetected.

The hospital had called him once, but it was barely an update. The nurse had told him they were still trying to figure out what McKinnon had consumed. He'd gone back to her house and done a more thorough search. There had been no evidence of what had happened. Now it was just a waiting game.

He could be patient when he wanted to be. However, Bear had spent the last several days on the defensive. It was time to make a move. He wasn't running from the problem anymore. And he sure as hell would not sit idly by while the sheriff deteriorated.

It was go-time.

Bear left his truck in a gravel parking lot near a river, almost two miles from the Bowser Freight's building. Even if someone saw it, they'd think he'd gone fishing or walking through the woods. It'd buy him some time and even an alibi if he needed it.

He waited ten minutes at the edge of the woods and watched over his truck to see if anyone rolled up to look at it. Best he could tell, no one followed him. Half the town against him and the other half looking the other way, he wasn't taking chances.

Satisfied that he'd done his due diligence, Bear hiked north to the building. The woods were cool and full of the sounds of nature. Every time a stick cracked, it sounded like a gunshot, and he ducked his head. He'd grabbed his pistol from the glove compartment for some security. Still, he was a sitting duck if someone was watching him.

It took him twenty minutes to work his way through the woods, and another ten to pass the building and double back. The rest of the journey offered no cover. A pair of headlights swung in his direction just as he rolled behind the nearest vehicle. He waited and caught his breath while the van pulled to a stop in the next row.

From his hiding spot, he watched the van as two men jumped out.

"Yo, this day was cray," one said. "They sent me to Buffalo *and* Syracuse. They gotta give those routes to two different drivers."

"You're complaining about the overtime?" the other guy asked.

"I'm complaining about my time being wasted. Got things to do, man."

"I'm sure your mom won't miss you too much. Come on, let's lock up and get out of here."

The other man's response was lost in the wind as they made their way to the building. Bear had to be quick. He sprinted from one van to the next until he was a few feet from the door. The two men entered. Bear stayed low and reached for the handle before the door clicked shut. He waited a minute, then peeked through the window. When he saw no one in his direct path, he slipped through and let the door fall closed behind him.

Bear wished he had the layout of the building. There hadn't been time for research ahead of the mission. He took in what he could as he ducked behind machinery and ran along the wall. He made out voices on the other side of the room.

The warehouse was one large room. On the far end, there were offices. The rest was full of aisles of boxes and packing machinery. There were several roll-up doors that opened onto the loading docks.

An emergency exit if he got trapped. No guarantee he could easily open them.

The plan didn't feel like it was worth the risk anymore.

As one man rounded the corner, Bear caught sight of his face. Or rather, the tattoo on his neck. Red and blue. Eagle. It was the tattooed man he'd fought off the other day. The same one who had tried to kidnap Mandy.

Every muscle in his body ached to pounce. To jump out and grab the guy and beat him. Bear's brain wrestled for control. Satisfying as it would be to teach the guy a lesson and smack that ever-present smug look off his face, Bear had a job to do. Several people lay in limbo while he searched for answers.

He repeated the numbers Weinberger had given him like a mantra. Seventy-two. Thirteen. A hundred and six. Ninety-seven.

Five minutes passed. The other guy grabbed his belongings out of his locker and the two left. The door slammed shut behind them. Bear waited another five minutes. The building remained dead silent. The lights were off. Everything was powered down.

He was alone.

The flashlight on his phone illuminated enough space for him to navigate the warehouse without too much trouble. He walked the perimeter to ensure he was alone, and then headed to the offices.

The first office door he tried was unlocked. Bear pushed through and shut the door behind him. The room was bare. A couple generic paintings on the wall spruced the place up. Not that he cared. Bear only had eyes for the computer. He plopped down behind it and wiggled the mouse. The monitor flickered to life. This one booted up faster than Dr. Sing's. In fact, everything in the warehouse looked new and barely used.

To his surprise, the computer didn't require a password. Bear carefully navigated the desktop, knowing he'd recognize what he was looking for when he found it. There were icons for programs he'd never heard of, as well as countless folders all in shorthand. He clicked on everything he could until he ran into a program that kept track of inventory.

Bingo.

Bear clicked on the menu. A pop-up box asked for an authentication code. He tried to click around it, but it wouldn't let him through. He opened desk drawers and riffled through papers, looking for a pin or something that might work. Nothing.

Bear pulled out the phone and called Mandy. She answered on the first ring.

"Everything okay, Mandy?"

"Yeah. You?"

"Put Marcus on the phone."

He heard the cell transfer between hands. Marcus' voice sounded even higher than usual. "Uh, hello?"

"I need to get into a computer. An application on the computer."

"Okay."

"It requires an authentication code. How can I get past that?"

"Um."

"You're a hacker, aren't you?" He couldn't believe he was asking a fourteen-year-old for help. "Can you hack into it?"

"I'm going to need a lot more information than that. What kind of computer? What kind of authentication code?"

"I don't know." He wanted to slam his fist on the table. "It's for a program called Inventorious. It keeps track of the company's inventory. I'm looking for specific lot numbers."

"Okay, so a program on the computer." He heard pounding feet, like Marcus was running up the stairs. "But you're on the actual computer? You just can't get into the program?"

"That's right."

"Is there a mail icon on the desktop?"

Bear closed the window and moved his mouse around until he found one. "Yeah."

"Is it logged in? Can you access the emails on the computer?"

Bear double-clicked the icon, and a window opened. The inbox was empty, but as he clicked through the folders, he saw he had unrestricted access. "Yeah, I can get into that."

"All right, read me the email address. I'm going to send a virus that allows me to get into the system. Then I can get you the code."

Bear did as he was told. When the email came through, Marcus instructed him to click on the link. He did. A few silent minutes later, Marcus was controlling the mouse, clicking through various programs, and typing various commands. Then he let out a contented sigh. "You should be good to go. Try opening the program now."

Bear did. When it was time to put in the authentication code, it auto populated. All he had to do was hit enter. He had access.

"Thanks, kid. Close out of this and pretend you never saw it. You got me?"

"Yes, sir."

"Good. I'll talk to you two soon."

Bear hung up and turned his full attention to the computer screen in front of him. He might not have known exactly how Marcus had done what he'd done, but it didn't matter. He had the information he needed at his fingertips. Now he just had to look for it.

The search function proved adequate, and Bear started putting the lot numbers in. Seventy-two was a drug called Hydroxaprone. Thirteen was for Femaproxine. A hundred and six? Norethelene. And ninety-two was simply Varaxa. They all sounded like medications, but none of the information in the system told him what they were used for.

It didn't matter. He had what he'd come for. Bear hit print and waited for the pages to land in the tray, then he backed out of everything and shut the computer down, leaving the mouse where he had found it. Tucking the pages into his back pocket, he reentered the warehouse and turned to close the door behind him.

Before it fully shut, a heavy object came crashing down on the back of Bear's head, sending him sprawling across the floor.

36

BEAR LAY ON THE FLOOR. HE SHOOK OFF THE COBWEBS AND WAITED TO see what the assailant would do. If they'd wanted him dead, he'd be gone by now. Yet here he was. Alive.

This person wanted a fight. And Bear planned on giving them one.

He heard his attacker panting just a foot away. He stepped closer and chuckled. Big mistake.

"The bigger they are,"—Bear recognized the voice— "the harder they…"

Bear struck with his right leg. His shin connected with the guy's knee cap. The man yelped from the pain and stumbled backwards. Bear scrambled to his feet and faced his opponent. His suspicions were confirmed.

"We gotta stop meeting like this," Bear said. "Don't even know your name."

Neck tattoo swung his bat up and let it rest on his shoulder. His smug grin infuriated Bear. He kept his anger hidden.

"Jeremy Olsen. Happy to make your acquaintance."

"Olsen, huh? We've been looking for you." Bear stood tall. "Wish I could say the same, but you're a piece of garbage."

"Got you good last time, didn't I?"

"I remember it differently. Without your buddy, you'd already be in jail. Or worse."

Olsen spread his arms wide. "It's just you and me now."

Bear liked his odds. He was bigger than Olsen and just as fast. Besides, Bear still had his gun tucked into the waist of his jeans. He wouldn't hesitate.

This wasn't just about surviving. This was about revenge. For Mandy. For all the people dying in this town.

Olsen lunged at Bear. He swung the bat up and over, going straight for the cranium. Bear anticipated the move. He moved back and to the side. Olsen would need to step up to reach him. Bear would capitalize if the guy tried.

"Pretty spry for a guy your size." Olsen cinched up on the grip.

"A talker, huh?" Maybe Olsen would give up a few secrets. "How'd you know I was here?"

"Saw your truck down the road. Think you could hide that beast?" He stalked forward a step. "I see you got it all fixed up. Shame about that accident."

"It was you, wasn't it?"

He shrugged. "I plead the fifth."

"You will." Bear backed up and bumped into the corner of a table he thought was further away.

Olsen took advantage of the stumble and lunged again, this time bringing his bat down twice. Bear dodged left, then right, and followed with a jab at Olsen's cheek.

"Swing and miss. What's your batting average?"

"Better than yours." Olsen sounded light, but Bear could tell he was getting to him.

"You don't know a thing about me."

"Don't need to. Boss tells me to take care of someone, I do it."

"Who's your boss?" Bear backed around a corner, venturing deeper into the warehouse.

Olsen chuckled again. "You don't get to know that."

"Worth a shot." Bear shrugged. "Your boss sounds like a dick. What kind of asshole tells someone to kidnap a little girl? What kind of asshole *kills* a little girl? I knew you were weak. That's just pathetic."

Olsen sneered. "I never killed a little girl."

"Katie Lamoureux disagrees."

Olsen shook his head. "You really don't know what's going on here, do you?"

"Enlighten me." Bear took a few more steps back.

"You think I'm that stupid?"

Bear didn't hesitate. "Yes."

"Your mistake."

Olsen charged. He swung the bat several times and pushed forward. Bear threw up a defending arm. The bat crashed near his elbow. His entire arm tingled. He worked his fingers into a fist. Nothing broken. Olsen went for speed instead of strength. That's where Bear would get him. He'd only need to land a couple punches to get this guy on the defensive.

Bear moved in for the kill. Olsen didn't give him a chance. He brought the bat down on Bear. He moved his head at the last second and the bat connected with his ear. The burst of pain was enough to distract him. Bear missed Olsen swinging for his gut. The bat knocked the wind out of him. He stumbled back. Olsen swung again. Head shot. Three points.

Bear landed on the floor.

Olsen didn't bother checking if Bear was unconscious. He brought the bat down across Bear's left knee. There was a sickening crunch. Bear howled in pain. The jolt shot up his leg and into his hip and radiated to his toes. His entire leg was on fire.

"Fair is fair," Olsen said.

Bear didn't bother responding. He launched himself upwards, despite the shooting pain in his leg, and tackled Olsen. He drove his forearm into Olsen's neck. They smashed into a pallet full of boxes. The bat flew across the floor with a clatter.

"Fair is fair." Bear said. "Let's see if you've still got that smart mouth when I'm done with you."

Olsen grinned. Bear threw two punches to his face and another to his stomach. Only one punch connected. From the guy's form, he was using to fighting on the street. Bear only needed one good shot to knock him out.

Olsen stayed defensive, ducking and weaving to avoid most of Bear's blows. The few that he didn't avoid elicited a grunt. Olsen kept his balance. Frustrated, Bear swung a wide right hook. Olsen leaned back to avoid the blow. He kicked Bear in his injured knee. Bear grunted and tipped forward as he lost his balance. Olsen used Bear's momentum to push him. Bear caught himself, but not before he felt Olsen move behind him and pull his pistol from his waistband.

"I thought we were playing fair?" Olsen asked. "Didn't know this was a gun fight."

Bear turned in time to see Olsen aim for his skull. One bullet between his eyes. That's all it would take to end this. Bear had envisioned himself on the other end of the gun, deciding whether he could live with one more dead body on his conscience. Instead, he stared death in the eye.

And the only thing on his mind was Mandy.

She'd lost so much already, and she'd hardly even lived. At fourteen, she'd seen and experienced things most adults couldn't even conceive. Bear would've given anything to have shielded Mandy from those nightmares, but they had made her stronger. She could survive without him, but surviving wasn't living. Hadn't that been his mistake all these years?

Bear threw himself to the right just as Olsen squeezed the trigger. A bullet whizzed by Bear's head and tore through the boxes behind him. He tucked and rolled, popping up a few feet away. Olsen followed him, slowly and methodically lining up the shot before he squeezed off another bullet. This guy wasn't in a rush. Olsen was toying with him.

Bear dove behind another pallet of boxes and sprinted down an aisle, turning this way and that. His goal was to distance himself from Olsen as much as possible. Olsen laughed. Bear could hear his footfalls trailing after him.

"Come on, man. You're not going to win this one. Let me make it quick for you."

Bear stayed moving, maintaining the distance. He had to find the upper hand again. It's not like he'd never been outgunned. This felt different, though. *He* felt different. He was angry. That emotion elicited a spark in him. Now it felt like suffocating coals. The flames never went out. They ate him from the inside out.

What would killing Olsen do? What would it solve? Bear was still strong and fast, but his body had seen a lot of combat over the years. How long could he maintain this? Mentally, he was checked out. He'd told Noble to stay away so he could live a quiet life with Mandy. Yet here he was, stirring up trouble because he couldn't just walk away.

Bear knew he wasn't at the top of his game physically. But that meant he had to be smarter.

"Come on, man. The cat and mouse game ain't fun. Look, if I *promise* to put the gun away, will you come back out and play?"

"Sure thing, boss. Let's settle this."

Bear heard Olsen change trajectories, pinpointing Bear and moving to him. Bear was already on the move himself. He made for the outside wall, then circled around behind Olsen. He tossed a few boxes to distract and misdirect the other man.

By the time Bear came up behind him, Olsen was so turned around, he had no idea where Bear was. Bear grabbed him from behind. Pinned him against a rack with a chokehold. Olsen swung wildly and fired a shot into the ceiling.

Bear didn't flinch. He drove his knee into Olsen's groin, then knocked the gun free. Olsen scrambled against the hold on his neck. He dug his nails into Bear's forearm. Bear squeezed harder. He worked his fingers around Olsen's trachea. Olsen passed out in thirty seconds. Bear slammed him to the floor, then threw a few punches to his face.

As Olsen lay on the floor moaning, Bear slipped a pack of zip ties from his back pocket. He'd seen them laying on one of the random pallets and snatched them up. Figured they'd come in handy. Death wasn't on the menu tonight. But hell if he was going to let Olsen go.

With Olsen secured to one of the structural pillars inside the warehouse, Bear retrieved his gun and the bat. He slipped the Glock back into his waistband and kept the bat ready. He wasn't opposed to forcing some answers out of the other man.

Olsen stirred.

"Let's try this again," Bear said.

That smug expression had been wiped from Olsen's face. He spat blood on the floor between them. "I'm not telling you a thing."

Bear brought the bat down on the man's knee. He waited for the screaming to stop. "I'd rather not kill you. But you've done a good job of pissing me off this week. I'm liable to change my mind at any minute. That's how this works. I'm going to ask you questions. You're going to give me answers. I promise you'll end up in a prison cell instead of a grave."

"Go to hell."

"Who's your boss?"

"Screw you."

"Why did you kill Katie Lamoureux?"

"I didn't."

"Who did?"

"Why don't you go off yourself?"

"Is it the same people who poisoned the Weinberger's? I know HealTek is behind this."

"You have no evidence."

Bear gestured to Olsen. "I have an expert witness. If you cooperate, I'll make sure McKinnon goes easy on you."

"You're lying to yourself if you think she's still alive."

Bear ground his teeth together. He hadn't gotten any calls from the hospital and figured no news was good news. "Come on, man. Give me something. Or you're going down with the rest of them."

"All right, I'll give you something." Olsen smiled up at him, his eyes beady and his teeth bloody. "I'd like to report a crime."

"Come on, man."

"No, no. You'll want to hear this one." He chuckled, like he couldn't wait to tell Bear the punchline. "You remember my friend? The one who whooped up on you the other day?"

"The guy who jumped me? Yeah, I remember him."

"Well, I think he's about to do something bad. Really bad." Olsen's smile broadened. "Your daughter, what's her name again? Mandy, right? And her friend. His name is... Marcus! Well, my buddy has paid them a visit. And if I don't come back alive, he's got instructions to make you regret ever moving to this town."

"I already do. In a second, you're gonna regret it, too."

Bear swung the bat like he was trying to clear The Green Monster at Fenway. It connected with Olsen's temple. The guy's head snapped. Blood and saliva sprayed from his mouth. His head collapsed under its own weight. Maybe he was dead. Maybe he was barely alive and would suffocate while hanging from the railings. Bear would let fate decide if the man ever regained consciousness. He chucked the weapon and sprinted out of the warehouse to his truck. He'd be at Marcus' house in less than ten minutes.

He only hoped he'd make it in time.

37

As soon as Mandy heard the knock on the door, she knew something was wrong. She and Marcus were sitting in the living room with their homework spread between them, the TV on mute so it wouldn't distract them too much. He'd gotten them a bowl of popcorn to share. The smell of butter saturated the air. Mandy had spent the last five minutes practicing throwing pieces up and catching them in her mouth. Marcus watched in bemused silence.

As soon as they heard the knock, they froze, eyes wide. They remained still as the seconds ticked by. There was no noise from the other side. Mandy hoped the person would just go away.

Knock, knock, knock.

Marcus looked toward the door, then back at her. "Should we see who it is?"

"Bear said not to," Mandy whispered. "Don't answer it."

"Not to answer it." Marcus sounded defensive. "Just to see who it is."

"I don't think it's a good idea."

Knock, knock, knock.

The sound was louder now. More frantic.

"Doesn't seem like they're going away," Marcus said.

He rose. Mandy pulled him back onto the couch.

"Stay here. I'll check." It went against all her instincts. If one of them was to do it, it had to be her. She didn't trust Marcus to be discreet. "Don't move."

Marcus nodded his head. His wide-eyed stare followed Mandy as she made her way around the room. There was a window on either side of the door, and she pressed herself against the wall and made her body as flat as possible. As she inched closer, her heartbeat drummed against her chest. Every fiber of her being screamed at her not to do this.

Turn around.

Go upstairs.

Hide.

Using her index finger, Mandy moved the curtains a half inch to peer out the window. There was no car in the driveway. Their mystery guest had walked the whole way or left their vehicle down the road. It was too late to be the mailman or a salesperson. Perhaps it was a neighbor. At this hour, though? Most neighbors had the decency to not disturb a family later in the evening.

She pushed the curtains open another inch and leaned her head closer to the window. It had been silent for a minute. Had the person given up? Had they walked away? Or were they circling the house to find another way in? She and Marcus had closed and locked every door and every window in the place. Even on the second floor. Panic gripped her spine like a boa constrictor. What if they'd missed one? What if someone found a way in?

"Do you see anything?"

Marcus' voice was too close. Mandy jumped. Her arm flailed out and pushed him away. He stumbled backwards, caught himself, and looked up at her as though she'd attacked him.

She scowled. "I told you to stay over there."

Marcus looked ashamed.

Mandy walked up to the door and stood on her tiptoes to look through the peephole. It was rash and stupid, but when she saw open air, she breathed a sigh of relief.

It was a nice respite from fear. She turned back to Marcus and guided him back to the couch. "Stay here." She pushed him down onto the cushion. "I'll be right back. *Don't move.*"

He glared at her but didn't protest.

Mandy made her way around the house. She tested the doors and windows. At each window, she peeked outside to glimpse whoever might've knocked on the door. The yard remained empty. She hustled up the stairs and checked the view from each room. Even with the better vantage point, she saw nothing.

Why was her heart still pounding so hard?

Mandy bounded down the stairs. She still felt on edge.

"All clear," she told Marcus. He'd stayed put. "I don't know who it was."

"Maybe—"

The jiggling of the door handle interrupted him. Mandy jumped the rest of the steps and landed halfway across the room. She grabbed Marcus' wrist and pulled him off the couch. When the door opened, a haggard-looking woman greeted them.

Marcus' mother.

"Hey, sweetie." She pulled her keys from the doorknob. "Sorry I'm late. Have you eaten yet? We can order—"

When she looked up, she caught sight of Mandy and Marcus frozen in the middle of the living room, holding hands and looking like they'd seen a ghost. Mandy had the wherewithal to drop Marcus' hand and take a step back. She looked down at her shoes.

"Hello, Mrs. Moore."

"Hello, Mandy." Mrs. Moore's gaze shot to Marcus. "This is a *surprise.*"

"I'm sorry, Mom." Marcus took a step forward. "The sheriff got sick, and her dad didn't have a choice—"

"The sheriff is sick?" Mrs. Moore's eyes darted around the room as she grabbed her stomach. "What happened?"

Before either could answer, a man stepped into the door frame and shoved Mrs. Moore forward. She stumbled to her knees. Her purse flew out of her hand. The contents slid across the floor. A violent scream erupted from her mouth.

For a split second, Mandy feared it was the tattooed man but she didn't see the splotch of red and blue on his neck. This guy was about as tall as the other, but his hair and eyes were lighter. He had tattoos along his left arm. In his right hand, he held a knife.

The man mule-kicked the door closed without taking his eyes off the trio. "Everyone shut up. Sit on the couch and do not move unless I tell you to." When none of them started for the couch, he yelled. "Now!"

Mandy helped Mrs. Moore to her feet. The woman convulsed in between sobs. She grasped for Marcus and shielded him with her body. The hysterics annoyed Mandy. She stuffed the feeling down. Not everyone was used to this level of violence. Crying wouldn't help them, but it was natural. Maybe it would even garner sympathy from their attacker.

The trio sat on the couch. The man remained in front of them. His stare and twisted smile turned Mandy's stomach. She resisted the urge to look away. It would only aggravate him. She had seen Bear use the tactic to put an adversary off their game. Mandy was too small to do that. She'd have to catch him off guard.

Mrs. Moore continued to cry, and soon Marcus joined her. Mandy felt bad for them. They'd never been through something like this before. When Mandy told her about the sheriff, Mrs. Moore's expression made Mandy think the woman knew more than she let on. She was friends with Dr. Sing, so maybe...

"Shut up!" The man smacked the coffee table with an open palm, making all three of them jump. "Shut up before I really give you something to cry about."

Mrs. Moore's crying intensified. She tried to keep it quiet, but she was beside herself with fear.

Mandy had to come up with a distraction. She twisted in her seat and propped herself up on a knee. "What do you want?"

"For you to shut up." He sneered at her. "Now sit back down."

"Tell me what you need and I'll get it. Money?" She pointed to the spilled contents of Mrs. Moore's purse on the floor. "Her wallet's right there."

"I'm not here for money."

"Drugs?" Mandy knew Mrs. Moore was a pharmacist. Maybe she was involved in this whole HealTek business, too. "I can't help you if you don't tell me what you want."

"I don't want you to help me." The man stepped forward and snatched Mandy by the arm, dragging her over the back of the couch. She knocked over a vase. Water spilled onto the side table and dripped to the floor. He held the knife to her throat. "I want you to shut up."

Fear gripped Mandy. She steadied herself. Bear had trained her for this. She had to stay still. She raised her hands to show she was unarmed and not a threat. She kept direct eye contact in order to hold his attention and see if his expression changed. Most people couldn't help but telegraph their moves ahead of time.

"I'm sorry." Mandy didn't bother to hide the way she shook. She needed him to feel like he was in control. "Are you here for me?" She kept her voice small. "Because your friend couldn't kidnap me before?"

She heard a gasp behind her. The guy looked over at Mrs. Moore, who was twisted in her seat now.

"Please," she begged, "she's just a kid."

Mandy lunged forward. She knocked his hand away and kneed the guy in the crotch. While he bent over in pain, she looped both her arms around the back of his neck and drove his face into her knee. He grunted and stumbled backward. She gripped both hands together and slammed them down on his wrist. The knife fell to the floor. Mandy twisted toward Marcus and locked eyes with him. "Upstairs. Now." When he didn't move, she yelled. "Go!"

Marcus took his mother by the wrist and dragged her upstairs. The woman dug her heels in. Marcus kept pulling. He might not have been big for his age, but he had a weight advantage over his mother.

"She can handle herself," he yelled. "Run!"

Mandy's attention was pulled away when the guy in front of her grabbed a fistful of hair and yanked her around. His face was too close to hers.

"You're going to regret that."

She didn't bother responding. The pain in her scalp distracted her. Mandy gasped for air. The oxygen was enough to clear her mind. She pushed past the sting and drove her fist into his bloodied nose. It wasn't enough to make him let go of her hair. She twisted around and bit his arm as hard as she could. She felt the skin tear. Blood flooded her mouth as she ground her teeth together.

Finally, he let go.

Mandy kicked back. Her foot connected with his knee. Before he could react, she was sprinting up the stairs, taking them two at a time, until she reached the landing. She heard Mrs. Moore crying behind the door at the end of the hall. Mandy skidded to a stop in front of it. She beat her fists against the door and yelled, "Let me in! Let me in!"

Marcus swung open the door. She bowled him over as she pushed through. He got up and slammed and locked the door behind her. She used her shirt to wipe out her mouth, ignoring the way her stomach twisted.

"What is going on?" Mrs. Moore yelled. She was half furious, half panicked. She pulled Marcus into her arms and held onto him for dear life.

"It's a long story." Mandy didn't even know where to start. "The other day—"

Banging on the door. All three of them jumped. The door handle jiggled, but it wouldn't open. There was a solid thump, like the guy was trying to kick the door in. Luckily, the door was solid, and the lock was a deadbolt. He'd have to split the entire door or take it off the hinges to get through. Chances were, he would eventually. But they had bought some time.

Mandy rushed over to the window, trying to gauge whether they could drop from the second floor and make a run for it. If this guy was alone, they might be able to do it before he'd noticed their escape. But if he had any buddies, they wouldn't make it very far, and they'd be back to square one. If he wasn't alone, why hadn't they come in when they heard yelling?

Mandy was still trying to work out a solution when they heard a different kind of roar. Another set of footsteps pounded up the stairs. The thumping went quiet. There was a scuffle on the other side of the door. Then a grunt as a body hit the wall.

A different voice spoke. The door muffled it, but there was no mistaking what he said. "You're going to regret that."

Mrs. Moore's crying intensified.

A smile swept across Mandy's face. "We're going to be okay."

"How do you know?" Marcus asked.

Mandy's smile widened. "Because that's my dad."

38

An hour later, the police were leaving Marcus' house. They'd arrested the intruder and taken the trio's statements. Mrs. Moore had been cold toward Bear and Mandy over the last week. Now she couldn't thank them enough. She'd hugged Mandy at least three times and told Bear if he ever needed anything to let her know.

"There is one thing," Bear said. "Mandy tells me you're a pharmacist?"

"Yes, that's right."

He pulled the pieces of paper from Bowser Freight out of his back pocket. "Can you tell me what these are?"

The woman took the papers and studied them. She looked back up, afraid. "Where did you get these?"

"A friend helped me get them," Bear said. Marcus had the good sense to stay silent. "Why? What are they?"

"They're the components of an experimental drug that HealTek is trying to develop. It's not on the market yet."

"What does it do?"

"They're pitching it as a miracle drug that cures cancer. But the FDA won't approve it because the side effects are too severe."

"What are the side effects?"

"More virulent forms of the cancer. Untreatable."

Bear didn't want to point fingers in front of her kid, but if she knew more than she was letting on, he could use that information to put a stop to this. "How do you know all this?"

Mrs. Moore handed the papers back to Bear and sat on the couch. She placed her face in her hands and cried. After a minute, she pulled herself together. She straightened her shoulders and looked him in the eye. "Dr. Sing was a good friend of mine. She trusted me. Not with everything. But I understand how drugs interact with the human body. She would pick my brain."

"Did you know?" Bear tried to keep the accusation out of his voice. "About what's been going on?"

"No." She wiped wetness from her eyes. "I still don't understand it all. And if I'm being honest, I don't want to." She looked away. "I know that makes me a terrible person—"

"We all make mistakes." Bear joined her on the couch, aware that both Mandy and Marcus were watching them like hawks. "Trust me, I've made some pretty big ones in my life. But it's never too late to do the right thing. To try to fix something. I need you to tell me what you know."

Mrs. Moore took a deep breath. She looked at Marcus and smiled, but it was sad. Like she hoped this wouldn't make him see her in a different light. "Aimee—Dr. Sing—had been working with HealTek for about twenty years. She had her practice at the hospital, and she was a consultant with the company. They paid her good money for her opinion. She said at first, it was simple stuff. Easy things. Like which drugs they needed most. Which would be more profitable. She didn't have a problem telling them. After all, it'd benefit her in the end. She got paid to tell them, and they'd make sure she was one of the first to have the medication."

"There's no shame in helping people and getting paid for it," Bear said. "But you mentioned this was the easy stuff?"

She nodded. "After a while, they started asking her strange questions. Like if it were possible to induce diseases in people. Make them sick at an accelerated rate. She told me that, at first, she believed they were thought experiments. You know, a think tank. This was right after nine-eleven. People talked about biological weapons. She thought she was helping them fight against those things. The questions got more specific as time went on. Her contacts at the company would leave and come back a week or a month later with more questions. She felt like they were using her expertise for their experiments. Every time she asked what was going on, they'd cut her out of the conversation. Eventually, she learned to not ask."

"Then what?" Bear asked.

"Things went quiet for a while. They still consulted her, but not on anything big. Those questions in the back of her head never got answered, you know?"

"When did they start consulting her again?"

"About five years ago." Mrs. Moore rubbed her hands together like she was cold, then crossed her arms and hugged herself. "Now, they were asking the opposite questions. How to cure diseases. Not just treat or manage them. Eradicate them from the human body. The big question was about cancer."

"How did she feel about that?"

The woman shrugged. "Every pharmaceutical company is looking to cure cancer with a pill. That's the dream. The golden egg. She told them what she knew, and they'd come back every week with new questions."

"I'm sure she felt better about that line of questioning."

"She did." Mrs. Moore smiled. "She was excited and thought they'd be able to do something together. She was a brilliant doctor. And they had a lot of resources. It was a match made in heaven."

"Until it wasn't?"

She nodded. "Aimee was naïve. Innocent, almost. She liked to believe the best in people. I think that's part of what made her a good doctor, you know? She didn't judge. One day, she told me she'd done something terrible. She wouldn't tell me what, just that she needed to fix it. She asked my opinion on two scenarios. The first was that she would go to the authorities, but she'd go down with HealTek. I didn't know in what context." She blew out a breath before she continued. "The second scenario was that she would attempt to fix it herself.

While it might have taken longer, she'd save a lot of lives. And keep hers."

"I'm guessing she went with the second."

Mrs. Moore nodded. "That's what I told her to do." A sob escaped, and her voice shook with emotion. "I didn't know what she was talking about. I didn't want to lose my friend. Whatever she had gotten caught up in, it was because she was trying to do the right thing."

Silence filled the room as Mrs. Moore sobbed. Mandy walked up to her and placed a hand on the older woman's shoulder. "It's not your fault. She made her choice. You were trying to protect your friend."

The woman looked up at her, tears still in her eyes. "Thank you."

"Do you have any idea what was going on?" Bear knew more now than he did earlier in the day, but he still didn't have the whole picture. "Do you have any idea what HealTek has been doing?"

She shook her head. "I've never talked to them directly. I fill prescriptions and answer questions about drugs. That's all I ever did for Aimee. Occasionally, I'd set something aside for her, but I think she got most of her resources from HealTek directly."

"Do you know if she was participating in any clinical trials?"

Mrs. Moore shook her head. "In the last year, we haven't really talked about it. Maybe I should've asked what was going on. I could've been—I could've been a better friend. I could've asked. But I was afraid."

"She made her choice. That's not your responsibility." Bear's phone buzzed. He got up from the couch, his head swimming with information. "Hello?"

"Is this Mr. Logan?"

"Speaking."

"This is Anna from the hospital. Sheriff McKinnon is stable and would like to talk with you. She'd like to see you immediately."

He felt a hundred pounds lighter. McKinnon was stable. He turned to Mandy and smiled. "I'll be right there."

39

BEAR STEPPED OUT OF MRS. MOORE'S HOUSE JUST AS SOMEONE WAS pulling into the neighbor's driveway. It was dark enough that the head-lights blinded him. He put up a hand and waited for the driver to cut the engine. After a few seconds, the car shut off and Bear blinked away the spots in his vision.

It wasn't until the man climbed out of his car that Bear realized it was the councilman who had threatened him and McKinnon. "Good evening, Mr. Logan."

"The hell are you doing here?" Bear said.

"Picking up my son." He straightened his jacket, smoothing a crease along the front. "Tell me, how's Sheriff McKinnon doing?"

Bear didn't care that Mrs. Moore and the kids were at the door. Or that this was a sitting member of the town council. He didn't know what kind of power Henry Richter had, and he didn't care. Even if he shared a name with one of the founding fathers of this town and even if he had all of HealTek to back him up, Bear wasn't afraid of him.

And when he launched himself over the garden fence dividing the two properties, he enjoyed the petrified look that crossed the other man's face. Bear grabbed his tie and yanked him closer. "What did you say?"

The man sputtered. "What are you doing? Let me go." Bear shoved him back so hard, Richter landed on his backside with a grunt. He looked up at Bear with terror and embarrassment. "Who the hell do you think you are?"

"I'll tell you what I'm not." Bear stepped closer. He towered over the other man now. "I'm not afraid of you. But you need to be afraid of me."

Richter stood up. His hands were shaking. He covered it up by brushing the dirt from his pants. "You're going to regret that. I've already given you one warning, Mr. Logan."

"Like you gave McKinnon?"

The man shrugged. "I told her to wrap up the investigation. She refused. I was trying to help her."

They were toe to toe now. "What did you do to her?"

"It's what she's done that matters. It's what you're doing. If you'd just left well enough alone—"

Bear didn't bother letting him finish the sentence. He reared back his arm and punched the man in the face. Richter fell for the second time in as many minutes. Bear heard Mrs. Moore gasp behind him. The neighbor's front door opened and a teenager peered through the screen door. It took Bear a minute to place him. Mandy had shown him a picture of the kid who had been bullying her. It was him.

Pete.

"This makes a lot more sense now," Bear said. "You're a piece of work, Richter. And you've turned your kid into a bully." By this point, Pete had made his way out and was standing next to the passenger door with his backpack slung over one shoulder. Bear glanced over at the kid. "Don't turn out like him. You might bully your way through life for a while, but one day you'll come up against someone bigger than you. And you'll regret wasting your life chasing power and prestige."

Richter started to get up. "Don't you *dare* talk to my son..."

Bear pushed him back on his ass. "Sit down." He bent over and stuck a finger in the man's face. "You're lucky the sheriff survived whatever you tried to do with her."

"What are you even talking about, Logan?"

"It's only a matter of time before we nail everyone else involved. And I look forward to seeing you hang there with your buddies."

"You've got nothing." The councilman sneered. "By the end of the week, you'll be gone. And no one will remember you. No one will miss you."

"We'll see about that." Bear turned to leave. He cast a glance over his shoulder. "If I were a betting man, I wouldn't bet on you, Richter."

After Richter and Pete backed out of the driveway and drove off into the night, Bear walked up to Mandy and kissed her on the forehead. "I'll be back in a few hours. Stay here. Lock the doors. I don't think anyone else will bother you tonight, but stay vigilant, okay? You protect these two, got it?"

Mandy's face was set in stone. She stared into the darkness. "Got it."

Bear hugged her and looked at Mrs. Moore. "She's a good kid. Listen to her."

"What are you going to do?" the woman asked.

Bear turned back to his truck. "I'm going to end this." He ground his teeth together. "One way or another."

40

BEAR KNOCKED ON THE DOOR AS HE ENTERED THE HOSPITAL ROOM. A nurse was checking on McKinnon's vitals, and when she saw Bear, she frowned. Patting the sheriff's hand, she walked toward the door, making direct eye contact with Bear. "She's still weak. Don't get her worked up, you hear?"

Bear put a hand to his chest. "Me? Never!"

The nurse scowled and left the room. When Bear turned to McKinnon, she smiled. He doubted she had the energy to laugh. He pulled a chair up to her bed and gave her a once over. She looked pale, but otherwise the same. Her eyes drooped, like she could use nothing more than a good night's rest.

"One of the great ironies of a hospital," Bear said, "is that they want you to rest and relax so you can heal, but they'll wake you up twenty times during the night."

"Yeah, they don't really like it when I fall asleep," she said. "Then they can't ask me the same questions over and over again."

He chuckled. "How're you feeling?"

"Good." She grimaced. "Well, not good, but better. Thanks to you." When Bear waved off the comment, she scowled. "Seriously, Riley. You saved my life. I owe you big time."

"I might have to cash that in sooner than later."

For the first time, McKinnon took Bear in. He knew his face was already bruising and he still had flecks of blood on his shirt.

"What the hell happened to you?"

"I found Jeremy Olsen." When her eyebrows went up, he continued. "He's the same guy who tried to kidnap Mandy. And the guy who tried to run us off the road. He works for Bowser. Pretty sure it's off the books."

"How did you find that out?"

Bear had the good sense to look sheepish. "I may have reexamined Bowser's part in all of this."

McKinnon nodded. "And?"

"They're in bed with HealTek." He handed the pieces of paper detailing the drugs to her. "Our good friend Mr. Weinberger tipped me off that they make him leave the room when certain shipments arrive. He told me the lot numbers. I pulled this info from their computers."

"I won't ask how you did that." She sifted through the papers, then looked back up at him. "Weinberger? Really?"

"Really. Didn't even have to rough him up for it."

She shook her head. There was a small smile on her face. "What are these?"

"According to Marcus' mother, they're components of a so-called miracle drug. She learned bits and pieces from Dr. Sing, but she doesn't have the full picture. It looks like Sing had been involved since the beginning. First as a consultant, then more directly."

"Did Moore know anything about the clinical trials?"

"No. We need to find Sing's notebooks. That'll give us more information. Maybe enough to make an arrest."

The sheriff looked through the papers again, and then handed them back to Bear. She looked more drained than when he'd first entered, and for a second, he was afraid the nurse would come back and kick him out. But when McKinnon spoke again, her voice was clear. "We're so close. We have the dots. Now we have to connect them."

There was a knock on the door, and Bear twisted around to find Weinberger standing there. "Maybe I can help?"

Bear didn't bother hiding the skepticism from his face. "What changed your mind?"

"My daughter. Laura Lynn. She's... getting worse. I don't know what else to do."

Bear was still trying to reconcile the Weinberger he had met a few days ago with the man who seemed to have found a healthy dose of humility. "Thought you didn't know anything."

"I don't. But I know where you can get some answers." The man nodded and entered the room. There was only one chair, and Bear wasn't going to give it up. It forced Weinberger to stand with his arms dangling at his side. "The company houses its labs below the building. Most employees aren't allowed down there. As the warehouse manager, I have access for deliveries. I can get to four out of the five floors."

"And the fifth?"

"I think that's where you'll find your answers."

"You think?" McKinnon asked.

Weinberger shrugged. "Best I can do. I'm not allowed on the fifth level. It makes sense. Besides, I've seen Dr. Sing get off on that floor a hundred times. She was working on something big for them."

"What else do you know about Dr. Sing's projects?"

"Not much." Weinberger looked up at the ceiling as if the answers were written there. "They escorted her in and out a couple times a month. Sometimes she left late at night, looking like she'd spent hours pulling her hair out. She didn't talk to the rest of us. There were rumors, but I don't know how true they were."

"What were the rumors about?" Any information might point them in the right direction.

"That she was working on some fancy new drug that would get us all a big paycheck."

Bear handed Weinberger the papers from Bowser Freight. "These are the drugs they don't want you seeing. Do you recognize any of them?"

Weinberger looked at the pages but handed them back. "No. I couldn't tell you what they were for if you had a gun to my head."

"Could arrange that," Bear muttered under his breath as he pocketed the papers. "They're for a miracle drug. Something that could cure cancer. Dr. Sing was doing clinical trials. I don't know whether she was trying to fix a problem she created or make it worse. Either way, HealTek has our answers. And the evidence we need."

"That place is like a fortress," McKinnon said. "You need a keycard. There are cameras everywhere."

"I've got a cousin in security," Weinberger said. "He's pointed the cameras in another direction once or twice. I can get you down to the fourth floor."

McKinnon clicked her tongue a couple of times. "They'll find out you helped us. You'll be fired."

"It doesn't matter." Weinberger looked resigned. "I have to do something to save my daughter."

"When does your cousin start his shift?"

"Midnight every night."

"Let him know we're coming."

McKinnon's mouth pressed into a hard line. "I'm going with you."

"You're too weak." Bear laid a hand on her shoulder. "Besides, I'll need someone to bail me out if I get caught."

She didn't laugh. "Bear—"

"We need to hit them hard and fast. Take them by surprise." He looked up at Weinberger, who had his phone out, and nodded. "We're doing this tonight."

41

Bear and Mr. Weinberger pulled into HealTek's employee parking lot five minutes after midnight in Weinberger's car. Bear's truck would have attracted too much attention. It had to be on some internal HealTek BOLO by this point. Weinberger had insisted it wouldn't matter either way. There were no cameras in the lot.

Bear surveyed the structure. Five stories tall. Weinberger had said the layout was basic. The upper levels consisted of offices, meeting rooms, a cafeteria, and a lounge. Everyone from number crunchers to board members and their lawyers were housed inside during work hours.

The scientists lived on the lower floors. Five levels below ground. Offices and laboratories and who knew what else. Weinberger had spent little time down there. He dropped items off and never stuck around to chat. The HealTek bigwigs kept scientists away from other employees so they wouldn't spill company secrets.

"Two minutes." Sweat lined Weinberger's brow.

Bear nodded and remained silent. Weinberger's cousin pulled through. He had provided them access to a side entrance and pointed the interior cameras in the opposite direction. According to Weinberger, his cousin had done this before. For employees who wanted to raid the cafeteria for food after a drunken night out. Employees who wanted to have sex who-knew-where. Employees brave enough to skim a couple bottles of pills off the top of the stack in the supplies room.

Bear slipped five hundred dollars from his pocket and handed it to Weinberger. "You'll get your cut after." He trusted the man—his motivation to save his daughter was as altruistic as it would get—but he wasn't taking any chances.

Weinberger didn't seem offended. He glanced at his phone. "Sixty seconds. Ready?"

"Let's roll."

Bear climbed out of the car and shut the door behind him. They darted across the parking lot. Bear stuck to the shadows. Weinberger followed suit.

The pair pressed themselves against the outside wall of the building, then made their way toward the side entrance.

Weinberger leaned closer and whispered, "Ten seconds."

Bear moved faster.

As soon as they were within a foot of the entryway, the door buzzed. Bear pushed it open and stepped inside. Weinberger followed. The lights inside the building were dim, both in Bear's favor and against it. It'd be hard for someone to spot him, but he'd also have to keep his eyes peeled.

Weinberger took the lead. He navigated his way to the stairwell. They climbed two floors and headed straight to the security offices. He knocked twice on the door, paused, then knocked again.

The man who opened it to greet them looked nothing like Weinberger. He was at least ten years younger, fit and attractive. He had a well-manicured beard, and hair that swooped to one side.

Eddie sized Bear up. After a few seconds of staring Bear in the eye, he nodded, then turned to his cousin. "Payment?"

Weinberger handed over the wad of cash and watched as Eddie counted it. "It's all there."

"Just habit, man. Don't be offended." Eddie stuffed the money in his pocket, then looked back up at Bear. "You're a big guy."

"That a problem?"

Eddie shrugged. "Not for me. I don't suffer from Gigantasophobia." He turned and grabbed a pile of clothes off a shelf, tossing them to Bear. "But these might be a little snug."

Bear inspected the security uniform. He hadn't expected to go in with a disguise. This could buy him a few more seconds if he ran into trouble. He peeled off his clothes. "Thanks."

"No problem. You've got ten minutes before my partner comes back. After that, don't bother knocking on the door again. Got it?"

"Where is he?"

"Who?"

"Your partner. Where is he right now?"

"Number two." Eddie grinned. "Every night, like clockwork. Tell you the truth, I think he jacks off in there or something. No one is that regular."

"How do I—"

"No." Eddie plugged his ears with his index fingers. "No, no. I don't want to hear it. I don't know you, where you're going, or what you're trying to do once you get there. I get you in. The rest is up to you. The uniform was for the extra hundred you threw in." He checked his watch. "You've got nine minutes. Do what you gotta do. Discuss it amongst yourselves."

Bear watched as Eddie turned his back on them and walked the length of the room. He settled in front of a pair of monitors and put on his headphones.

Bear finished putting on the security uniform. It pinched at the shoulders but otherwise fit. He handed his clothes to Weinberger. "Take these, get back to the car, and get out of here."

"Don't want me to wait for you?"

"Appreciate the thought. Not worth you getting caught."

"They'll catch me, anyway." He produced his keycard and handed it over. "If not tonight, then tomorrow, or the day after."

Bear approached Eddie and tapped him on the shoulder. The man took out one earbud and looked up at him. "You got seven minutes."

"Yeah, yeah." Bear pulled another hundred out of his pocket and waved it in front of him. "Can you wipe Weinberger's logs for tonight so no one knows he was here?"

Eddie glared at him. "I told you, I get you in, the rest—"

Bear pulled out another two hundred. "It's a hell of a bonus, man."

Eddie snatched the money from Bear. "Six minutes. Get out of here."

Bear figured that was as good as it was going to get. He pushed Weinberger back toward the door, grabbing a roll of duct tape on the way out. It always worked for MacGyver.

"Go ahead of me," Bear said. "Head straight for the car. Take my clothes to the sheriff. I'll pick them up from her later. Then stay with your kid."

"Should I go to work tomorrow?" Weinberger asked.

"Just act like everything is normal unless you hear otherwise, got it?"

The man nodded, then hurried down the hallway and through the doors to the stairwell. Bear gave him a sixty-second head start before following him back down to the first floor. There was a special elevator to the lower levels, only accessed by passing in front of the main security desk at the entrance. He would have to time everything perfectly.

A bolt of excitement clawed through his body. It'd been a while since he'd done an undercover gig. He pulled the hat labeled SECURITY over his brow to obscure his face from the cameras.

Bear pushed through the doors and jogged down the stairwell. He collected his thoughts before exiting onto the first floor.

It was go-time.

42

Bear preferred knowing a building's layout before he broke inside. This time, he was flying blind.

He spotted the cameras along the hallway and ducked his head low. He had a general sense of where the front door was. He walked north. Whenever he was forced to take turns, he'd correct his trajectory as soon as possible. There were few navigational signs. And dressed as a security guard, he needed to pretend to know where he was going.

A squeak of shoes down the hall caught his attention. He didn't hear any banter. Another guard doing a solo round. Weinberger had told them there were two dozen guards at all times, working in pairs on each floor. They switched off and searched the building every hour. Bear had avoided them so far. His luck had run out.

Bear was a quarter of the way down the hall when the other man turned the corner. Bear noticed when the guard spotted him. The guy tilted his head forward as if to get a better look at his face. The hat was a godsend as much as the uniform. If Bear could avoid the man's gaze long enough, he could pass him by without any trouble.

When the guard sped up, Bear knew that wasn't possible. A camera was in the middle of the hall. Someone would notice if he neutralized the man here. He needed to be smart about his next move.

That's when he spotted the bathroom halfway down the hall. If he could make it there before the other guy, he'd be able to slip in without being held up. And if he couldn't, he'd use the bathroom's lack of cameras to his advantage.

Bear sped up. He tried to not look suspicious, but he also wanted to seem like he was on a mission. As long as you looked like you knew what you were doing, most people didn't question it. A wave of panic crashed over him. What if the guards had already been warned? What if they were on the lookout for him?

The other man was ten feet away. Bear pushed through the door to the restroom and barreled into a stall. He slammed the door and latched it. He sat down and didn't bother dropping his pants. If this guy knew what he was up to, it wouldn't do him any good to be caught with his boxers around his ankles.

Bear heard another squeak of the man's sneaker as he halted outside the bathroom. A few seconds ticked by. The door opened. The guard stepped up to the urinal. "Hey, man. What's up?"

This dude was breaking the most sacred rule of the men's room. Don't make conversation. "Hey, man."

"Busy night?"

"Not so far." Bear remained seated and leaned forward to get a glimpse of the guy through the cracks. All he saw was the left side of his body. "You?"

"Quiet, as usual." There was a beat of silence, and then the man pulled up his zipper. "Hey, do I know you? Didn't recognize you."

"Yeah, man. Been working here for a year." Bear forced a laugh. "I work up on three."

"What are you doing down here?"

"Someone blew up the bathroom on the third *and* the second floor. Had to find a new one."

"Ah, man. That sucks. But you know you're not supposed to be down here, right? You could get written up."

Bear shifted as the man walked to the sink and washed his hands. He was peering at Bear's stall with a funny look on his face. "I know. Look, don't tell Eddie, will you? He's been on my back for the last week."

"Eddie? That dude's chill. You just got to slip him a twenty every once in a while."

"Really? All right. I'll take your word for it."

"You really shouldn't be down here, though. If Jamison catches you—"

"I know, I know. Look, I just really gotta go. Can't do it with an audience, you know? Soon as I'm out of here, I'll head back up. Drinks are on me next time we go out, all right?"

The man shook the excess water from his hands, then grabbed a paper towel. "Yeah, all right. But you owe me."

"You got it, chief."

Bear waited for the guard to leave before breathing a sigh of relief. Then he waited an extra two minutes. If Bear ran into him again, he doubted he'd be so lucky. The guy seemed like a nosy prick.

After the two minutes had elapsed, Bear waited another thirty seconds before pushing through the door, back into the hallway. It was clear. He kept his head down and walked toward the main security desk. And when he turned the corner, there it was.

Two men sat behind a bank of computers. One was reading a book while the other was playing on his phone. Neither of them noticed when Bear slipped behind them. He stuck to the wall and headed for the far end of the entrance. He only dared to take a full breath once he reached the elevators. According to Weinberger, these were the only ones that went downstairs.

Bear used the man's keycard to call the elevator. It arrived with a *ding*. The sound reverberated around the room. There was no way the guys at the front desk didn't hear that. Bear stepped inside the elevator without looking up and hit the close door button. Then he pushed the button for the fifth floor.

Nothing happened.

He pushed it again. Even waved the card against the reader as he pushed it for a third time. Nothing. Weinberger had told him he didn't have access to the fifth floor. Bear had been hoping he'd never tried kind of like he'd never tried to go looking for those lot numbers he wasn't allowed to see.

As Bear went to press the button for the fourth floor—he hoped he'd figure out a way to the next level, even if it meant crawling through air ducts—the doors to the elevator opened and a guard stood there. He stared at Bear with an inquisitive look. Thank God it was someone other than the guy from the bathroom.

"Having trouble?" He was a little older than Bear. Short, thin, and gangly. Like he'd never really grown into his body.

"Yeah, man. Sorry. Trying to get to the fifth floor. Pass isn't working."

"You're not allowed on the fifth."

"Normally, I'm not." Bear pulled out the empty envelope he had stashed Eddie's money in. "This guy gave me this letter to deliver to the fifth floor. Told me if I didn't screw it up, he'd give me an extra two hundred bucks. I could really use the money, man."

"What guy?"

"Huh?"

"What guy gave you the letter?"

Bear scrambled for a name. "I can't remember. It was a weird last name. Started with a P? Or a B? I'm terrible with names."

"Pachulski?"

Bear was sweating now, which added to his performance. It would be all over if they caught him this close to the fifth floor. The other guard at the security desk would sound the alarm. Bear'd be screwed. "Yeah, that's him."

"Pachulski trusted you to go to the fifth floor and didn't even give you a pass for it?" There was an awkward silence, then the guard cracked a smile and started laughing. "Sounds like him. He's such a douche sometimes. I can get you to the fifth floor, but I can't let you out of my sight. You give me fifty bucks and we'll call it even."

"You got it, man."

The guard stepped into the elevator and held his pass to the reader. It blinked green, and he hit the button for the fifth floor. The elevator started to move. Bear tipped his head back in relief. Almost there. Just a few seconds longer.

The doors opened with another *ding*. Bear scanned the barely lit hallway. He didn't see any cameras. Didn't mean they weren't there. HealTek had plenty to hide, but they sure as hell had this floor covered.

"Thanks again, man," Bear said. "Really appreciate this."

"No prob—"

Bear didn't let the guy finish. He wrapped an arm around the guard's neck and held tight while the man struggled. After about twenty seconds, the guy went limp, and Bear used his recently pilfered roll of duct tape to bind his hands and legs and tape his mouth shut. Then he dragged the unconscious man down the hallway and threw him into a janitor's closet.

Weinberger's knowledge had helped him get this far. Now Bear was on his own. It wouldn't be long before the other guard realized his partner was missing. Bear checked every room on the floor until he found what he was looking for.

And now the real work began.

43

The door had a placard with Dr. Sing's name on it. Above the handle was a keypad, which Bear pried from the door. He yanked the wires free. The doorhandle twisted under his hand. He had to work fast. What if the keypad had triggered an alarm upstairs?

Bear shut the door behind him. This office was much bigger than the one Sing had at the hospital, and it came with its own lab. Beakers and Bunsen burners and boiler plates lined the table.

Sing's desk was covered in leather-bound notebooks, just like the ones Mandy had seen locked away in the secret compartment in the doctor's hospital office. Bear and McKinnon had found Sing dead an hour later. She couldn't have brought the notebooks here. Was it Jeremy Olsen? His buddy? Or someone else?

Whoever it was, they were suspect one in her murder.

Bear searched the room until he found a pair of latex gloves. He squeezed them over his hands, and then went to work flipping through the notebooks. They were in no discernable order, so he looked for dates until he had lined them up sequentially. There were over twenty notebooks spanning from 2002 to present day. If these didn't hold their answers, he didn't know what would.

As much as he wanted to sit down and read every page, Bear moved on. He didn't know how much time he had and there was plenty left to explore. Sing's desk drawers contained office supplies, a few snacks, and an uneaten bagged lunch. Going through a deceased's belongings was never easy. He was conflicted about Sing. She was undoubtedly at the center of whatever was going on in this town. However, Mrs. Moore seemed to believe the doctor was trying her best to help people.

Bear skimmed the bookshelf against the far wall. It was mostly full of medical textbooks and journals. They were for posterity or research purposes, and he needed something concrete. He moved to the lab table in the center of the room.

Sing had been in the middle of something before she died. He snapped as many pictures with his phone as he could. Slides containing drops of blood. Solutions of various colors in the refrigeration unit. Charts and drawings with numbers and symbols written all over them. It all mattered, even if none of it did. McKinnon could find someone to decipher this stuff.

Bear found what might have been the holy grail. A box full of pills. They were capsules, white with either a blue or red end. Were these the drugs making people sick? Or were they the cure?

Bear pocketed the box. The room went dark. After a few seconds, red emergency lighting switched on, casting an eerie glow. A shrieking alarm blared. Bear's time was up. He grabbed a plastic bag from one of the desk drawers and dumped Sing's uneaten lunch onto the table and replaced it with the notebooks from earlier. They barely fit, but Bear wasn't about to leave a single one. He was certain the information within would bring HealTek to its knees.

As soon as he pushed his way out of the office, a bullet slammed into the wall next to his head. Debris pelted his face. He ducked and rolled, then sprinted down the hallway and around the corner. He took cover to collect himself. Alarms continued to scream. Red lights strobed. He could hardly hear the commotion behind him. When he poked his head out again, the hair on the back of his neck stood on end.

Bear ducked back behind the wall as another bullet whizzed by.

There had to be another exit. Maybe there was only one way to get down here, but there'd be another to get outside. Especially with all this equipment.

Bear only hoped that the HealTek board members cared about being up to code. They clearly didn't care about the townspeople. He was betting they wouldn't want their scientists to go up in flames even if they were willing to kill Dr. Sing.

As another bullet crashed into the corner of his protecting wall, Bear scrambled to his feet and dashed down the corridor. At the other end, he slowed down before rounding the corner. A pair of armed guards headed toward him.

Halfway between Bear and the guards was an exit sign. He sprinted for the door. If they had somehow overridden the system, he'd either wind up dead or in jail.

Bear was eighty percent to the door when pain ripped through his shoulder. He glanced down. Flesh wound. He'd survive. He burst through the exit and stumbled as the door shut behind him. The tunnel was lined with red lights. He didn't look back as he sprinted down the corridor with the bag clenched tight to his chest. At the end of the tunnel was a ladder. He climbed to the top, where he found a door that opened with the turn of a wheel.

He burst through the door. The cool night air chilled his sweat-soaked body. He was two hundred yards from the building. Guards flooded the yard. They sprinted toward him with their guns raised and shouted for him to stop. Bear ignored their warnings. He sprinted through the woods to the street on the other side. He didn't slow down when he hit asphalt and was almost wiped out by a passing car.

The driver slammed on the brakes. Tires squealed. The smell of burning rubber pervaded Bear's senses. He launched himself in the other direction and hit the ground hard on his injured shoulder. The passenger side window rolled down. Bear saw a familiar face.

Weinberger leaned across the seat and popped the door open. "Get in!"

Bear didn't hesitate. He scrambled across the street and crawled into the front seat. "What are you doing here? I told you to leave."

"Felt guilty." Weinberger barely gave Bear enough time to get in and close the door before he pinned the accelerator to the floor. "Find what you were looking for?"

Bear looked down at the notebooks and smiled. "Yeah. We've got everything we need."

44

It was amazing what a group of pissed off people could accomplish.

Bear gave Weinberger most of the credit. He had put Bear's plan in place. He had gathered enough people together. The truth had been revealed. More than half the town was on their side now.

Weinberger had led the march through the front doors with Bear and Mandy at his side. Behind them were more than a hundred parents and grandparents, brothers and sisters, aunts and uncles. People who had been long-time employees and supporters of HealTek. People who had once kept their heads down in order to protect themselves.

No more.

Once they'd heard about Dr. Sing's research, they realized keeping their heads down had done nothing more than encourage HealTek to walk all over them. Weinberger had hand selected the families he thought would listen to what Bear had to say, and by mid-afternoon, they had a small army.

All in time for the board meeting.

Weinberger led them to the elevator and scanned his keycard while a pair of men detached themselves to stand guard at the security desk.

Bear entered the elevator first, Mandy by his side. She had insisted on being there. Bear felt certain they weren't walking into danger. They outnumbered the board almost ten to one. And it's not like HealTek didn't know Mandy existed. Besides, Bear needed her help with the technology side of the plan.

Mrs. Moore hadn't let Marcus attend, so he was at home running the backend. He'd make sure enough people saw what HealTek really was.

Marcus promised he'd broadcast it anonymously. Bear could tell his mom was proud of him for doing what she'd always been afraid of doing herself.

The first elevator full, Bear pushed the button for the sixth floor. Weinberger stayed behind to give the next group access to the elevators. He'd ride up with the last of the parents, ensuring everyone got a seat at the table.

The anticipation in the air electrified Bear. The elevators opened with a *ding*. His group parted to let him lead the charge. Mandy had her phone out and was recording. She looked up at him with a smile on her face. For the first time since he found Katie Lamoureux's body, Bear was certain he'd made the right choice.

The board didn't see them coming. When Bear pushed through the doors into the dark meeting room, all eight members around the large oval table looked to the small army, surprised and angry. Bear flipped the light on to reveal who had entered their private meeting. All eight faces turned to disbelief.

"Evening, folks." Bear went to the front of the room and allowed the crowd to join him. Even if the board members wanted to escape, they had no outlet. The only exit was blocked. "I have an announcement to make."

"Who do you think you are?" The man at the head of the table asked. He had a shock of white hair and bright eyes.

"Don't pretend like you don't know me, Mr. Anderson." Bear had studied their faces on the website. Anderson was the head honcho.

Anderson didn't bother arguing. "What's the meaning of this? This is a private—"

"It's not private anymore," Bear said. "We've called a town meeting. And we decided to have it right here."

"You can't do that."

"We just did." Bear spread his arms open and gestured to the crowd. He knew they had a lot to say. He wanted to paint a picture for their online audience first. For effect, Mandy scanned the crowd, making sure not to include Bear's face. They were still trying to lie low, after all.

Bear waited until Weinberger entered the room and closed the door behind him. He stood with his arms crossed like he was their appointed bodyguard.

"I'm giving you a chance to come clean," Bear said. "Who wants to start the explanations to your fellow townspeople?"

Caplan looked directly at the camera with his bright blue eyes. "What's with the theatrics? None of this is going to save any of you in the end."

"Shut up," Anderson snapped. He turned back to Bear. "You'll be hearing from our lawyers. In the meantime, we're not saying anything."

"Good." Bear let the grin he'd been holding back spread across his face. "That means I can do all the talking." He pulled out one of Dr. Sing's notebooks and saw a few of the board members' faces darken with recognition. "I see you know what these are. For those of you who don't, let me explain."

Bear stepped forward, holding the notebook high. Most of the townspeople in the room had received the watered-down version of what had been going on. This would be the first time they had seen the whole picture.

"On September 11th, 2001, America experienced a horrific attack on our own turf. Just a fledgling company at the time, HealTek saw an opportunity to develop a drug to use as a biological weapon against those who wished to see our demise."

Anderson got to his feet. "Lies."

"Say what you want. I have the proof. Dr. Aimee Sing was a consultant for the company back then. She has written, beginning in June 2002, several questions she was asked by high-ranking members of HealTek. She also kept track of the answers she provided. I've read every single one of these journals. Sing had concluded HealTek attempted to develop a drug that could be fed into the water supply to kill off entire towns without a trace of evidence."

The crowd was murmuring now, unable to help themselves. It spurred Bear forward.

"HealTek used their employees as guinea pigs. First in small doses, then in larger quantities once they realized they weren't getting the results they expected. What HealTek created was a drug that accelerated the rate of cancer in its recipients. Not everyone developed the disease in response to the compounds they ingested through the water supply. Those who did were dead within a few years. Sometimes it happened quick. Others, it dragged on for months. They all died in the end."

One of the board members—Bear recognized him as Abraham Irons —stood and attempted to make his way through the crowd. Two heavyset men stood in his way and pushed him back until he was sitting again. Anderson shot the man a look of disgust, but he didn't dare say anything.

"Having realized their weapon was too slow-acting to be useful to the United States government, HealTek gave up on the project." Bear opened the notebook so the camera could see Sing's scribbles along the pages. "Then they started a new one. They developed a drug that caused cancer. So, why not reverse-engineer their technology to come up with a cure? If they could cure cancer with a single pill, they'd be rich. Beyond rich. A foolproof plan."

Bear paused, hoping a board member would say something. He wanted them to defend their actions—it would be damning to have that caught on tape—but they were too smart to say a word.

"Members of the town continued to get sick. Dr. Sing studied their cases, hoping to come up with a miracle cure. According to her journals, she was on the precipice of discovery when I uncovered the body of a twelve-year-old girl in my backyard. Katie Lamoureux. She'd been dead for over fifteen years. Her father had been close to talking about what he knew went on in the company, in the town. So they killed her. And it worked. Her parents moved away within a couple months. Another loose end had been tied off."

Bear stared at Anderson. "Your first mistake was thinking you could bully me and Sheriff McKinnon into submission. Your other mistake was thinking the people in this town would stay afraid forever."

"You have no proof," Anderson spat. "Just the journals of a dead woman."

"We have proof, but you'd find a way to cover that up, too. Men with money are dangerous, and you've proven you'd go to any length to save your own asses."

Bear turned to a pair of women behind him. One carried a pitcher of water, the other a tray with eight empty glasses. They went around the table and set a glass in front of each board member.

"This is the same water parts of town have been drinking for close to two decades. We know you have ways of expediting the effects if you wanted someone to get sick quicker. We've used the same methods on this pitcher of water. If you've done nothing to the water supply, then you have nothing to worry about. Go ahead. Take a long drink."

"You can't make us. It doesn't mean—"

"Oh, it does. If you don't drink, it's incriminating. Maybe not in front of a judge, but the court of public opinion will have plenty to say about it."

When Anderson didn't reply, Bear nodded to Mandy, who cut the feed. The two of them walked out of the room, their steps lighter than they had been in weeks. The rest of the townspeople stayed behind. As Bear and Mandy stepped onto the elevator, they saw a team of the sheriff's deputies marching down the hall, handcuffs ready.

Bear looked down at Mandy. Whatever happened next, he knew he'd done his part to make her proud. And that was reward enough.

45

Bear met McKinnon outside the hospital. It had been two days since the video of HealTek's most recent board meeting had gone viral. McKinnon had spent the better part of her recovery filling in the State Police and FBI on everything she knew. She also handed over all the evidence Bear had collected. When they'd asked her where she had gotten it, she said an anonymous source had provided it.

"Thanks for picking me up." McKinnon hoisted herself into the front seat of the truck with a grunt. One hand was full of paperwork. "I appreciate it."

"The least I could do for keeping my name out of this."

"You act like I don't owe you more than a thanks for figuring all this out."

Bear shrugged and put the truck into drive. "Didn't have much of a choice, really."

"You did." McKinnon eyed him from the passenger seat. "Something tells me you're good at disappearing. You could've left town if you'd wanted to."

"Almost did."

"What kept you here?"

"Mandy. Her friend, Laura Lynn. You." He looked over at her and smiled. "Couldn't let you have all the glory."

"Glory." She scoffed. "More like mountains of paperwork."

"The Feds say anything promising?"

"They're all over this. Especially with rumors that this was government sanctioned. They're gonna try to cover this up as much as possible."

"Sounds about right."

"I think they're here to help. The notebooks sealed the deal. Combined with testimony from all the HealTek workers, they'll be able to paint a significant picture."

"I see Weinberger hasn't backed down."

McKinnon smiled. "He's become quite the unlikely hero, hasn't he? The State Troopers told me he's doubling down on everything. And he's got a lot to say."

"Good for him. Good for his daughter."

"Everything's about to change."

Bear glanced over at her. "What do you mean?"

"Dr. Sing was so close to finding a cure for cancer. Someone out there will finish her work. We'll be able to cure the people who've been sick. Laura Lynn. My neighbor's kid. All of them. If they can just hold on a little longer, they'll have a real future ahead of them."

"And HealTek won't get any of the credit. That's a reward if I've ever heard one."

"Speaking of rewards," McKinnon said. "I've got a surprise for you."

"Oh?"

"Trust me, you're gonna love it."

"Last time I trusted someone..."

McKinnon waited for him to finish. She didn't press when he didn't.

She instructed Bear to drive out of town until they were winding their way along a country road. Just as Bear was about to question where she was taking him, they saw a group of police cruisers lined up along the street with their lights flashing.

"Pull over here."

"You sure?"

"Yeah, they're expecting us."

Bear pulled over. The two of them hopped out of the truck and walked up the driveway just in time to see a group of officers pulling a struggling man out of his house. He was kicking and screaming, but when his eyes landed on Bear, he stopped. Spit dribbled down his chin. He looked deranged.

"You."

"Jeremy Olsen." Bear chuckled, happy to see the man in cuffs. "We've been looking for you."

Bear had left Olsen tied up in the middle of the Bowser Freight warehouse, knowing full well someone would set him free by morning. When the news broke of HealTek falling under and the board—who had been cutting checks for him for decades—being arrested, Olsen ran. As much as it pained Bear to think about it, he figured they'd never find him. If he were smart, he would've put as much space between him and HealTek as possible.

Turned out Jeremy Olsen wasn't all that smart.

"He tried to lie low at his girlfriend's house." McKinnon pointed at the woman who had stepped onto the porch in a robe and slippers. A cigarette dangled from the woman's lips. "As soon as she heard what happened, she alerted the authorities. Poor bastard didn't even see us coming."

Bear tipped his head back and let out a guttural laugh that brought tears to his eyes. He locked gazes with Olsen. The smile that formed on Bear's face was one of the most genuine he'd ever felt in his life. "What's he being arrested for?"

McKinnon watched as her deputies loaded the screaming man into the back of one of their cars. "Attempted kidnapping. Attempted manslaughter. Assault with a deadly weapon. I'm sure we'll find a few more. We're reexamining Katie Lamoureux's case. He had something to do with that, too."

Bear couldn't help himself. Before the officer shut the door on Olsen, Bear called out to him. "Karma, right?"

46

Marcus and Mandy sat in their usual spot in the corner of the crowded cafeteria. It felt strange without Laura Lynn, but Mandy was glad to have Marcus by her side, even if it was only for the morning.

"I can't believe you're leaving." Marcus pushed a pile of mashed potatoes around his plate. He'd been doing it for the last ten minutes. They had to be cold by now. "Couldn't even stay the whole day?"

"We have to get on the road. My dad wanted to leave earlier. I convinced him to let me say goodbye first."

Marcus wouldn't meet her gaze. "Do you even know where you're going? Will I ever see you again?"

"I know we're heading South, but that's all I know." As sad as she was to leave her new friends behind, Mandy was ready to start over. She'd learned a lot from Marcus and Laura Lynn, but something felt tainted about this town now. There was no way they'd be able to lead a normal life here. "I don't know if we'll ever see each other again, but you have my email." She smiled. It felt sad, even to her. "And my phone number. We can keep talking. You'll have to keep me up to date on how things go around here."

"Yeah, all right."

Mandy opened her mouth to tell Marcus he'd probably forget about her in a couple of months. She was surprised by an apple that went whizzing by her head. It hit the back wall and exploded. The whole cafeteria went quiet.

To no one's surprise, Pete stood up and stalked toward the table. Mandy hadn't seen him all day. Marcus said he'd spent the morning in the principal's office. Unfortunately, there wasn't much they could do to him, considering he was the councilman's son. That was another reason Mandy was excited to leave. They might've shaken things up with Heal-Tek, but some things would never change. If Councilman Richter didn't end up going down with the rest of them, he'd use the power vacuum to his own ends.

And if he ended up going down? Well, Mandy was pretty sure Pete would be even more insufferable than he already was whatever happened to his dad. Sometimes bad genes just can't be overcome.

She rolled her eyes and went back to her lunch. "What do you want, Pete?"

"Heard you were running away with your tail between your legs like the bitch you are."

"There's a difference between *choosing* to leave and running away. Just because you're scared of your father doesn't mean I am."

Pete's face darkened. "You're going to regret everything you did to us."

"No, I'm not." Mandy climbed on top of the table. Anyone who hadn't already been paying attention to their confrontation was now completely tuned in. Even the teacher meant to monitor them for the lunch period didn't bother to intervene.

Mandy stood. "Hey, everyone. Listen up."

Marcus hissed from below her. "What are you doing?"

"If you don't already know who I am, my name is Mandy Logan. My dad is the one who took down HealTek and saved the people of this town, including my friend Laura Lynn Weinberger. And Sheriff McKinnon. But he didn't do it alone. He did it because he had friends who wanted the same thing he did. People brave enough to stand up to bullies."

Mandy glanced down at Pete, who was looking around the room, trying to figure out where she was going with this. "One of those bullies is Mr. Richter, Pete's dad. He's a real piece of work. If you don't know him, I'm sure you've heard rumors. For Pete's sake, I won't repeat them here." She looked out at the crowd and saw a few grins. "Remember, he only has power because you gave it to him. That's how town councils work. And Pete only has power in the school hallways because you let him take it from you. He's just as scared as we are. Maybe even more, since he has to go home to his father."

There were a couple of chuckles and a few murmurs.

"But Pete can't be a bully if there's no one to push around. And if he can't be a bully, he's just like the rest of us. Maybe once that happens, he'll figure out it's better to have genuine friends than a group of people to bully into doing his dirty work. It didn't work out for HealTek in the long-run." She looked down at him. "And it's not going to work out for you."

Mandy hadn't expected anyone to cheer after her speech, and they didn't, but they started talking amongst themselves, pointing at Pete and shaking their heads. If she accomplished one more thing before she left, she hoped it was to show Pete that there was a better way.

As she jumped down from the table, Pete took a step forward. "You think you're so much better than me, don't you?"

Mandy shook her head. "No, I don't. But I do have a better dad, and he taught me to always do the right thing. I wish your dad had taught you that. But guess what? You don't have to be like him. Maybe he gets out of his mess this time, but one day, he's going to get caught. Because the good guys always win. And your dad? He's not one of the good guys."

Pete scowled, but Mandy didn't give him a chance to talk again. She grabbed Marcus' hand, and they walked through the cafeteria with their heads held high. As soon as they were out in the hallway, they sprinted toward the exit, laughing and whooping the entire way.

They burst through the doors just in time to see Bear pull up to the curb with his truck filled to the brim with their belongings.

Mandy turned to Marcus. "I'm sorry I have to go. And I'm sorry you have to deal with Pete."

He shrugged. "It sucks, but I've survived this long. Who knows, maybe he'll actually listen to you."

"Maybe." Mandy grinned. She didn't believe it, but she still liked the idea. "So, this is goodbye."

"Yeah." Marcus scuffed his shoe against the sidewalk. "Goodbye, I guess."

Mandy wrapped her arms around him and squeezed. She waited long enough for him to return the gesture before she spun around and hopped into the front seat of the truck. Before she knew it, they were turning onto the highway and heading south.

Bear looked over at her. "How are you holding up?"

"I'm good." She meant it. "How about you?"

"I'm doing all right." Bear twisted his face into a smile. "Bittersweet leaving them behind, isn't it?"

Mandy thought of Laura Lynn, who she'd said goodbye to the day before, and Sheriff McKinnon, who she'd hugged just that morning. "Yeah. But they'll be okay without us. Besides, I'm ready for a change."

"Me too." Bear turned back to the road. "Any idea where we should head next?"

Mandy rolled down the window and let the cool autumn breeze flow through her hair. Then she turned back to Bear with a big grin on her face. "Yeah, I've got a few."

BEAR & MANDY'S story continues in Book 2, UNDER THE SURFACE! Order your copy today!
https://www.amazon.com/dp/B09N1Z1LM1

Join the **LT Ryan reader family** & receive a free copy of the Jack Noble story, *The Recruit*. Click the link below to get started:
https://ltryan.com/jack-noble-newsletter-signup-1

ALSO BY L.T. RYAN

Find All of L.T. Ryan's Books on Amazon Today!

The Jack Noble Series

The Recruit (free)

The First Deception (Prequel 1)

Noble Beginnings

A Deadly Distance

Ripple Effect (Bear Logan)

Thin Line

Noble Intentions

When Dead in Greece

Noble Retribution

Noble Betrayal

Never Go Home

Beyond Betrayal (Clarissa Abbot)

Noble Judgment

Never Cry Mercy

Deadline

End Game

Noble Ultimatum

Noble Legend

Noble Revenge (Coming Soon)

Bear Logan Series

Ripple Effect

Blowback

Take Down

Deep State

Bear & Mandy Logan Series

Close to Home

Under the Surface

The Last Stop

Over the Edge (Coming Soon)

Rachel Hatch Series

Drift

Downburst

Fever Burn

Smoke Signal

Firewalk

Whitewater

Aftershock

Whirlwind

Tsunami

Fastrope (Coming Soon)

Mitch Tanner Series

The Depth of Darkness

Into The Darkness

Deliver Us From Darkness

Cassie Quinn Series

Path of Bones

Whisper of Bones

Symphony of Bones

Etched in Shadow

Concealed in Shadow

Betrayed in Shadow

Born from Ashes

Blake Brier Series

Unmasked

Unleashed

Uncharted

Drawpoint

Contrail

Detachment

Clear (Coming Soon)

Dalton Savage Series

Savage Grounds

Scorched Earth

Cold Sky (Coming Soon)

Maddie Castle Series

The Handler

Tracking Justice (Coming Soon)

Affliction Z Series

Affliction Z: Patient Zero

Affliction Z: Abandoned Hope

Affliction Z: Descended in Blood

Affliction Z : Fractured Part 1

Affliction Z: Fractured Part 2 (Fall 2021)

ABOUT THE AUTHOR

L.T. Ryan is a *USA Today* and international bestselling author. The new age of publishing offered L.T. the opportunity to blend his passions for creating, marketing, and technology to reach audiences with his popular Jack Noble series.

Living in central Virginia with his wife, the youngest of his three daughters, and their three dogs, L.T. enjoys staring out his window at the trees and mountains while he should be writing, as well as reading, hiking, running, and playing with gadgets. See what he's up to at http://ltryan.com.

Social Medial Links:

- Facebook (L.T. Ryan): https://www.facebook.com/LTRyanAuthor
- Facebook (Jack Noble Page): https://www.facebook.com/JackNobleBooks/
- Twitter: https://twitter.com/LTRyanWrites
- Goodreads: http://www.goodreads.com/author/show/6151659.L_T_Ryan

Made in the USA
Columbia, SC
07 May 2023

16206148R00162